Finding Peace
A Medieval Romance

The Sword of Glastonbury Series

Book 2

Lisa Shea

Cover design by Lisa Shea
Book design by Lisa Shea
Visit my website at LisaShea.com

In 2013, Finding Peace earned a Silver Award from the Independent Publisher Book Awards.

First Printing: June 2012

- 11 -

Print ISBN-13 978-0-9855564-1-9
Kindle ASIN B008FQZ8JY

Treat yourself with compassion.

You deserve it.

Finding Peace

Chapter 1

England, 1174

"Anger is short-lived madness."
-- Horace

"God's Teeth, next the badgers and wolves will march by two-by-two," scowled Elizabeth with vehemence as she lugged the soaked saddle off her roan and dropped it in a sodden heap on the cracked bench. The fierce November storm crashed down all around her, hammering off the thin roof, reverberating through the small stable's walls. The lantern hanging in the corner guttered out dense smoke, barely holding off the deep gloom of the late hour.

She worked quickly in the flickering dark to bed down her horse, the familiar routine doing little to soothe her foul mood. She was drenched to the bone – her heavy cloak and hood had done little to shield her after the first ten minutes in the torrent. Her stomach was twisting into knots with hunger. Exhaustion and cold caused her fingers to fumble as she finished with the bridle. She hung it on the wooden peg, then turned to walk the few short steps toward the stable entrance.

The small inn's door was only ten steps away, but it seemed like ten miles through the deluge. Elizabeth took in a deep breath, pulled her hood up over her head, tucked in her glossy auburn curls, then sprinted across the dark cobblestones. It felt as if she were diving into a frigid stream, struggling against its strong current, and she reached out a hand for the thick, wooden door. In another second she had pulled open the latch, spun through the door, and slammed it heavily behind her.

The inn looked like every other hell hole she had stayed in during this long, tiring trip. Six or seven food-strewn oak tables filled the small space, about half occupied by aging farmers and rheumatic merchants. A doddering, wispy-haired barkeep poured ale behind a wood plank counter. The only two women in the room were a pair of buxom barmaids, one blonde, one redhead, laughing at a round table in the back with a trio of men. Two of the men appeared to be in their early twenties and were alike enough to be twins. Their dusty brown hair was the exact same color, the same periwinkle blue eyes gazed out from square faces. Like every other pair in the room, they swept up to stare at her the moment she came to rest, dripping from every seam, against the interior side of the door. After a moment of halfhearted interest, the farmers, merchants, and twins turned back to their pints of ale and their conversations on turnips and wool prices.

All except one. The third man, sitting somewhat apart from the preening twins and the flirtatious waitresses, held her gaze with steady interest. Her world slowed down, her skin tingled as a drip of water slid its way down her neck, tracing along every inch of her spine.

He was in his late twenties, a dark brown mane of hair curling just at his shoulders. He was well built, with the toned shoulders of a man who led an active life. It was his eyes that caught her and held her pinned against the wall. They were a rich moss green, a verdant color she remembered so strongly that her breath caught, her left hand almost swung down toward her hilt of its own accord.

She shook herself, turning to the row of wooden pegs running in an uneven line next to the door. That man was in the past, and by God, he would stay there. Why did she have to keep seeing that foul bastard's eyes everywhere, in every tavern, in every stranger she passed on the road? She pushed the hood of her cloak back, then shook its damp embrace off her body, revealing the simple, burnt-orange dress she wore beneath and the well-used sword hanging on her right hip.

Now, to get some stew, or gruel, or whatever mystery meat this cook had to offer, and get some sleep.

"You, woman!" came the growled order, plunging the room into immediate silence.

Elizabeth blew out her breath in an exasperated huff. Just for once she would like to have her food and rest without going through this ordeal. Sometimes it was just a snide comment, a mention of the dangers of a young woman traveling alone, or a sly joke about the "oldest profession." Sometimes the greeting cut with its chill edge. One solemn innkeeper had served her meal brusquely, informing her that she would have to find somewhere else to sleep.

All she wanted was food and a bed. She took in a deep breath and closed her eyes for a moment. If she could just rein in her temper she could get through this and snatch a few hours' reprieve from the torrential deluge.

She turned around slowly, holding her features in what she hoped was a neutral gaze. The twins were on their feet, their eyes sharp on her, their faces twisted in anger. They wore matching outfits of fine leather jerkins. Behind them the green-eyed man stood more slowly, his eyes scanning her with careful attention.

Twin number one shouted in rage. "You! Woman! I cannot believe you simply strolled in here and expect to be fed and cared for!" His eyes nearly bulged from their sockets. "What, did you expect a pint of ale?"

Elizabeth blinked in surprise. She had certainly encountered people in rural towns who thought little of her traveling alone – but she had reached new lows in hospitality with this outpost from Hades. Still, the hammering of the torrential downpour just outside the door encouraged her to press her case.

"Please," she bit out, her rising anger sharpening the edges of her attempted civility, "all I want is something hot to eat and a place to sleep. In the morning I will be out of your town and on my way."

Twin number two took a step forward. "Maybe you did not hear my brother, John," he snarled, his voice perhaps even a few notes higher than his double. "I think we should step outside."

His brother's voice was almost like hearing an echo. "Absolutely, Ron," agreed the clone with heat.

Elizabeth couldn't help herself. John and Ron. Twins. The rhyming duo. Her laughter bubbled up within her, emerging from her exhaustion, her frustration, her hunger and weariness with the world. It was the final straw in the long carnival which had made up these past few weeks.

The brothers glanced at each other, fury boiled their faces crimson, and her left hand dropped to her hip, doing the twist – latch – release to free her sword hilt from its clasp in one smooth movement. She had her weapon sliding smoothly from its sheath in the same moment that the pair launched themselves across the spellbound tavern toward her. Her steel rose in an arcing block as John brought a haymaker drive down toward her skull. She deflected his blow easily, sliding it off to her left, turning and whipping the sword – flat first – against his kidney with the full force of her momentum. He screamed in pain and sprawled back on the rough wooden floor, his face contorted in agony.

She continued her spin, remaining low, the whistle of Ron's blade skimming over her head. She kicked her boot hard against his kneecap. He buckled backwards, screaming in fury, and she rose, whirling her sword in a circular motion, preparing to give him a welt to remember her by.

There was a dark figure before her. Her moving blade slammed into a block, was held, and she looked up into moss green eyes. Her breath caught, and she leant her sword against the tension. Her blade pressed in an X against his, their hands nearly touching, his body presenting a barrier now between her and the two young men.

"My name is Richard." His voice rumbled out deep, steady, and serious. He gazed at her face for a long minute. "I would call your eyes a deep brown, would you agree?"

Elizabeth shook her head in confusion. "What? I suppose," she ground out, continuing her press against his sword. The man had excellent balance; his arm did not move one breath.

Richard turned his head slightly, calling down to the two at his feet. "Certainly not ice blue," he calmly informed them.

His focus came back to her. "I apologize for these two impetuous ones, and would ask that you choose to stay at the Traveler's Inn, a scant mile east. To be truthful, they are much cleaner than this location."

A hot flare of fury burst through her. She was attacked, and now *she* was the one who had to leave? It was the second coming of the Flood out there! She snapped her sword free of his and sidestepped to the right, determined to finish what she had started.

Richard moved easily with her, brought his sword hilt back against his hip, and pointed the tip between her eyes. His body remained evenly between hers and the sprawled men. "I will defend them," he added in a cool, steady voice. Elizabeth could see the steel settle into his gaze. She remembered being sheltered by that same style of fierce protectiveness, remembered being sprawled, herself, on a cold floor, her guardian angel standing resolutely between her and danger.

God's teeth, she missed her brother.

The burning flame of fury ebbed within her, and she sighed. It was not worth it, not for a flea-bitten mat in this God-forsaken hole in the ground.

She took a step back, slid her sword smoothly back into its sheath, then turned on her heel. She pulled the soaking wet cloak over her shoulders, shivering as its damp caress sucked the warmth out of her body. She half kicked the door open. Outside the rain pummeled the ground as if to beat it into submission, and she nearly turned back, nearly took on all three.

"Here," came a call behind her. She turned, and Richard tossed her two golden coins. She caught them easily as they came near her, and the corner of his mouth twitched up in appreciation.

Now she was being paid to leave.

She turned back toward the rain, took a deep breath, and walked steadfastly into the torrent, leaving the door wide open behind her.

Chapter 2

A movement to her left caught her eye, and a young boy, perhaps eleven, scurried down from a box where he'd been squinting through the crack between the dingy shutters. He peered, at her half curious, half afraid. Rags of clothing were plastered against the rail-thin bones of his body. Elizabeth looked down at the coins in her hand and, without a second thought, she tossed them over to the lad. He caught them nimbly, gazed down at them, and his eyes widened in surprise. As she continued her way through the maelstrom toward the stables, she heard the soft splash of feet following behind.

"Thank you, miss," came the high voice, "this is a gift beyond measure! Let me be of service to you!" He came alongside her as she moved to her saddle. He carefully held out the straps as she lifted it from the table and carried it over to her roan. "What a fine steed this is, too! Well cared for, that is clear to see." He stood nearby as she strapped the saddle on securely, then brought over the bridle for her to fasten.

"You must be going to the Traveler's Inn, I warrant. I can be your guide, to get you there safely in this deluge."

Elizabeth shook her head. "Surely you want to get home to your family, especially in this weather," she replied.

The boy shook his head. "I have no home," he stated simply. "I am an orphan. Michael the orphan. For now, I am your navigator!" Without further ado, he stood by the horse's head, holding the reins, waiting for Elizabeth to mount.

Shrugging, Elizabeth climbed onto the saddle. In a moment they were off, Michael leading the way out into the pitch dark night.

Elizabeth found she was thankful to have a guide. There was no moon, and the thundering rain made it nearly impossible to see the road ahead. Michael knew the way with sure attention, leading the horse around potholes and crevasses in the road. Elizabeth had several questions for him but the noise of the rain hammering against the road drowned out all conversation. She bided her time until they made their way out of the village, across several farm areas, and into the outskirts of the next rough collection of buildings, where a small stable stood aside a quiet inn.

Michael's face was dark as he helped her get the roan settled into a stall. "I would have not chosen this place willingly," he commented in a low voice. "Except for the storm, I would have suggested you go on several miles to the next outpost." He glanced toward the door, then dropped his voice even further. "The owner here is a pig."

Elizabeth shrugged, hanging the bridle on a peg, shaking a circle of water out of her cloak. "Most men are pigs," she responded evenly. "I will deal with him. All I need is some food and a dry place to sleep."

Michael's stomach rumbled audibly at that, but he looked around the stables, nodding in resolution. "I will stay here for the night."

Elizabeth shook her head. "You have been a help to me, and I appreciate it," she commented. "Come and stay with me; I will get you some food as payment for your assistance."

Michael patted the pouch at his waist. "Those coins were more than payment," he pointed out.

"That was a gift," corrected Elizabeth. "If you come in you can keep me company while I eat."

Michael glanced again at the door. "I would rather the inn-keep not see me," he admitted, his voice tight.

Elizabeth's interest piqued. Just what had the lad done? "Fair enough," she responded. "I will let you in the window once I get the food set up in the room. Give me about ten minutes."

With that, she turned and strode through the waterfall to the main door, slipping within. Richard had spoken truly. The main room here was better cared for, although only a lone, elderly man sat in a chair by the fire, his eyes half closed. The inn-keep was a portly, pink faced, middle-aged man with wisps of grey amongst his dark brown hair. His eyes lit up with greedy delight as he saw her, and instantly he was trundling to her side, his eyes sliding unctuously down her form, sizing her up.

"Shall you be staying with us, miss?" he wheedled in delight.

"Yes," she agreed shortly. "A private room. Bring me two pints of ale and two servings of stew. I am very hungry and have no desire to come in and out tonight."

"Of course, of course," he agreed, rubbing his hands together with glee. "The last door on the right, and here is the key." He fumbled at a pouch at his waist, withdrew the small, iron item, and deposited it in her hand. "I will bring the food down in just a minute."

She nodded, turned, and made her way down the hall. A quick twist of the key opened a small but serviceable room with a low bed in one corner, a stool and table, and a small window looking out over the stables. A candle glowed on the table, giving faint light.

She stood there for a long moment, the tumult sounding through the window, the steady drip-drip-drip coming from the edges of her cloak. Then there were footsteps in the hall and the inn-keep bundled in through the still open door, placing the two bowls of stew and two mugs of ale down onto the table with clinks and clunks. He looked at the spread, and then back at her.

"I would be more than glad to sit and keep you company," he offered in a reedy voice. "You must be in need of companionship after your long ride."

"I am fine," she responded shortly. "Please leave me."

"If you need anything – anything at all – you have but to call for me," he offered. "Hyde is my name. I am here to serve you."

"I am sure you are," offered Elizabeth, her eyes sharp.

The man seemed caught between truculence and eager anticipation, but finally he was in the hallway and she closed the door firmly in his face. She slid the bar across the channel, then sighed, shrugging the sodden cloak from her shoulders. She hung it on the peg by the door before moving to give a wave at the window.

Michael had slid his way through it before she could finish stepping back, and she pulled the shutters closed over the opening. He ran a thin hand through his sandy hair, then his eyes lit up with delight as he spotted the food. In a moment he was sitting on the stool, shoveling the stew into his mouth, barely pausing for moments to drink.

Elizabeth smiled at his enthusiasm. The poor lad had probably not eaten properly in weeks. She took her own bowl to sit on the edge of the bed, and after the first bite her pace was nearly as quick as Michael's. She was starving. It had been a long ride today, but her journey was finally coming to an end. By tomorrow – or perhaps the day after – she would be with Claire at the nunnery. Her trip would at last be over. She could finally rest and give some thought to her future.

She laid her hand on the hilt of her scabbard, and, as she did every night, she offered a heart-felt prayer to Kay and Reese who had gifted her with this sword, *Andetnes*. Its very name meant honor and mercy. That sword, the horse, and other gear had made her journey possible.

Elizabeth had not fully understood the story behind the sword's origin, but she accepted Kay's request. Elizabeth could use the sword as long as she needed it. And then, at some point in her life, when she had found true contentment, her sword would be passed to another whose life hung in the balance.

Elizabeth's mouth quirked. If true contentment was what it took to part her from the sword, she might be its owner for a very, very long time.

Michael had finished scraping the last bits of stew from his bowl. The waif was now licking every remnant with focused attention, getting the last tiny drips out of the cracks in the wood.

"I can get another bowl," offered Elizabeth with a smile. The emaciated thing must have been starving.

He shook his head. "I am full," he commented steadily. "Just making sure nothing is wasted."

Suddenly he froze, cocked his head at an angle, then swiveled to look at the shuttered window.

"That is Richard's horse," he stated firmly.

Elizabeth could not hear anything through the pounding rain, but she did not doubt the lad. She put a finger to her lips, then moved to the door, sliding it open a crack, looking down the hallway. It was dark, and ahead the main hall was now lit only by the flickering light of the fire. The inn-keep was putting out the candles in preparation for night.

She could not see the main door from her angle. She worked her way down the hall, leant against its right hand wall, and crouched down to peer around into the central room. There was the sound of quick footsteps from outside, and then the front door was swinging open. Richard stepped through and shook the rain off his cloak, creating a growing puddle.

Elizabeth almost laughed at the instant change in Hyde's demeanor. Gone was the delighted, ingratiating inn-keep. In his place was a surly, taciturn face lit by two glowering eyes.

"What do you want," he growled. "We are full up for the night."

"Of course you are," answered Richard evenly, his eyes scanning the nearly empty room with sharp focus. "For I am not female and comely. Speaking of which, did a young woman just come in and ask for a room and board?"

"No," snapped Hyde without a moment's hesitation.

Richard's eyes swiveled around to hold his steadily. "And would you tell me if one had?"

"No," repeated Hyde, his eyes shrinking even smaller.

Richard pursed his lips. "Hoping to press your client for a favor, as a token of her gratitude?" he asked with displeasure.

"You have no business here," snapped Hyde, "and your family's influence stops two miles hence. This is my inn, and I can run it any way I please."

"Some day you will slip up," reminded Richard coolly, "and when you do, I will be pleased to help haul you in."

"It will be a cold day in Hell before I let a *bastard* teach me about morals," snarled Hyde, his pink face darkening into crimson.

Richard went still at that, and Elizabeth could feel the ice sliding down his spine, sense the control that kept his hand still, prevented it from dropping to the hilt of his sword. Then he gave one last sweep to the room, turned, and headed out into the pounding inkiness beyond the door.

Hyde's eyes lit up in triumph, his face beamed with pleasure, and he turned toward the hall where Elizabeth still crouched. She stood at once, taking a step forward into the half-light, her left hand dropping easily to the hilt of the sword on her hip.

Hyde staggered to a stop when he saw her there, as he took in the sword and her stance in one long sweep. A surly frown moved across his features, but he pushed it away.

"As you can see, I protected your privacy," he offered ingratiatingly. "I took care of you."

"Yes, you did," she agreed coldly. "I think it is quite clear why."

His eyes sharpened slightly. "It is not unfair for me to ask for some measure of thanks for my protection," he snapped. "Richard is an exceptional swordsman. I stood up to him in order to keep you safe. I risked my life for you. Is it that much to ask that -"

She wrapped her fingers around the hilt, gave it a slight tug to ease it an inch out of the sheath, her eyes focused on his. "I have been itching for a fight all night," she warned him. "You try to lay one hand on me, or get anywhere near my room, and I may just get my wish."

He pressed his lips together in displeasure, and when his voice came, it was low and guttural. "Ungrateful wench," he spit out, then his shoulders sagged and he turned, making his way back toward the other side of the room.

Elizabeth waited until he had closed the door with a sharp click. She turned, and stopped. A pair of bright, glowing eyes was peering at her from the crack of her bedroom door. She smiled slightly, then moved forward, stepping in past Michael, pulling the door shut behind them. The bar was slid home with a solid thud.

Michael's face was wreathed in smiles. "You were amazing!" he crowed. "You stood up to Hyde! I want to learn how to do that."

"To stand up to a bully? That is certainly a good skill to learn," agreed Elizabeth, settling herself down onto her bed. She unstrapped the belt, laying the sword and then her dagger alongside her. "But right now, I am exhausted and need to get some sleep." She glanced around the room. "What will you do?"

He immediately settled into a corner, pulling his knees up tightly against his chest, wrapping his arms around them. "I am perfectly fine," he stated, dropping his head, laying it atop his knees. And, indeed, it seemed that within a few minutes he had fallen sound asleep.

Elizabeth chuckled, then lay back, hearing the steady pounding of rain outside the window. She was beyond worn out. It seemed only a moment had passed before she, too, was lost to the darkness of night.

Chapter 3

Elizabeth blinked her eyes open, getting her bearings. She was in a small, barely furnished room. The faintest hint of pre-dawn light was edging in past the corners of closed shutters. The occasional sounds of drips and patters came from the eaves of the building, but it seemed that the main part of the storm had passed.

She started. Two bright, round eyes were staring at her from the corner of the room, encapsulated by the thin, wiry frame of a child. The previous day's events returned to her.

"Good morning, Michael," she offered wearily, giving a long stretch.

"We should be out soon, if we want to stay ahead of Richard," he offered evenly.

She arched an eyebrow as she drew herself into a seated position. "Oh? And should we be worried about doing that?"

Michael shrugged, tugging his knees in more closely to his chest. "I do not trust anyone," he offered.

Elizabeth smiled at that. "You seem to trust me," she pointed out.

Michael's face relaxed slightly. "You are different," he stated firmly. "You stood up to Hyde."

Elizabeth pushed herself up to standing. She moved to the window, eased the shutters open with a creak, and gazed out over the rolls of mist which wafted between the inn and the stables. "It sounds like someone should have done that years ago," she commented dryly.

"*That* is for sure," affirmed Michael in a growl.

Elizabeth reached down, drew on her belt, and strapped it into place. "Well, then, let us be off."

A short while later they were making their way down the mist-shrouded lane, Michael still in place by the horse's head, picking out the path, leading the way without hesitation. Slowly the sun rose and began to burn off the swirling mists, revealing a landscape of rolling hills and clumps of elm. Elizabeth could sense a slight tang of salt in the air the further east they moved, and a shiver danced through her. She had grown up in a bandit-ravaged land, knew what to expect from their attacks, had become well versed in the ebb and flow of their activities. But pirates and slavers who could vanish on the ocean would be an entirely new breed of monster.

"So, how far are we going today?" asked Michael with idle curiosity. She chuckled softly. The poor lad had no idea where he was going or what dangers he was getting himself into. He was simply happy to be on the move and have the potential of food waiting for him at the end of the day.

"Not too far," she responded. "My friend, Claire, has been stationed at the nunnery at Kilnsea. I am visiting to lend her a hand."

Michael smiled with pleasure. "I hear they have fantastic gardens at Kilnsea," he mused. "And that is but ten miles ahead. Even with this sodden ground we should easily make it there by nightfall."

The tension began to ease out of Elizabeth's tight shoulders. That was good news. She had been on the road for two weeks, and the dismal reception at each town had only compounded the dreary weather. It would be a relief to settle somewhere welcoming and warm.

"Just so you know," added Michael. "We are in fact moving closer to Richard's lands ... or, more properly, his father's lands."

"The inn-keep mentioned that Richard was a bastard," responded Elizabeth, pondering. "So he was being literal with that charge?"

Michael nodded, his eyes on the road ahead. "Yes, indeed. Everyone knows the story. It's almost a legend around here. Richard's father was Lord Corwin, and as a young man the Lord fell in love with a local farm-girl named Bliss. He had two children with her – two boys – but his outraged family refused to recognize their union. No priest would agree to marry them for fear of upsetting the family."

He glanced off toward the right, and Elizabeth wondered if that was the direction of the family estate. The lad continued after a moment. "Eventually Lord Corwin gave in to the pressure and married a "proper" lady. Lady Lauda took over control of his keep and gave him twin boys. They are only seventeen, but they now run the keep and lands."

"I assume that means the parents have passed on? Do the twins rule as a pair?"

Michael nodded. "Technically John is the elder, by a few minutes, but they are rarely seen apart."

Elizabeth pursed her lips. "So Richard is acting as an advisor?"

Michael shrugged. "Richard seems more of a bodyguard, to keep them out of serious trouble. I hear they have priests and other functionaries to do the work of managing the keep." He gave a snort. "From what I see at the local inns, the boys seem to spend most of their time drinking and wenching."

They came over a rise and Elizabeth smiled with delight. A grey-green river lay before them, bending just in front of them. It gurgled with the heavy flow from the rain, running fast before diving to tumble over a series of rapids. A grassy patch lay immediately alongside the bend, and a pair of weathered logs facing a fire pit indicated that other travelers had found this an ideal place to rest.

"Here we go, the perfect place for a late breakfast," offered Elizabeth. "I imagine you must be hungry."

"Am I ever!" agreed Michael with delight. In a moment they had hobbled the roan near the patch of grass. Elizabeth spread her still-damp cloak out on a bush to dry, and she and Michael sat down on the two logs. She pulled open a leather pouch and dug through it, drawing out a hunk of cheese. She deftly carved a piece off for herself, then handed the remaining wad over to Michael.

He looked at it for a long moment, almost seeming as if he would simply stuff the entire thing into his mouth, before exhaling slightly and looking up at her. "I do not have a dagger," he admitted quietly.

Pity eased through Elizabeth. A dagger was critical for so many things – for eating, for dealing with snags in leather, for fending off wild dogs. How had this poor child lasted as long as he had? She handed over her own dagger, holding her tongue as he adjusted the grip in his smaller hand, as he carefully wriggled the blade against the cheese and worked off a piece. His proud smile when he accomplished the task was worth the wait.

He held both back toward her, but she waved him off. "You go ahead," she offered. "I will just enjoy our rest for a little while."

Michael did not need a second prodding, He was working on the cheese again, his skill with the knife improving with every new attempt, and after ten minutes he was cutting his way through each piece with ease, his eyes glowing with joy.

Elizabeth watched the icy waters race down alongside them, wondering what type of fish she might find in this river. Its steady tumbling gave her a sense of peace, one she had not felt in a long while.

"Wow, I am stuffed," offered Michael with a groan. Elizabeth looked over, then chuckled. The lad had eaten nearly two thirds of the hunk and his stomach was visibly distended. She took the offered items back, cutting a last chunk off for herself before tucking the rest into the leather bag.

"I think I need to wash my hands," Michael commented, trying to wipe the many bits of yellow cheese from his fingers. He turned and made his way toward the water's edge.

"Just be careful," called Elizabeth after him. "With all the rain, those green rocks are probably -"

There was a yelp, and a swish, and a high splash as Michael's body cartwheeled into the stream. Instantly he began to be pulled downstream by the fierce current.

"Michael!" cried out Elizabeth in alarm, darting diagonally toward the bank. "Grab that branch!"

He saw the long, snaking branch sticking out from the center of the stream, caught at the head end of the rapids. He twisted with agile intensity, lunged, and grabbed a hold of it with one hand. He hung there, his thin body in the frigid water up to mid-chest, his breath coming in long heaves.

"Hold on!" Elizabeth called out, looking for a way to get across to him. She tried one of the rocks and nearly spun into the water herself, its surface was so slick. The next was as smooth as ice. She stretched her arm out but there was a good foot of distance between them still. She knew if the lad jumped that he was likely to pull them both in and straight toward those jagged rocks.

Michael's fingers slipped, and he re-wrapped them around the branch. "I do not know how much longer -"

A strong, firm hand slammed shut on Elizabeth's right arm, and a deep, steady voice assured her, "I have you."

Elizabeth did not hesitate. She lunged forward, balancing on one foot, calling out, "Jump! Now!"

Michael looked at her for a long moment, then he was launching himself with all his energy. Her left hand clasped his solidly, and she was being hauled back on shore, collapsing down onto the ground, landing on a warm, broad chest. Michael's soaked, light frame crumpled in against hers.

For a long moment she just lay there, her breath coming in long draws, her heart hammering in her chest.

Michael scrambled up, wide eyed, staring at the rapids. Elizabeth's breathing began to return to normal, warmth rising up against her, the aroma of musk and sweat and leather surrounding her, and something else. It felt familiar and comforting.

Michael turned and looked down at her with concern. "Are you all right?"

She blushed, then rolled over to her feet, brushing herself down, watching as Richard gained his feet. He looked Michael over, then in a moment he had swept off his dark brown cloak, wrapping it around the lad who was now beginning to shiver.

His voice was low and even. "The first thing we need to do is get your clothes dry."

Michael's eyes lit up in panic. "I am not taking my clothes off; they are all I have," he insisted.

Richard raised an eyebrow at that, but he nodded in agreement. "A fire should do quite nicely to dry you from without, while your body heat does the trick from within," he agreed. He glanced at Elizabeth, and in a moment the two had gathered up enough kindling to create a small tent form within the ring of rocks. He retrieved a small box from the saddle on his dappled grey horse. Before long a cheerful blaze was sending off heat. Michael settled himself down immediately at the edge of it, drawing the cloak tightly around his body, carefully holding various body parts as near to the flame as he dared.

Elizabeth glanced at Richard. "Lucky you just happened to come by then," she offered, half serious, half cynical.

Richard nodded at her, accepting both parts of her statement equally. "I doubt the lad knows how to swim," he mused.

"Nope," agreed Michael without turning. "Never saw a need for it."

Elizabeth found herself smiling slightly. "Maybe now you see that preparing for every eventuality can bring you a longer life," she commented gently.

"That is for sure," sighed Michael, the pink tone beginning to return to his cheeks.

Richard's eyes twinkled. "Maybe that extra five pounds of cheese helped him to float more easily."

Elizabeth brought her eyes over to meet his. She was struck again by the moss-green color, the rich depths. She forced herself to look away. "Just how long have you been watching us?"

"I was keeping an eye on things," agreed Richard. "Luckily for the young lad here."

His gaze wandered down the quiet path, following it as it wended its way along the river. "So, where are we heading next?"

An invisible shield closed in around Elizabeth, sealing her off, and her voice was cool and emotionless. "This is an ideal spot, I think. We will camp here for the night."

Michael's eyes flicked up to hers for a minute, but he said nothing, returned his gaze to the fire evenly.

Richard was not so quick in his acceptance. He held her gaze for a long minute. "The boy is chilled through," he pointed out. "Surely if you were to continue further along your way, toward an inn -"

Elizabeth shook her head. He wanted more of a sense of where they were heading, and, as it happened, this road led further into his own domain. She was not willing to give him the slightest hint, the tiniest inkling of where they were going.

"I think Michael is doing quite well, thanks to your cloak and the fire," she commented.

"Yes," piped up Michael immediately, turning his arms so another angle was presented to the fire's heat. "I think I am nearly dry already. We will be fine here."

Richard looked between the two, considering. "If that is your decision, then I am happy to help by -"

"By providing us with some privacy," finished up Elizabeth firmly. "I am, after all, a woman caring for a child. It would be highly improper for a strange man to spend the night with us. We appreciate your assistance, and Michael will be more careful around the stream from now on. I think it would be best if you continued on your way and let us finish our daily activities in private."

Richard pursed his lips, but after a long moment he nodded. His eyes moved to Michael. "Please keep the cloak," he offered. "You need it more than I do." Then he was mounting, turning, and riding back along the path, quickly becoming hidden over the rise.

Michael's voice came in a low whisper. "Shall we ride out as quickly as we can?"

Elizabeth shook her head, kneeling down beside him. "I have no doubt he will set watch on us just over that hill," she mused. "We still do not know why he is so interested in pursuing me." She glanced out over the landscape. "How well do you know this area?"

Michael looked down. "Not well," he admitted. "I rarely made it far out of the main village. This was probably the boundary of my explorations."

She patted his shoulder gently. "Never you mind. The rain has stopped, and there should be a full moon tonight. As soon as night falls, we will head out and go cross country. The nunnery is on the coast. We can hardly miss the ocean if we head straight east."

***

The orange sun shimmered as it slipped below the horizon, and Michael and Elizabeth finished up their handiwork. They had fashioned two piles of twigs on either side of the fire, creating shadows in roughly human shape. It would be a while before Richard felt the darkness would let him draw that close, to realize he had been watching decoys. By then they would be long gone.

She took her dagger to the lower ends of Richard's cloak, forming small boots for her horse's hooves. The fabric would mask their print as they moved over the damp soil. Then, with a final glance back toward the rise in the road, they set into motion.

They went slowly, carefully, picking out the more rocky areas where they would leave no mark of their passing. Soon they found a place where she felt they could ford the river, and they climbed on the roan's back, encouraging him through the icy water. He made it without having to drop into a swim, and Elizabeth breathed a sigh of relief when they reached the other side. If there was ever a path which left no trace, it was crossing a waterway.

She allowed them to pick up speed then, to move more surely east, always east, following the constellations and the path of the moon. It was rising now, shining a silvery light down on them, turning their world into a glistening fairyland. It seemed that dew danced on the edge of every blade of grass, every small bush.

She and Michael walked on either side of her horse's lead, their eyes searching forward for trenches or hidden branches. She smiled, looking over at him. He had not complained once, not offered any resistance to her plan. He was resolute to see through what she had put into motion.

They stopped occasionally, listening intently, but there was never the slightest sound of pursuit, only the keening of the wind and the soft huff of her horse's breath.

The sun was just starting to send a dappled softness to the world when they came over a rise and saw the spread of the ocean out before them, the low waves, the glistening green-blue.

Michael's eyes went wide, and he gazed along its length. "I have never seen the ocean before," he breathed. "I could not have imagined it was so large."

"I have not seen it either," agreed Elizabeth. "It is certainly beautiful, but it is also quite dangerous. It provides easy access by great numbers of troops. There is no way to seal off a pass here."

Michael glanced left, then right, then back over at Elizabeth. "So, which way now?" he asked with the simple trust of youth.

Elizabeth's gaze followed the coast in both directions. She had a fifty-fifty chance, but she decided that it was most likely that the nunnery lay to the north. "Left," she stated firmly, and in a moment they were moving their way along the edge of the beach, breathing in the sharp tang of the air, immersing themselves in the sound of the rhythmic pull and release of the waves.

Chapter 4

Elizabeth exhaled in satisfaction, her shoulders slowly unknotting as the nunnery loomed before her. It was just as Claire had described it, tucked into a small cove against the ocean. It was serene, strong, isolated, and beautiful. The curtain wall was nestled close around the inner keep, and a single, large door stood open on the side opposite the ocean. A pair of soldiers waved down a greeting as they wearily made their way in through the wooden doors.

A young woman came forward to take the horse, and Elizabeth hesitated a moment. "Do you have a separate stable, perhaps one where you keep infirmed horses?"

The woman paused, chewing the edge of her lip in thought. "I suppose there is the small stable alongside the blacksmith, where he keeps horses he is preparing to shoe," she commented.

Elizabeth nodded. "Yes, please stable my horse there," she agreed.

The woman furrowed her brow. "But surely these stables are more comfortable -"

"It would please me to have my horse separate for now," requested Elizabeth firmly.

The woman acquiesced and led the horse across the open courtyard. Then there was a patter of running feet, and a nun came streaming across the grounds, bright red curls escaping from beneath her wimple.

"Claire!" called out Elizabeth in relief, drawing her friend into a warm hug as the woman drew near. They embraced for a long while before Claire drew back to look Elizabeth over critically.

"You poor dear! You look half dead. How long has it been since I saw you?"

"I think ten years, since we were both thirteen," mused Elizabeth. "A lot has happened since then."

"Yes," responded Claire, her voice dropping. "I was so sorry to hear about your brother, Jeffrey. He was a favorite of mine, as you know. A dearer lad could not be found anywhere. You must miss him terribly."

"I do," agreed Elizabeth, a shadow moving over her. He had been her rock, her protector, and now he was gone, and it was all her fault.

Claire drew her into a fresh hug, then looked to the side. "And who is this skeleton figure?"

"Claire, let me introduce you to Michael," offered Elizabeth, forcing a smile back onto her face. "This young lad was my guiding light these past few days."

"It is a pleasure to meet you, Michael," greeted Claire, bending down to shake his hand. "I would have to guess that you are hungry."

"Yes, indeed!" cried out Michael, his face brightening with pleasure.

"Well then," welcomed Claire, drawing an arm around each of them. "Let us get you inside, warmed up, and well fed."

They moved their way across the courtyard with its myriad of out-buildings and shops, then up the steps into the keep proper. The entry hall was laid out with long tables lined with benches. Most tables had already been cleared, and Elizabeth saw the sisters moving to and fro on their various duties, but the head table was still arrayed with a delicious spread of rich cheese, plates of pickles, and bowls of fragrant, warm gruel. Elizabeth dove into her meal the moment she was seated, and Claire laughed with warmth as her two charges devoured the offerings.

Elizabeth's eyes began to droop once she had finished, and she barely knew where Claire was leading her as they headed up a spiral set of stairs. She was taken toward a bed and tumbled into it, sword still on her hip.

* * *

A hand was shaking her awake. The sun was streaming brightly through the window; she guessed it could not be much past noon. She had gotten five hours of sleep at the most.

"What is it?" she murmured groggily.

Claire's voice was low. "You have a visitor."

Elizabeth sprang awake, and in a moment was following Claire over to the window. She had been given a room on the front of the keep, facing over the courtyard. Looking down into its well-lit square, she could see a dappled grey horse held to one side. A well-built man with dark brown hair was standing in the center of the courtyard, his eyes looking carefully over every corner of the area, searching.

Elizabeth quickly drew back from the window.

Claire chuckled. "Not a friend of yours?" she inquired dryly.

"I am not sure," replied Elizabeth warily. "And that enough keeps me from wanting him to know where I am." She brought her eyes to meet Claire's. "I realize you are a nun, but -"

Claire's eyes twinkled. "Say no more," she reassured her friend. "We have plenty of women here who are keeping away from fathers, brothers, and men of all varieties. We have no issue at all with sending them on their way. Let us take care of this for you. We are well practiced in the art."

With a friendly pat, Claire turned, heading from the room. Elizabeth carefully made her way back to the window, peering down. In a moment, Claire walked regally out from the main keep doors. She strode straight up to Richard and began talking with him. Richard seemed to protest, but she was even and firm. He motioned toward the stables, and she shrugged, offering an invitation with the sweep of her hand. He moved at a fast pace, vanishing within for a few minutes.

Finally he emerged, the frustration visible in his tense motions, and he remounted. He pulled his horse in a circle, and his eyes scanned across the buildings ... the windows ... Elizabeth pulled to the side, careful to avoid being seen. When she looked back out again, he was in motion, riding out through the open gates, heading down the coastline.

She watched him go, her shoulders easing in a mixture of relief and curiosity. Just what was it the man was after?

A loud yawn erupted from her mouth, shortly followed by another. She wearily tumbled her way across to the bed. She was impressed that he had managed to track them so quickly, but for now she was safe. And right now, the most important thing she needed was rest.

* * *

Elizabeth blinked awake, the gentle pre-dawn light dancing in through her window, tinting her trunk and low table with streaks of gold. She had slept straight through the day and night, and felt more rested than she had in months. She drew in a long, deep breath, relishing the feeling.

She climbed to her feet, moved to her door, and stepped out into the quiet hallway. She knew from Claire's letters that most of the keep's inhabitants would already be down in the chapel at morning vespers. Still, she kept her movements quiet as she headed down the hall, descended the spiral staircase, and moved out into the dew-laced courtyard. The main gates stood open, and a pair of soldiers waved to her from their watch over its entrance.

She waved back, then headed over to one side where a straw dummy was set up surrounded by a low ring of hay bales. She guessed this was where the small contingent of guards kept themselves in shape during the long, quiet stretches of their assignments here.

She began by doing a series of stretches and lunges, working the kinks and knots out of her muscles. When she was warmed up she began practicing her swordwork. She placed the hilt of the sword at her left hip, striking out left and down at the dummy's right shoulder. Being left-handed, she had a natural advantage against most other fighters. They practiced regularly against other right-handed opponents, but rarely faced a left-handed one. She, on the other hand, had ample experience dealing with right-handed fighters and knew exactly where they tended to have trouble.

She worked for a while on her high, arcing strike, then moved along to the low leg sweep. She drew her focus in, striving to hit the exact point where the blade would carve its way into …

A pair of bright eyes peered over a hay bale to the left, and she pulled in, startled. Michael climbed over the bale, staring at her in fascination. "Could you teach me how to do that?"

Elizabeth's first reaction was to ease him off, to remind him that his stay here would undoubtedly be short, that her own future path was uncertain. But his eyes were so eager, his face so plaintive, that she found she did not have the heart to discourage him.

"I am sure they keep practice swords around here somewhere," she agreed. They dug around in the piles of odd belts and leather which littered the back side of the ring. In a short while Elizabeth emerged with a pair of medium length wooden swords. She handed one to Michael and took the other for herself.

"We start with footwork," she instructed him, and helped him to position the sword at his hip, holding the point forward, aiming at an imaginary opponent's eyes.

"Your feet are the core; they support everything else you do," she instructed him firmly. For a moment she was Michael's age, and her brother was there beside her, his green eyes looking down at her in kindness, his hand rustling through her hair. She blinked away the vision, concentrating on the here and now. "Move the front foot forward a half stride, then bring the back one up to match. Always keep yourself balanced. Now ... advance."

Michael dutifully made a motion forward, his legs wavering.

"Imagine your feet must go straight forward, or straight back," suggested Elizabeth. "You want to maintain your balance. Your stance should not widen or narrow as you move. Now, again. Advance."

Michael moved more steadily, and Elizabeth smiled with approval. "Better," she encouraged. "Advance."

The soldiers on the wall noticed what she was doing and called out praise and suggestions as Michael moved through the basics of advances and retreats, of lunges and fades. Elizabeth found herself enjoying the process, watching as Michael became more sure in his movements, as his stance became more steady, as his head was held more high.

The guard's voice carried clearly across the courtyard. "Hey, down there, visitors," he warned.

Elizabeth dropped the wooden sword, grabbed Michael's arm, and in a moment they were both ensconced behind the back bales of hay, looking out toward the gate. There was a long stretch of time where the sound of hoofbeats grew ever closer, and then a dappled grey horse came in through the gates at a canter, his rider deftly drawing him in to a clattering halt in the center of the area. His eyes swept the courtyard, lingering for a minute on the wooden swords laying in the center of the ring, on Elizabeth's own sword laid carefully on one of the hay bales.

Elizabeth cursed beneath her breath. Damn the man and his sharp eyes.

Claire was walking smoothly out from the keep steps, her voice carrying easily across the courtyard. "What do we have to thank for your return visit, Richard?" she asked calmly.

Richard dismounted, moved forward to stand before her, and dropped his head in a short bow. "My family has been asked by your nunnery several times to open into discussions of patronage," he offered. "John and Ron would like to invite you to attend a dinner tonight, and begin those talks."

Claire's eyes were bright with amusement. "That is indeed a fortuitous invitation," she offered. "I believe tonight's dinner has been planned for several weeks, has it not?"

Elizabeth could not tell if Richard blushed, but his voice held a hint of contriteness. "The guest list has just been finalized," he commented roughly.

He handed a scroll to Claire, and she scanned it, pursing her lips. "It says here that I am allowed to bring one guard with me," she commented at last.

Richard nodded, his eyes glancing around the courtyard. "We would not want to compromise your safety."

"Of course not," returned Claire. "Well then, I shall give the offer some thought."

Richard seemed slightly startled at this response, then bowed. "Of course. We look forward to your presence tonight." He gave one last, long look toward the ring, and then he was wheeling his horse, heading out through the gates and across the coastline.

Claire watched him go for a long while, then she turned and strode across toward the ring. Elizabeth and Michael climbed back over the hay bales, moving to stand with her.

Claire's voice was light with amusement. "We have been attempting to get those two into talks for three years now, ever since their father passed on. The day after you show up on our doorstep, suddenly the invitation is presented to us. Does that seem coincidental to you?"

Elizabeth found she was still staring at the open gates, gazing at where Richard had vanished from view. "I want to go."

"Of course you do," agreed Claire. "But do you think it is wise? Surely we should learn more about what is going on before -"

Elizabeth shook her head. "The sooner we know what is happening, the sooner we can address it," she insisted. "By going disguised as your guard, I can ask questions and get answers that you would not. We can cover twice the ground in half the time."

Claire shrugged. "You were always headstrong, even when we were little," she chuckled. "Let us see what kind of an outfit we can rig up for you before tonight, then. We want to make sure you are properly dressed for your visit."

Chapter 5

The sun was just slipping below the horizon, tingeing the sky with streaks of orange and crimson, as Elizabeth and Claire rode side by side toward the main gates of the keep. Claire's modest garb was matched by Elizabeth's quiet leather gear, a close-fitting leather cap tucked down along her skull, her hair nestled up beneath. A dark cloak completed the outfit, hiding her completely from view.

Claire chuckled. "Here we go," she smiled, the freckles on her face glimmering in the light of the torches, and then they were through the gates, dismounting, handing their reins over to the grooms and heading across the courtyard. The area was gaudily decorated with bright honeybee-yellow banners. They moved up the steps toward the main keep door, and were guided by staff up the spiral staircase toward the dining hall.

They turned the corner and were immediately blasted with the rich aroma of spice, the jangled music of a group of musicians in a far corner, the bright combination of torches and fireplaces and braziers and glowing yellow banners on every wall. The room was crowded with well-to-do nobles, boisterous merchants, watchful guards, and modestly dressed religious folk. Servants weaved dexterously through the mob, delivering plates of fragrant meats.

Elizabeth inhaled deeply, overwhelmed by the cacophony. This was a far cry from her father's austere regime, from the firm grip he held over his own keep.

A shadow moved before them, and Elizabeth dropped her eyes, drawing in the scent of musk, and leather, and that other intangible, tantalizing hint …

"Good evening," welcomed Richard calmly, looking between the two. "I am so glad you could attend tonight."

Claire's eyes sparkled. "Your offer was hard to resist," she responded. "The hospitality of your home is renowned."

"Your guard may sit to the right," he offered, his gaze moving over to Elizabeth.

She resisted the draw to look up, forced herself to nod, to set into motion without being drawn into those emerald oases. She had only ever known two other men with eyes such as those. Why did it seem that in each case it portended some sort of heartache?

She found the table of leather-clad men, settled herself amongst them in the shadows of a corner, nodded in thanks as a mug of ale was set down before her. She sipped at it absently, watching as Claire was brought over to the head table and seated next to John … or was it Ron? She decided that it had to be Ron, the one with the wilder tuft of hair. Neither seemed much changed from the night at the pub. They were laughing with enthusiasm, grabbing at the maids as they passed, and downing prodigious amounts of ale.

Ron nudged against Claire at some sort of jest, and Claire stiffened slightly. Elizabeth dropped her hand to her hilt, her shoulders tensing. It suddenly occurred to her that her role here as guard might be called into actual use. She had thought that, once within the walls, she would be at leisure to -

Ron put his arm on Claire's shoulder, slurring some sort of comment into her ear, and Elizabeth could feel her shiver, feel her pull away. A cold cloak of focus draped over her, narrowed her world down to a pinpoint. The guards were in animated discussion around her, silver platters of chicken and goose were being passed around, but the fragrant aromas barely drew her attention.

Ron's hand slid down Claire's side, then went beneath the table, and Claire's eyes popped wide open. Elizabeth stood with a sudden movement. She'd had quite enough of this. She stepped back over the bench, moving through the crowded room with a firm press of her shoulders, her eyes dark with fury.

Bodies blocked her way and she ground to a halt in frustration, pressing her way between them. She could no longer see where Ron had gotten to. Damn the man. He should be in chains until he was thirty at least. She pressed forward. There was a dark shape before her, and she stepped left, her heartbeat quickening. What was he doing to Claire now? Her way was still blocked. She stepped right. The form before her stepped right. She looked up in exasperation.

Richard was standing there, his gaze steady on hers, his emotions hidden in the depths.

Elizabeth's throat went tight with anger. "Let me pass," she snapped.

"I think we should have a talk outside," returned Richard, his voice low.

Elizabeth glanced up toward the head table, and now both seats were empty. Her heart thudded in a panic. What had the lecher done with her?

She pressed forward. "I have to get to him before -"

"You need to -"

Richard put an arm out to grab her left shoulder.

She sprang back at that, reacting as if an adder had stricken her, her left hand dropping to her sword, pulling it out slightly, releasing it from its lock. The crowd instantly retreated back into a circle with a cry. In a heartbeat Ron was at Richard's side, looking wildly between the two.

"It is her!" he screamed. "Guards, grab her! Throw her into the dungeons!"

The circled crowd was staring at her in a hush, the hilt of the sword was in her hand, and suddenly she was back at the May Day tournament. She was standing in shock as her father had shouted those words in fury, the spittle flying across her face.

Throw her into the dungeons!

At her father's command, the guard she had grown up with, had sparred and laughed with, had instantly clamped his hand on her left arm and shaken loose her sword. He had hauled her down the long, stone stairs and tossed her into the dark, foul-smelling pit of rats and waste. She had been alone ... abandoned ... the silence and misery and dampness driving her absolutely mad.

She had sworn to herself that she would die rather than endure one minute of that again.

"Never," she snarled, drawing her sword in a long flourish. In an instant Richard's was held steadily before her, its point directed at her eyes. She slid her gaze up to his. To her surprise, his eyes held caution, concern.

She pushed the feelings aside. She knew how cold those green marbles could turn. She knew the jagged pain they could inflict. She drew in a deep breath, readying herself for the first strike.

A cool, even voice sounded from over her shoulder. "May I ask just what is going on with my guard? This hardly seems a hospitable way to treat invited guests," suggested Claire in a quiet voice which carried to all corners of the globe.

Ron's screech shook the walls. "It is her! She needs to be wrapped in chains!"

Claire seemed unruffled. "And why might that be?" she asked reasonably.

Ron's voice reached an even higher key. "She killed my mother!"

Elizabeth blinked in surprise. The charge was so wildly unexpected that she bit back the urge to laugh. Given their reaction to her previous episode of mirth at the inn, she doubted it would go over well. Before she could begin to formulate a response, Claire was speaking again.

"I am so sorry for your loss. When was your mother slain?"

Ron looked at her as if she was daft. "On May Day, of course!"

Elizabeth could not help it. May Day. The laughter escaped from her before she could draw it in, bubbling out of her in rich relief. Of all the days for her to be accused of some sort of skulking activity.

Ron's face had boiled over into a deep shade of crimson, and Richard was holding him back forcibly with one arm. Ron's voice cracked as he shouted, "How dare you triumph over -"

"I am not making fun," amended Elizabeth, dragging control over her emotions, taking in a long breath. "It is just that the ridiculous nature of your accusation boggles my mind."

"But you are a left-handed swordswoman," insisted Ron, his eyes bright with fury. "And an auburn one at that! How many of those could there possibly be?"

Richard's voice interjected in a calm tone. "But her eyes are brown," he pointed out. "The witnesses said the woman accused of pushing your mother had ice blue eyes."

Ron shook his head with vehemence. "Those peasants could easily have made a mistake there. What are the chances of two left-handed, auburn swordswomen being in this area?" His eyes burrowed into hers. "Throw her into the dungeons until we can get the peasants here to say for sure."

Elizabeth's fingers wrapped more tightly around the hilt of her sword, but she took in a long, deep breath. Ron's desire to seek justice for his mother was certainly understandable, and she did find the similarity fairly baffling. "Whether there are three or three hundred women like me, I still have an alibi which is unassailable," she countered. "I swear to you - it was not me who harmed your mother."

Ron scoffed. "What kind of alibi could we possibly trust from you?" he snapped.

An odd twinge coursed through her that the scene of her ignominy could now provide some slight benefit to her life. "I was at the May Day tournament in Hawes," she offered simply. "I am sure over five hundred people were there."

Ron's voice was snide. "Oh, and I am sure every one of those people saw you," he accused.

The day flashed into bright relief, and again she heard the roar of the crowd all around her, felt the thick mud beneath her boots, sucking her down, smelled the metallic tang of blood, the rich aroma of sweat and grime and leather. There was a sword swinging high, and the blinding flash of reflected light in her eyes … her foot slipped …

Her hand tensed automatically on her hilt, and Richard's gaze shot to meet hers. His gaze widened in surprised understanding.

"You are Elizabeth of Hawes," he stated, realization flooding over his face. "You came in second."

There was a rolling gasp of noise around her, but Elizabeth could barely hear it. She heard the echo of those same words, *you came in second*, shouted in furious outrage by her father as he stormed across the muddy field, as his mailed hand swung high, slammed down against her head, driving her face-first into the grime and muck.

She blinked, staggered by the force of his blow. After a breath, then two, her world slowly began to draw into focus. Her mind sought to piece together the sounds coming toward her. Her father was shouting his fury to the far corners of the field. She would be thrown into the dungeons. She would be disowned.

She fought against the throbbing of her skull. There had to be a way out. Her eyes sought out Corwin's, to find some small reassurance, some slight support from her fiancé. He was only a few years older than her. Surely he knew what it was to face challenges, to find a way through them.

He was looking at her with cold disapproval. And then, with a sudden motion he was standing, his moss-green eyes as sharp and emotionless as marbles.

Then he was turning his back on her. He stalked out of the stands. He was leaving her ... he was abandoning her to her doom.

Claire's voice was gentle at her side. "Elizabeth ...?"

She shook herself back to the present, to the same green eyes staring at her. She turned sharply, putting them out of sight. Tumultuous emotions swelled within her, and she would be damned if she allowed them to spill from her while surrounded by strangers.

She pushed her way out through the mob and down the stairs. In a moment she was in the stables, snugging her saddle securely on her mount.

Claire was by her in short order. Soon they were riding out at a canter, taking the streaming distance home through the crisp night air.

Chapter 6

The first golden glimmers of dawn were stretching across the courtyard as Elizabeth steadily, methodically reduced the straw dummy into small shards with each swing of her sword. Tension built up within her at each blow, the craving for release, the desperate desire for an easing of the anger, but it never came. Each slash only seemed to reinforce the simmering feelings within her, validate her fury with all the wrongs in her life.

She could see her father's face before her, his cheeks mottled crimson with rage, the spittle flying as he called her a lazy whore, a useless hag, a good-for-nothing female who had caused her own brother's death. The truth of it echoed deep within her soul, and she swung high, arcing circles at the target's shoulder blade, hammering again and again, seeking to sever it completely.

There was a clattering of hooves in the entryway, and she finished her furious swing, noting with satisfaction that only a thin tendril of straw held the arm connected to the body, before turning to see who had come in.

Of course.

Richard sat on his dappled grey, his gaze fixed on hers, his moss green eyes unreadable in the soft morning glow.

He swung off his horse, handed the reins over to the sister who came up to help him, and then strode quickly toward her. His gaze moved between the dummy and her sword before coming back up to meet her eyes. His voice was low and rushed.

"Elizabeth, I want you to know that -"

There was a pounding of hooves from the entry area, and a pair of wild stallions burst into the courtyard, spinning and snorting as their riders struggled to bring them under control. It was a moment before Ron and John could get their steeds to a stop, could prepare to dismount and hand the reins off to a pair of hesitant sisters.

As one they strode over to stand alongside their half-brother, their eyes bright with petulance and anger.

John piped up first. "We were supposed to be included in every step of this process," he insisted. "You should have drawn in and waited for us."

Richard's face shuttered. "You are free to proceed," he offered evenly.

John rounded on Elizabeth, his eyes sharp. "Where is the child you have kidnapped?"

Elizabeth's eyes snapped to meet Richard's; he gave the slightest shake of his head. Anger welled within her at yet another unjust accusation, and she forced it down with determined attention. She needed to figure out what was going on.

"Who is this child?" she asked through clenched teeth.

Ron waved his arms in outrage. "Why Michael, of course, the inn-keep's valuable helper! Hyde depends on him for everything he does. You have cost that man a pretty penny. He wants either the child back or a substantial sum to cover his loss."

Elizabeth's spine hardened. There was no way in hell she would let the child anywhere near that lecher. "You can tell that pig of a man that he can rot in a slaver's hold for all I care," she spat.

Ron's face flared brighter than a full-on sunset. "So you admit you stole the child?"

Elizabeth's hand clenched the sword which still waited ready in her hand. "I admit that man is a swine and no innocent person should be left anywhere near him."

Ron's cheeks mottled with fury, and he could barely speak. "You are resisting my authority?" he screamed, his voice cracking, his hand flailing for his sword, seeking to draw it.

There was a scurry of motion, and suddenly Michael was clambering over the wall of hay bales, running to stand beside Elizabeth. His face was timorous and tight, but he stood tall.

"I do not belong to Hyde," he insisted in a wavering but loud voice. "Hyde offered me food and a bed in return for cleaning the rooms and stables. I accepted. In the two months I stayed in that hell hole, Hyde tried three separate times to climb into bed with me. The last time was a week ago. I left that night and never came back."

Ron stared in disbelief at the thin waif before him. "Hyde would never do that," he insisted hotly. "He gives me free ale whenever I come by. He is a perfect gentleman."

Elizabeth snorted. "And when he lied to Richard, and told him I was not on the premises, the swine then attempted to pressure me into showing my *gratitude* by having me spread my legs," she snapped.

Ron's gaze swung up to meet hers, and something in her eyes made him take in a breath, glance between the two of them. He turned to look up at Richard, and his eyes narrowed as he stared into his face.

"You knew?" he asked his half-brother.

Richard shook his head. "I suspected, but I never had proof. Nobody would come forward against him." His eyes moved up to the woman and child who stood before him. "If you two would -"

"Absolutely," Michael huffed out instantly. "I will shout it from the rooftops, if it will bring him to an end."

Ron turned to look at John, and their faces brightened with fresh glee. "We can go bring him in!" cried out John with delight, and in a moment they were scrambling toward their stabled steeds.

Richard held his gaze on Elizabeth. "I am sorry for what you had to go through," he quietly offered.

Michael's eyes lit up with fierce delight. "You should have seen her," he crowed. "She stood up to that pig. She was a Valkyrie come alive on earth. It was amazing. I never felt as alive as I did in that moment, when she faced off against him."

Richard looked thoughtfully at Elizabeth, and she sensed a hint of pride, of approval in his eyes. "I wish I had been there."

Then he glanced over his shoulder at the noise coming from the stables, and, bowing to the two, turned to quickly join the pair. In a moment, the group was thundering out through the open gateway and down the road.

Claire came up behind Elizabeth and Michael, following their gaze. "I guess they know where you are now," she mused with a half-smile.

Elizabeth found herself looking out to where Richard had vanished from view. She wondered if she were hoping that he would not return again … or that he would.

Lunch was a simple meal of bread and cheese, washed down with freshly made ale from the nunnery's own brewery. Elizabeth tucked a half loaf under her arm and waved her thanks to Claire as she headed out across the courtyard and up the thin flight of stairs that flanked one of the main gates. She worked her way along the top of the wall, nodding at the guards she passed, until she came around to the side facing the ocean.

She sighed with pleasure, leaning against the cool stone. It really was quite a spectacular sight. The water was the dark color of a deep well, with waves rolling in with steady force. It went on as far as the eye could see. She had grown up with hills and vales, where the line of sight was always interrupted. The sense of distance was stunning.

A friendly voice came at her side. "Impressive, yes? Claire tells me you have never seen the sea before now."

Elizabeth turned, nodding to the man before her. He was perhaps in his mid-forties, his dark hair silvering along the temples, but his sturdy build showed he was still quite capable of wielding a sword. "You must be Simon, the captain of the guard."

He nodded, giving a slight bow. "At your service," he agreed. "I have manned these walls for five years now. The lads beneath me come and go, but I like it here. It is quiet and restful."

Elizabeth looked back out at the non-stop march of incoming waves. "It certainly seems peaceful now, but I hear pirates are a constant threat?"

"Yes, certainly," he agreed. "This keep was well constructed, though. They have never breached our walls." He gave a fond pat to the stone before him. "As long as we man them properly, I have faith that the sisters will be safe here for another hundred years."

She smiled at that. "That is quite reassuring. Back home, we would be happy to go ten years without bandits launching an attack on us. They did breach the walls, a few decades ago, but we have made improvements since then. So far, the reinforced defenses have held off all attacks."

Simon nodded. "Claire has told me some of what her childhood was like. A rough area to grow up in."

Elizabeth shrugged. "I imagine no place on earth is ever truly safe from those who would cause harm." She tore a piece of bread off the loaf, offering it to Simon. He took it with a nod.

"Here, watch this," he said, grinning. He ripped a small piece of crust and tossed it off into the air.

A seagull swooped in from nowhere and snagged the piece before it had fallen ten feet. Elizabeth's eyes lit up in delight. "That was amazing," she cried. She pulled a small piece from her own loaf and threw it as hard as she could toward the sea. Another seagull appeared, plucking the bread easily out of the sky.

Elizabeth laughed. "You do have quite a lovely post, I agree. I am glad to see that you are taking such good care of Claire and her flock."

Simon's eyes were serious for a moment. "It is my honor to serve here," he agreed. "I will not let anything happen to your friend."

"I am glad to hear it," returned Elizabeth with warmth. "I will do my best to be helpful during my stay here."

Simon glanced back toward the keep. "I saw you working with the young lad. You have skill, and the boy is picking it up quickly. We will be glad to have your help on the wall, and if you are ever interested in a sparring partner a bit more your own height, just let me know."

"I will," agreed Elizabeth with a smile.

She turned to lean against the sturdy stone, looking out across the vast expanse of ocean. For the first time in a long while, a sense of ease settled into her heart.

* * *

Elizabeth sat up in the early morning light, rubbing the sleep from her eyes, stretching, and climbing out of bed.

She slipped on her dress, strapped on her belt and sword, then made her way down the long spiral stairs. Her feet shuffled, one after the other, as she made her way groggily over toward -

She pulled up to a stop. Richard was sitting on one of the hay bales, a leather jerkin worn over well-fitting leggings, his sword at his side. His eyes held hers with calm regard.

Anger flared through her. What new foolishness was he after today? She stormed over toward him before she could formulate a response, and in an instant he was on his feet, holding out his hands in a placating gesture.

"Peace," he offered, his voice low. "I have come to make amends. These past few days have not gone smoothly. It is clear that you did not deserve what we put you through."

"*That* is for sure," huffed Elizabeth, fury spiking within her, sending a tingling down her fingers, calling her to draw … to draw …

"Your straw dummy is running out of limbs," continued Richard with gentle calm. "Let me offer myself in its place, as an apology."

Elizabeth stared at him as if he were daft. "You want to do *what?*" she burst out.

Michael was over the edge of the hay bale in an instant, looking wildly between the two. "Do not do it, Elizabeth," he insisted with concern.

Richard smiled at that, spreading his hands wide. "I did not quite mean that you should hack me bodily apart," he clarified. "Just that I could help as a target, for you to show blocks and sweeps to your young student here."

Michael's eyes lit up with delight. "Really?"

Richard nodded. "With Elizabeth's permission, of course."

Elizabeth still felt the anger surge through her, although it began to throb with a little less heat. "You would interfere with my lessons," she grumped.

Richard shook his head. "I swear I will only do what you ask, and only in the manner you request of me."

Elizabeth drew her blade, holding it with both hands, moving the blade until the tip drooped over and behind her right shoulder. "So if I were to tell you to deflect from a high left guard ..." She quickly brought the tip up, over, and down hard toward his left shoulder. In an instant he had brought his own sword parallel across the top of his head, lunging to his left, letting her blade slide down its length and skitter off to the side.

Michael's eyes went wide. "That was *amazing*!" he shrieked. "Do that again!"

A flush of warmth swept through her at the heartfelt praise. She looked up to Richard and saw the quiet acknowledgment in his own eyes. She almost smiled back, then reset, her blade laying down against her shoulder blade, and again she dove forward, more quickly this time. Again Richard was in perfect alignment with her swing, catching the blade well clear of his shoulder, sending it safely away and down.

Elizabeth broke the move down into slower sections, and worked with Michael on each part, showing him how to move his feet, how to swing the blade at just the right angle. To her surprise Richard was patient and quiet as she took her time. He seemed perfectly content to stand frozen in place as she circled him with Michael, pointing out the finer points of the defense. She knew his sword was heavy, but his arms did not waver as he held it across his head for the long minutes.

Finally Michael was worn down, his moves lagging, and Elizabeth gave him a fond pat on the back. "You are doing very well," she praised. "We may make a soldier out of you yet."

"I want to be a nunnery guard, like you!" cried Michael with pleasure.

Elizabeth chuckled softly. "I am not quite a nunnery guard," she corrected him gently.

Michael looked up at her in confusion. "Then why are you here?"

I had nowhere else to go.

The thought rang through her head, and her good mood deflated, as hopelessness and despair began to infiltrate again.

Richard's voice was even. "She came because her friend Claire needed help, preparing for the long winter ahead."

Michael's eyes shone. "You are a wonderful friend, to come all this way to help her out," he offered with a wide grin.

Warmth stole back into Elizabeth's heart, and she looked up at Richard with gratitude. His eyes held hers for a long moment, and then he was sheathing his sword.

"If that is all for today, then I am off," he stated, giving a low bow. "I thank you for the enjoyable morning."

Elizabeth found a smile creeping across her face. "Thank you for your help," she responded. "You were indeed far more useful than that straw dummy had been."

"I am glad to hear that," offered Richard, the corner of his mouth quirking into a grin. Then he was turning, heading toward the stables. He mounted his steed and soon he was moving down the path at a canter.

Elizabeth watched him go, and she found herself hoping he would return again tomorrow.

There was a friendly call from the wall, and she smiled, turning to head up and join Simon in the guard's steady watch.

Chapter 7

A nervous flutter of energy danced in Elizabeth's stomach as she pulled on her dress, buckled on her sword, and headed down the quiet spiral staircase. She refused to put a name on it, and yet when she stepped out onto the misty keep steps and saw him standing there waiting for her, his sword at his side, pleasure seeped through her entire being.

Richard nodded. "Good morning," he offered, and the richness of it flowed through her. She realized that it was, against all odds, a wonderful, beautiful morning. Wisps of cloud floated past an azure sky, and her breath came out in white puffs against the crisp chill.

She closed the distance between them with a few quick strides. "Low sweep!" she cried out in delight, pulling her sword free and low and across, and he was there in an instant, sweeping her sword to the side, holding his blade out and ready.

Joy thrilled through her, and she held her sword high, the hilt poised by her right ear.

"Well, come on!" she called out in glee. His eyes were bright with interest; he did not hesitate a moment. In a heartbeat he was in motion, drawing down against her, aiming for her left shoulder, and she danced across the attack, pulling her blade above and left, deflecting his attack down her right arm. He reset in an instant and spun back at her right hip, and she slammed her sword down on his, driving it into the dirt, flipping her blade to pull it in and against his waist as she drove forward and left. His blade came straight up, vertical, blocking the blow solidly, and she leapt back, resetting.

Michael appeared out of nowhere. "God's teeth!" he cried out in amazement, his face alight. "How did you do that?"

Elizabeth's face was wreathed in smiles. "Like this!" She dove in at Richard again, and she was turning, swinging, cascading, and always he was there moving with her, catching the blade, his moves sure, strong. She found herself laughing with delight as he foiled one of her twists, as she nearly got in against his thigh.

The man was simply amazing.

Finally she staggered back, waving to Michael, who came over with the skin of ale. She took a long draw on it, her throat parched. She offered it over to Richard, who took it with a nod, draining a portion down before returning it to her.

At last she smiled over at him. "I suppose we should get to the real purpose of your visit."

"And what do you suppose that might be?" he asked, his eyes twinkling.

She flushed and looked away, gathering up the pair of wooden swords, giving one to Michael, the other to Richard. She put Michael through a series of simple blocks and deflections, watching his actions, trying to focus on adjusting his form. But every time she turned it was Richard's lean body she found her gaze drifting toward, the firm strength in his arms, the steady focus of his gaze.

There was a noise behind her, and she looked up to find that Claire was there with the nun who had greeted her on her arrival. Both women were carrying wooden platters of food.

Claire looked over the group with a chuckle. "Susan and I thought you might be hungry after your long morning," she offered. "Perhaps a picnic in your ring would make the most of this fine afternoon?"

"You are very gracious," offered Richard with a bow. "I appreciate the kindness immensely."

The cheese, pickles, and dried meats were laid out, and in a moment the three sat down to dig into the offerings. Elizabeth noted with a fond smile that Michael was no longer voraciously devouring everything in sight as if it were his last meal on earth. He was still hungry, but eating more regularly brought him a more normal appetite.

Michael spoke between bites of bread. "Even if you do not want to be a nunnery guard," he offered, picking up yesterday's conversation as if not a minute had elapsed, "I think that would be the ideal spot for me. I can think of no better way of life."

"You just want to be surrounded by beautiful women with no other competition for miles," teased Elizabeth with a grin.

Michael flushed at that, and looked down at his meal, suddenly finding great interest in a hunk of cheese there.

Richard's eyes went to Michael and Elizabeth, a growing awareness spreading on his face. Finally he settled his gaze on Michael, and his voice was calm, reassuring.

"Michael, you really should tell her."

Elizabeth looked between them in confusion. "Tell me what?" she asked.

Michael slowly looked up at her, his face a mask of nervous tension. "You promise not to get mad?" he asked in a wavering voice.

Elizabeth blinked. "Of course not," she insisted. "Get mad about what?"

Michael grew pale, but at last he spoke. "I am a girl," the wiry creature finally squeaked out. "My real name is Michelle."

Elizabeth was taken completely off guard. She stared at Michelle, at first telling herself it couldn't be true. However, as she looked more closely at the eyes, the lips, she realized that in the child's prepubescent state it was more than a possibility. If the hair were longer, and a dress was added …

"I had to pretend to be a boy," Michelle spilled into the quiet void which had resulted from her confession. "It was the only way to be safe on my own. Nobody looks twice at a boy running around loose."

Richard's low voice chimed in. "When I went to find records for an orphaned child during the past year, I could find no boy," he explained. "I did, however, find a girl whose parents both died of a weeping sickness about eight months ago. She had supposedly been sent to live with a distant uncle, but there was no indication that she had ever arrived."

"The man was a lecher," snapped Michelle coldly. "I had only seen him once in my life, and once was enough. There was no way I was going to live in his house."

Elizabeth nodded. "Of course," she agreed, wrapping her mind around this new twist. "I am just surprised that I never noticed, all these days! I would have thought that something would have given you away."

Michelle shrugged, going back to gnaw on one of the hunks of cheese. "People see what they expect to see," she mused. "They expect to see a rag-a-muffin boy climbing about in pants, and they take it for granted."

"God's toenails, but you are right," laughed Elizabeth, giving her a toast with the skin of ale. "Good for you for finding a way to succeed on your own terms."

Two pairs of eyes swiveled to meet hers, and Michelle burst out in giggles. "God's toenails? What kind of a silly phrase is that?"

Elizabeth blushed. "It was a saying I picked up," she hesitantly admitted. "So many people say 'God's Teeth', that it seemed amusing."

Michelle was still chortling. "God's toenails," she repeated with a snort.

Richard's look was more serious, and Elizabeth worried that she had offended him somehow. "I only meant -"

Richard drew himself back from wherever his mind had drifted. "You meant that our lass is a brave girl," he agreed, and the trio gave a toast under the warm morning sun.

Chapter 8

Elizabeth found herself rolling out of bed the following morning with a smile, her fingers flying as she worked the buckle on her sword belt, as she ran a quick hand through her hair, then slipped down the stairs and came out to the keep steps.

He was there, that quiet smile on his face as he stood, ready, at the center of the ring. She strode over to meet him, drew her sword out into a salute, nodded as he returned it. Her feet went into motion as she began circling around the edge of the ring, and he matched her, holding his eyes on hers, waiting for her to make the first move.

She knew he had been holding back, had been staying at the level presented, and she smiled. Despite Michelle's delight, she had only been demonstrating simple deflections and blocks yesterday, giving her young student a taste of what she could attain soon. She wanted Michelle to see what the moves she was learning could be used for.

Now it was time to have a little more fun.

She spun her sword high and over, aiming for his left shoulder blade. He blocked, and she dove for his left waist. He deflected, and she sliced up from below at his left calf. He faded back with a leap, and she moved to start at his right shoulder blade. Block. Right waist. Deflection. She twisted her shoulders as if she was going to begin the sweep for his right calf, and his hands, his sword moved down to match.

She lunged forward, turning her hips, whipping the tip of the blade around, rotating it as she went so the flat of the blade would connect. There was no way he could -

Slam. His blade barely caught up with hers, but it was there, sending hers skittering to the side. She leapt back to give herself space, her mouth hanging open in surprise.

God's teeth, this man was amazing.

He smiled at her expression, gave the sword a spin to limber his wrist, then settled back into a low guard. She could see it in his eyes, in the way they shone, that he wanted more.

Here we go.

Then she was in motion, slicing high, drawing him into a deflection, wrapping her blade around his, and he ducked beneath the counter-cut, bringing his sword across to aim for her stomach. She leapt backwards, then instantly forward again, driving her sword down against his left calf, working on his weak side. Usually her opponents were slower here, and her left handedness brought her a sizeable advantage, but Richard was there each time, his blade securely in position, his arms barely flinching as he absorbed the blow, turned his blade to retaliate.

She lost track of time, of place, of everything except Richard's green eyes holding hers, of the lean of his shoulder, of the tremor of motion which ran along his bicep as he blocked, of the wrap of his fingers as he spun his blade to deflect her lunge.

She sought for the tell. So many fighters had one. They reseated their hand slightly before beginning an upper cut, they flexed their foot an infinitesimal amount before making that forward lunge. But with Richard, he seemed flawless. Nothing she did could draw him out of his easy response, his sure grace.

The morning sun slid the final inch over the keep wall and suddenly she had the full force of its glare in her eyes. She turned her head sharply, trying to track Richard's blade by its sound, twisting, and he pulled in roughly to avoid the hit. Her arm collided with his and she lost her balance, tumbling to the ground. The ring she wore on a chain around her neck spilled from beneath her chemise.

Richard was kneeling at her side in a heartbeat. "Elizabeth, are you all right?" He helped her to a sitting position. Michelle scampered over from where she had been watching behind the bales, looking her over.

"I am fine," Elizabeth promised them, bringing herself to standing, wiping the dirt from her dress. "If I ended a sparring practice without raised welts, my father would consider that time ill spent."

Richard pressed his lips together at that, but Michelle interrupted with bright interest. "Whose ring is that?"

Elizabeth flushed, looking down, and with a quick motion tucked the item back beneath her inner layer. "Time to get you practicing, before we lose the entire morning," she offered gruffly, putting her sword aside on one of the bales, taking up the two wooden ones instead. "Today we look at attacking on a diagonal."

Richard's eyes were near her throat, looking at where the ring had slipped, but he did not say a word. He took up the wooden sword and began moving through the drills with Michelle.

The ring against her chest seemed to have blazed into fiery heat. Over the past six months there were times she almost forgot it was there. Then other times it seemed a heavy weight, one which would drag her down into the darkest of depths. Now it seemed the tip of an iron-hot poker, searing at her, reminding her of the pain she had suffered.

Her hand almost went to it, to reassure her that it was the same cold, metal circle it had always been. She forced her hand to stay in place, to focus on the pair before her.

Then Claire and Susan were bringing out their lunch, along with three mugs of cider. They settled in on the fragrant bales of hay, and she cut even squares of her cheese, moving each into her mouth with careful attention. She could still feel the white-hot metal burning as if -

Michelle's voice rung in her distraction. "Really, Elizabeth, what is that ring?"

That girl was as tenacious as a wolf stalking a wounded doe.

Before she could rein it in, she found her hand moving to press against her chest, feeling its metallic presence, cold and dead. Finally she looked up at the pair. Both were holding her gaze with quiet curiosity.

"It is … was … my engagement ring," she admitted.

Michelle's eyes widened with shocked delight, but Richard's became distant, separated, and for a long moment he did not speak. Finally he asked, "you are spoken for?"

She shook her head, finding herself unwilling to look in those moss green eyes, turning instead to Michelle.

The girl's gaze was bright with interest. "Tell me everything," she insisted. "Did you have many suitors?"

Elizabeth snorted, taking a long draw on her cider. "Suitors," she repeated, putting a heavy dose of sarcasm into the word. "When my father put me on the market at age sixteen, it was the same thing every time. Every. Single. Time. The man would ride in mid-day, and I would be in my gear, sparring. The man would look at me with a gaze of utter disgust, but then I could watch as the avarice won over, pushed away those first impressions and molded his face into one of appreciation."

She took another long pull. "It got to be a game with me, to see how long it took before the eyes moved from one emotion to another. I would see if certain sword moves caused a greater reaction." She chuckled low. "The groin thrust seemed to be particularly effective in that area."

"I bet it was," chortled Michelle, her eyes bright. "So then what happened?"

Elizabeth looked down into her cider. What had happened indeed. She had seen those moss green eyes, so like her beloved brother's, and all sense had fled her mind. She decided that she had waited long enough, and that choosing someone at all had to be better than this endless round of feeling like one of the cattle at a market.

"After five years, Corwin arrived at our keep. He was good with a sword. He seemed interested in sparring with me, in testing and improving my skills. My father heartily approved of him. So, after six months of courting me, he proposed." She glanced down at where the ring lay. "I accepted."

Michelle was transfixed. "Was it romantic? Did he pledge his undying love?"

Elizabeth downed the rest of her cider. "Real life is not like that," she sharply corrected Michelle. "Marriage is a business transaction. Corwin and my father spent many long hours working out the precise details of my dowry. When they were done, they spent the remaining long hours drinking themselves into oblivion and congratulating each other on a deal well made."

Michelle seemed unperturbed. "Still, you must have felt *something* for him," she prodded, "to accept him after turning all those others down. Where is he now?"

A knife twisted in her stomach. She reached for her mug, found it empty, and Richard was offering his own without a word. She drew down a third of it, the welcome warmth easing within her.

"That May Day tournament," she stated quietly, grinding the toe of her boot in the dirt, "I was sprawled face down in the mud. I had just been defeated, and my father in his fury had laid me out. He announced to the stands that he was completely disowning me."

She could still feel the power of the moment, the taste of blood in her mouth, the shooting pain in her side, the sticky texture of the mud against her cheek and neck.

Her voice trembled. "I looked up for the one man I could rely on. The one man who would stay by my side; the only one since my brother Jeffrey who I could trust."

Her mouth quirked at the memory, seared into her brain. "He was looking at me, all right. His eyes held that same mixture of disgust and greed that every other suitor's had, and mixed in was the strongest of disappointment. Then he stood, turned his back on me, and strode out of the stands."

Michelle's voice was a whisper of shock. "He left you there to lie in the mud?"

Elizabeth downed another long draw of her cider, and her voice became guttural. "He left me to rot in the prisons, which is where my father had me tossed. They are the darkest depths of hell, with not a glimmer of light, not a hint of fresh air. It was a week before I could cajole one of the guards to let me into the hall to stretch my legs. Another week before my walks included the whole floor. A third week before I was allowed near the stairs."

Her eyes shone as she remembered her escape. "Once there, I had my hands on a dagger, then a sword, and then I was in flight. I had a small bag packed with my horse at all times."

Michelle was staring at her, transfixed. "Where did you go?"

Elizabeth smiled. "Once outside the keep walls, I moved from house to house to stay ahead of my father's fury. I had numerous friends in the tournament circuit willing to lend a hand. I was waylaid out on the western coast, but then kind strangers took me in and equipped me afresh."

She nudged her head toward the walls. "I had heard that Claire needed assistance, and here I am."

Michelle's eyes looked down toward the ring. "But if your betrothed was so cruel to you, and abandoned you like that, why do you still wear his token?"

Elizabeth's hand went again to the round metal, and she cynically chuckled. "Maybe to remind myself never to go through that agony again."

Michelle's voice was a squeak. "Really?"

Elizabeth shook her head. "No. I wear it because I want to find Corwin, to hand it back to him personally, and to tell him he did not break me. That it was better I discovered his true nature before I was irrevocably forced to remain by his side. That I have grown, and changed, and that I do not need to settle for men like him any more. I am no longer any man's chattel."

Michelle's eyes were shining. "You are my hero," she sighed. "I want to be you when I grow up."

Elizabeth drained the cider, stood, and looked down at the innocent girl with her too-short hair and her dusty men's clothing. "No, you do not," she warned the lass. "You do not want to be anything like me."

She could not bring herself to look at Richard, to see the pity or disgust or disapproval which could be showing in his face. She turned, taking the narrow stairs by the main gates in long strides, not stopping as she reached the top.

She strode along the wall to the back of the keep. She leant heavily against the sturdy stone, staring out at the distant horizon, becoming lost in the rhythm of the never-ending cascade of waves.

Chapter 9

Twists of unsettled feelings ran through Elizabeth as she rose in the pre-dawn softness. She carefully buckled on her sword belt and slid the familiar length of steel into its scabbard. She stood before the window for a long while, brushing her hair with slow, thorough motions, finally drawing herself to plait it into a braid.

She had no idea how Richard had reacted to her flustered eruption. She knew she should have said nothing, but the words had burst out of her before she could stop them. The emotions had been burning a hole within her brain just as the ring had been searing a hole into her chest.

The tale had been told. It could not be drawn back in now.

She sighed. If he was not waiting for her below, then maybe it was fate warning her that she was not intended for any man. Maybe this, too, was a way to learn of a man's failures before she became too fond of him. Maybe it would be better if the sparring ring were empty when she walked out into the gentle golden glow.

She forced herself to believe that, to anticipate it, to look forward to the empty sparring area. Now she could focus on working with Michelle, two women against the world. They could stay here at the nunnery together, taking their turns on the walls, keeping an eye out for danger, escorting the sisters on their various trips. It would be fine. It had to be fine.

She came to the end of the spiral stairs. Her steps slowed as she came out to the keep doors, pressed them open, stepped out into the grey light ...

He was there.

A wave of relief flooded over her so powerfully that she drew to a stop, caught in his moss-green gaze, and the corners of his mouth turned up in an understanding smile. She drew in a breath, stepping into motion again, coming down to stand before him, to look up at him, her eyes shining.

"You came back," she found herself saying before she could rein in the words.

He ran his eyes down her form, lingering on the sword, and then returned his gaze to hers, his eyes steady.

"Yes. Always."

His words were a vow.

A burst of joy spread from her very core, and she was drawing, saluting, swinging into action, but not with a drive to best him, simply with the delight of moving, of dancing, of weaving in and out, of lunging and retreating. He was there with her at every motion, his eyes on hers, his mouth relaxing into a smile. She threw her head back and laughed out loud. His face warmed, he eased up for a moment, and then they were spinning, weaving, dancing in the morning light.

Elizabeth's eyes twinkled as she retreated and looked him over. He had handled everything she'd thrown at him, but she had one more trick up her sleeve. The twisting undercut Corwin had taught her had been useful in numerous matches.

She circled slowly, balancing the distance, watching for just the right combination of stance and light and hold. It was coming ... now!

She drove in hard, her hilt high, the sword tip down, then leant in, rotating it out, spinning it high and around and down to …

SLAM. His blade was there, in place, solidly, and her mouth fell open in shock. How in the world could he have been so ready for that?

He stepped back, his eyes sharp on her. "How -"

There was a clattering of hoofbeats on the cobblestone, and Elizabeth spun in surprise as the twins came barreling in on their stallions, heaving hard on the reins to draw them in. The steeds circled and stamped as they settled down. The men clambered off, tossing their reins to the sister who scurried out to meet them, then turned as one to stare at her, their eyes drawing down her form, staring with open interest at the sword in her hand.

She could see it in their faces. Their looks went through incredulity, a shade of distaste, an edge of disapproval, and then, coming in stronger and stronger waves, the bright gleam of avarice.

There was a movement at the front of the keep, and Claire was sweeping her way down the stairs, moving to stand before them. Elizabeth found that her feet were in motion before she had conscious thought of joining them, and in a few long strides she had come up to the group, Richard close at her shoulder.

John was talking animatedly. "... and with our previous session with you being cut short, we felt it only proper to invite you back out for a quieter dinner. This time we could truly put the effort into discussing the patronage you had been interested in. We hoped tonight might be convenient?"

Claire's mouth tweaked into a faint smile. "Tonight, you say? That is rather sudden."

Ron burst in. "We should have invited you back sooner, we realize that," he wheedled. "We have been busy hauling in the lecher Hyde. We are sorry for not coming to apologize before now."

John's eyes sidled over to Elizabeth, his gaze going to the sword still in her hand, before returning to look at Claire. "And, of course, your companion is quite welcome to come. This time she may wear more appropriate clothing, of course. No need for her to hide in that rough disguise at our home. We would be honored to have her as well."

Ron chimed in at once. "Yes, quite honored," he chorused, eyes gleaming.

Claire's voice was even. "That would be up to Elizabeth."

All eyes swiveled to her. A roil of confusion and fury and frustration swirled within Elizabeth's chest. This had to be the work of her father. Only he could turn her world upside down like this, wreak havoc just when she thought she had escaped him. She had a mind to scream at the men to go away, to leave her in peace, to turn away with their eyes that judged and found her wanting.

She drew in a deep breath. She knew how important this patronage was for Claire. If she could help be a part of making it happen, then she would do that. Besides, she was curious just what her father was up to. Hopefully by the end of the evening she could pry the details out of these two jokers and map out a counter-plan.

"I am free," she responded shortly, nodding to Claire.

The twins' eyes lit up with delight. "Perfect!" cried Ron, giving a sweeping bow to both women. "Just after sunset then? We shall see you soon!" They turned and raced each other to the stables. In a few minutes they were streaming out through the gates, calling out with their delighted enthusiasm.

Claire turned her gaze to Elizabeth with bright curiosity. "Just what was *that* all about?"

Elizabeth had a sense that she knew *exactly* what that was all about. She turned sharply, striding toward the straw dummy which hung limply to one side of the ring. She gave a swirl to her sword, loosening her wrist, and then she launched a high attack down at the creature's shoulder blade.

SNAP - she severed the arm, watched it fall into the mud, and a shaft of angry joy burst through her. That was for her father. She whirled the sword above her head, then landed the blade hard against the other shoulder, hacking her way through the shoulder, visualizing him ... the fury building ...

"Does that help?" asked a calm voice by her side.

She slammed her blade down into the shoulder, feeling it sink in half way, relishing the surge of anger and release and power cascade through her. "Yes," she ground out gutturally, pulling the sword free, staring at the stray bits of straw and twine.

"How does it make you feel?" he asked quietly, not judging.

"Furious," she snapped, spinning the sword high over her head, bringing it down with a gratifying *thunk*. Bits of straw spewed in a fountain.

"And you want to feel furious?" he pursued.

"No," she retorted as if he was daft. She wound up again, slamming the blade down into the shoulder joint. She was nearly separating it now, nearly ripping the man apart.

"When you are done dismembering this thing, what do you think you will feel then?"

She spun to face him, annoyed with all the questions. She just wanted to destroy, to maim, to drive away the pain which throbbed through her. "I will be exhausted, and frustrated, and spent, and what the Hell is it that you want from me?"

"Follow me," he replied simply, then turned and began walking toward the main gate of the curtain wall.

Elizabeth stared after him open mouthed, shaken out of her focus, and after a moment she found herself following behind him, half angry, half curious.

Richard didn't look back as he passed through the gate, made his way through the grassy tufts of a path which led along the outer wall and around toward the ocean side. He crested the small rise, and they were descending through the brush and sandy soil until they reached the quiet beach. The ocean waves rolled in, easing out, and a small group of shore birds were dancing at the water's edge, their short legs moving in quick rhythm as they skittered along each wave, following the movement.

Richard settled himself down in the sand, facing out at the ocean. Elizabeth looked at him in disbelief, but he did not say anything further. After a moment she felt foolish just standing there, so she slid her sword into its scabbard, then plunked herself roughly down beside him.

"Now what," she snapped grumpily.

"Breathe in," he suggested calmly.

Elizabeth almost laughed. The man was clearly daft. She wanted to hurt, to destroy, to bash out her rage on innocent objects. And here he wanted her to breathe? Well, she would prove to him just how wrong he was. She glared at him and drew in an exaggerated long, deep breath, filling her lungs as fully as she could.

The scent of rich salt air filled her, the tang of the sandy soil, the faint fragrance of the wild roses which edged the water. She heard more clearly the soft peep of the scattering birds as they followed the waves, their small feet moving in rapid steps, watching for small bugs to eat with apparent delight.

"Now let it out," came the soothing voice at her side.

She released the air, feeling it ease out of her, feeling her shoulders relax, her spine ease, the muscles unclench as her body drew in on itself. The whoosh of the ocean waves filled her ears, and the soft sand beneath her cradled her gently.

"Breathe in."

She drew in the breath, longer than before. The air pressed out her chest, filled her soul. It was as if a cleansing force were drawing through her bones, scrubbing her clean, shaking loose the dirt and darkness that dwelled there. She took in air until she was completely full, and then she held it, almost floating up off the dense sand.

"Breathe out."

She released, and her body eased, the toxins were swirling and departing, the stress was sliding from her muscles, and she was buoyant, cleansed. It was as if she were a child again, somersaulting with glee through a pile of autumn leaves, or sluicing through the fresh water of the fish pond on a glorious summer afternoon.

"Breathe in."

His voice was barely a whisper now, a hum at the edge of her consciousness, and it blended in with the rolling susurration of the waves, with the gentle pressure of the sand beneath her, with the call of a seagull as it soared high above, changing direction with the barest movement of its wing tips. Each breath seemed longer than the last. Each seemed to latch onto hidden remnants of darkness and grime within her, to gather it up in a golden light, to release it with gentle understanding on the next exhale.

The minutes drifted on, and she lost all sense of place and time. She was renewing, refreshing, restoring, the waves a constant presence. Richard's warmth by her side was her steady rock, a sturdy promise that she would be safe. She was more alive than she had in years, more aware of all that was around her, more at peace with herself.

Richard's voice, gentle and low, drifted into her cocoon. "How do you feel?" he asked, almost tenderly.

Elizabeth was at a loss for words. She was not sure she had ever felt like this before. She searched her mind for an appropriate response.

"I feel ... utterly content," she finally offered, feeling that even that phrase could not adequately explain her frame of mind.

He was standing, putting a hand down to her, and she accepted it, awash with the strength and sureness in his grasp as he easily lifted her to her feet. She found she could not draw her hand free once she was settled, that she was soothed by the texture of his fingers around hers, by the warmth, by the strength there. He smiled gently, and then he turned, leading her back toward the keep. She wrapped her fingers more tightly against his, remaining at his side.

They came in through the gates, and he slowed as he neared the stables. She turned to gaze up at him, and was caught by the look in his eyes, a mixture of tenderness and pride and something gentler as well.

"I will be back at twilight to escort you both to the keep," he offered in a low voice.

"As you wish," agreed Elizabeth, a hitch twinging her heart at the thought of him leaving her now.

He smiled then, lowering his head to her hand, pressing the softest of kisses against it. The sensation thrilled through her, coursed through her veins, sending sparks of delight into her fingers and toes. Then he was turning, striding into the stables, and a moment later he was heading out through the gates, fading into the distance.

* * *

Elizabeth smoothed down her deep purple dress for what must have been the eightieth time. It was the only other outfit she had brought with her on her departure, the one nice dress she owned. It had been made for her engagement party with Corwin, done in his favorite color. Her father, pleased with her long-awaited marriage, had spared no expense on its creation. It fit her curves perfectly, tracing its way along her hips and spreading out in soft waves around her ankles. A delicate constellation of embroidered wildflowers skimmed along her neckline and hem.

She had been scrubbed, rinsed, brushed, and braided by the sisters who took great delight in the process. Now she stood alongside Michelle and Claire on the keep steps, watching as the streaks of orange drifted across the sky.

Michelle's eyes were alight in excitement. "You look beautiful," she whispered. "I wish I could go with you."

Elizabeth glowed with the praise, and a skittering of nervous energy swirled in the pit of her stomach. So many times she had willfully pushed off any attempt to neaten her appearance. And here she was -

There was a movement by the gates, and Richard trotted in on his steed, dressed in a dark brown tunic, his dense hair skimming his shoulders. A wave of pride and desire swept through her. His eyes came up to meet hers, and he drew in a long breath, his gaze fixed on hers, pulling on his reins absently, seeming to barely notice as his horse drew in to a stop. He dismounted, left the reins, and moved up to the trio, his eyes locked on Elizabeth's.

"You are a vision," he breathed out, and Elizabeth was not sure if he realized that he had spoken the words aloud.

Elizabeth reached her hand toward him, and he took it gently, bringing his head down to meet it, pressing his lips. Warmth spread through her, along with a sense of joy, of completion.

Claire's voice was low at her side. "Michelle, why not go bring our horses out." In a moment the girl was scampering toward the stables. Elizabeth barely noticed the movement. Richard was drawing her down the stairs, and she went alongside him, her hand still in his, breathing in his rich scent as the sky drifted into reds and crimsons.

"That dress," he offered in a low voice. "The color ... it is stunning on you."

Elizabeth flushed brightly, and she turned away, grateful that Michelle had arrived with the steeds, giving her something to focus on. He was at her side, helping her up into her saddle, and then the three of them were mounted, heading out together through the gates.

Claire's voice slid into her awareness. "I think I will ride ahead of you two, so you can keep an eye on me," she offered. With a gentle prod her horse was soon in the lead, and Elizabeth and Richard were riding side by side, their horses ambling through the approaching dusk.

Richard's gaze was warm on her, and his eyes slid down her dress, pausing as they looked at her saddle. "The leatherwork on your saddle is exquisite," he commented. "There are wildflowers there, too. Did you have the saddle made to match the dress?"

Elizabeth chuckled softly. "The other way around," she conceded. "This is the only fine dress I own, while I made this saddle years ago."

His eyes came back to meet hers, widening in surprise. "You made your saddle?"

"Not the whole thing," amended Elizabeth promptly. "I designed the leatherwork part of it. A craftsman at my father's keep handled the basic construction, but I did the carving and imprinting to shape it, sew it, and work the design into it."

"That is an exceptional talent," offered Richard in a rich voice.

Elizabeth blushed again. "Most men would say that embroidery was more fitting for a female to take on. But I always wanted to do whatever my brother did. He was my idol; I absolutely worshiped him."

Richard's eyes were tender. "Tell me about your brother," he encouraged.

Warmth eased through her as she thought of Jeffrey. "He was five years my senior, and the most amazing man in the world," she reminisced. "He was my guardian angel, mentor, playmate, and so much more. The minute he picked up a sword, I wanted to have one as well. When he took on an apprenticeship with the leather worker, I was at his side every minute, working with the scraps they would drop. It did not matter what he was doing. I wanted to be there with him."

"He sounds like a paragon of a brother," murmured Richard.

Time slipped away from her, and she was young again, basking in the warmth of Jeffrey's love, feeling his sure hand holding hers. "He was always there to defend me from my father, always quick to speak up in my defense," she murmured. "If I was feeling hurt, or sad, just one look at those moss green eyes of his and I knew everything would be all right. I was blissfully happy, until -"

The shaft of pain pierced her heart as if his death had happened just yesterday. The dense blackness closed in, and Richard rode at her side, not prodding, not asking, simply lending her strength with his presence.

Finally Elizabeth felt able to continue. "I had just turned thirteen, and my father was becoming more insistent that I leave off with my swordplay and other interests so I could focus on cultivating more marriageable skills. He told me it was my duty as his daughter.

Her mouth quirked up in a wry grin. "My brother defended me, of course. He blocked my father's efforts at every turn."

Her throat grew tight. "My father had finally had enough of this. My father sneered at Jeffrey; told my brother he was wrapped around my finger and that he needed to become a man. He forced my brother to volunteer in the King's guard. My father sent him off packing with a group which was heading through France."

Her eyes welled, and she forced the tears away. "I still remember the day Jeffrey rode out. He made me promise to stay true to my heart and to pursue the dreams I held within me. He promised to come home to me soon. Then he moved out through our main gates, and he was gone."

The dusk was drifting into darkness, and the deep, inky night wrapped into a thick blanket around her, muffling her.

Again Richard did not ask, did not push, simply remained by her side, patient to wait while she took in long, deep breaths.

"It was two months later when the message arrived at the house. I was out sparring with one of the guards when my father strode into the courtyard, his face mottled with fury. He grabbed up the quarter staff that one of the men was holding, drew down on me, and swung it with all his might at my right arm. The bone snapped as he hit. The ground came up to slam into my body, but I think the shock of it held off the pain. I could only stare up at him in confusion."

She could still feel the stunned paralysis that enveloped her. "He screamed down at me that it was my fault, that I had better become the best fighter in the land, because now it was all up to me. His rage and disbelief and fury were all focused down on me. It was as if he were drilling a hole through my skull, sending a stream of venom directly into my heart."

Elizabeth could still hear the echoes of her father's harsh words, but was no longer surprised by the way they rang ceaselessly in her ears.

You killed my Jeffrey.

She could only whisper the words now, and even so her eyes welled with tears. She shuddered with how the four words had slammed into her with the force of a stampeding bull. The pain in her arm had throbbed into fury. She had begun screaming, screaming, her world crashing to a halt around her. Amidst it all her father had turned, stalked off, leaving her writhing on the courtyard floor, utterly alone.

A hand was twining into hers, and she realized that tears were streaming down her face. She brushed them away with her sleeve, feeling the warmth of his fingers, drawing strength from his presence.

Finally she was able to bring her breathing under control. "After that, there was no question about my swordplay," she offered. "He pushed me every day to perfect my skills, and personally oversaw some of the sessions. My arm was barely healed when he fractured my calf, and then it was a twisted ankle, a dislocated shoulder blade. He pushed me ever harder, never letting up. The best I could hope for was a slight abatement of his fury, a gentler hit when I had performed to his satisfaction."

"You came to find his attacks were the only form of attention you would receive," mused Richard, his voice rough.

"I suppose so," agreed Elizabeth. "There was no one else left. My mother had died in childbirth when I was barely able to walk, and I had no one else to turn to. My whole life became a vain quest to meet his exorbitant expectations."

She looked out into the inky blackness ahead. "When I came of age, he decided I was ready to be courted. He seemed surprised at first that men were upset by my skills with a sword, and his fury turned on me, redoubled. He felt I was not good enough; that they were upset because I was still inadequate in my abilities. He trebled the pressure on me, pushing me morning, noon, and night to improve."

She drew in a long breath. "He entered me in tournaments to prove to the world that I was a prize worth capturing. Even when Corwin had agreed to his terms, he did not feel satisfied. He felt the May Day tournament was necessary to prove I was the ultimate catch."

Richard's voice was low. "You did come in second," he offered.

Elizabeth's heart dropped into a black chasm. Her jaw ached with the power of her father's fist; her ribs throbbed with the slam of the ground into her body. "Second," she echoed, her voice hollow.

Richard's hand was warm on hers, and she was bolstered by the strength flowing through it. His voice was low but sure. "Coming in second in a field of seasoned soldiers is a feat to be proud of."

She turned then, bringing her gaze to meet his eyes, and she was lost in their depths. There was a distant thawing in her core, the tenuous melting of an inner reserve.

A row of torches came into view, and she looked away, bringing herself back to reality.

Soon they were moving beneath the keep's outer wall, drawing to a halt, and a trio of servants came forward to take their reins, help them down. Then they were making their way up the steps and into the main hall. It was more sedate than the last time, with perhaps half the tables occupied by staff and soldiers. Ron and John were waiting at the head table and waved the group over with excited delight.

"There you are," called out Ron. "You are right on time. Come, join us!"

The two brothers seated Claire between them at the head table, placing Elizabeth immediately opposite them. Richard sat himself to her right, and in a moment servants bustled to and fro, setting down mugs of mead, baskets of rosy apples, wooden platters of steaming duck.

The two men began making polite conversation with Claire. Elizabeth let the words roll beyond her awareness, watching their sidelong glances at her as they inquired about the welfare of the sisters, as they discussed the general gossip of the town. Finally Elizabeth could not take it any more.

"So. What did my father say?" she snapped out.

All eyes turned to her, and a shaft of fury drove through her at the inanities that were being laid out. "Surely you got a message from him," she continued harshly. "Just tell me what it said." Her eyes narrowed. Maybe these twits worked better with carrots. "When I hear the news from someone else, *they* will be the one to receive my full thanks."

Ron and John tumbled over each other to be the first to share the details.

"He said he reinstated you as his heir," sputtered one.

"After long and deliberate thought," chimed in the other.

"But you need to return home soon," they both finished, nearly in unison.

Elizabeth snorted, taking a long draw of her mead. "Of course I do," she grumbled. "He wants me back under his thumb as quickly as possible."

John's eyes widened in surprise. "But he is your *father*," he argued in disbelief. "Surely this is wonderful news, that he is welcoming you back into his fold?"

Elizabeth's eyes blazed. "As he is the one who nearly broke me while driving me out, I hardly find that welcoming."

Ron's eyes creased with confusion. "He was angry!" he called out, as if it explained everything. "People get angry. He has gotten over it, and now he wants you back."

"As he might want back a prize heifer who had run from his whip," snapped Elizabeth.

Claire's voice was warm and rich over the table. "Here comes the apple tart, and what a delicious aroma," she commented with delight. "Shall we enjoy this before it cools?"

All eyes turned to the approaching servants, and the conversation hushed as the dessert was distributed. Elizabeth fought to hold her tongue. She had already ruined one evening for Claire. She owed it to her to allow this night to finish in peace.

She managed to stay silent during the closing conversation, during the goodbyes, as they headed out to the stables. However, as the trio passed beneath the arches and headed out into the inky night, the last of her reserves unraveled. She barely saw as Claire again moved ahead of her. Her limits had been more than reached; the fasteners on her mouth ripped off due to stresses far beyond their endurance.

"And he reaches out his hands to interfere with me *here*, after I had finally escaped his grimy grasp?" she ground out, bursting out loud with the running dialogue which had circled her mind for half of the evening. "I had at last found some small haven of quiet, and his corrosive breath has to contaminate me even here?"

Richard looked over, his eyes gentle. "It is only whispers he can send toward you," he soothed. "You control your own destiny."

"Hah," snorted Elizabeth, her fury cascading into ever larger waves. "He contaminates everything he draws into contact with. You saw how your brothers turned into the mirror image of the suitors I had dealt with. Disgust and greed. Disapproval and avarice. How soon until a fresh flood of carrion beetles wash over me here, drowning me in their reproach?"

Richard's presence was calm at her side. "The world can be full of wolves and blizzards, of plagues and lightning storms," he mused. "Through it all, we always have control over our choices and actions. Whatever the world throws at us, we have the final say."

Roiling darkness drew in around her, and she did not answer.

Chapter 10

Elizabeth spun into a high block, the warm morning sun beaming down on her, the freshness of the air thrilling through her lungs. The sturdy ground was solid beneath her feet, the firm wrap of her hilt was steady in her grasp, and there was nothing more she could want out of life. Richard's sword rang strongly against her own, and she laughed in delight, leaping back a step, reseating herself on the balls of her feet before lunging in toward his calf. She would get him one of these turns. If only she could twist, could just get him to -

There was the clicking of light hooves on the cobblestones, and she drew up in annoyance. If it was those twin twits ...

But no, it was a dandy in light sea-green, a high feather in his hat, his pale brown hair arrayed in elaborate curls. The sword at his hip seemed more for decoration than anything else, judging by the lack of wear along its length. His eyes were limpid powder blue. They swept around and took her in. She watched as they retreated in horror, shivered in disapproval, then blossomed slowly into a growing sense of avarice.

She'd had enough. She spun her sword high and stalked toward him, her eyes glowing in fury.

"You want this swordswoman before you?" she challenged him hotly. "If you think you are going to get anywhere near me, you will have to beat me first in my

Ring of Death. You get two blows before I start taking my swings at you, and once you have lost half your blood -"

The man blanched, wheeled back, and in a moment he was at a full gallop back out the gates, streaming south toward the coastline.

Fury coursed through her, and she was half disappointed that he had fled. It would have felt so good to pummel him, to show him just how wrong he had been.

Her eyes swiveled toward the gates. It was still early. There could be yet some fresh meat preparing to present itself for her dismembering blows.

Richard was moving past her toward the stables, his stride steady. "I think we should head out on a ride for the morning," he offered, disappearing into the shadowed depths.

"What? Where?" asked Elizabeth, pulled after him despite herself. He did not say another word. She found herself saddling her roan, drawing on the bit and bridle beside him, following at his side as they headed out the gates and turned south, angling away from the coast.

The sharp tang of salt in the air faded into a gentler aroma of wildflowers, and the hint of something else which Elizabeth found soothing. Her shoulders eased as their horses picked their way over the rise and fall in the ground, moving along the path, as they headed inland and down a series of hollows. Soon they were nestled into a cup-shaped depression, the gentle grassy walls sheltering them from the surrounding world.

Richard dismounted, holding out a hand to her, and in a moment she was at his side. He tucked the pair of reins around a bush, and then lay out a cloak. He sat down on the ground, and she found she was lowering herself to sit at his side, drawing in the rich scents of loam and grasses and fragrant wildflowers.

Time drifted by in silence as they sat side by side, as a ponderous bee moved inquisitively from flower to flower, as a fluffy cloud drifted lazily across the delicate blue sky. At last his voice, gentle and warm, eased into her thoughts.

"I grew up near here," he murmured, his eyes moving across the fields. "This hollow was a quiet retreat for me, hidden from all else. It gave me a chance to think and be by myself."

"It is beautiful," praised Elizabeth. She was soothed by the serenity of the place.

His voice became distant. "It is a shame it is not spring," he murmured. "When the weather gets warmer, this whole landscape bursts into a sea of columbine, the flowers carpeting as far as the eye can see, their purple flowers creating wave upon wave of fragrance." His eyes tracked to the east for a moment. "It was my mother's favorite time of year."

Elizabeth wondered for a moment what it might have been like to grow up with a parent who adored her, who took her hand and walked out into fields of flowers, drawing in their luscious scent.

The reality of her situation cascaded down on her like a wagon-full of stones releasing its cargo. "My father has more concrete desires," she snapped. "I cannot stay out here forever. The moment I return to the nunnery, the agony will start again. The parade of men will march by. Each man will stare at me with disgust and disapproval. Each will weigh my worth and find me wanting."

She ran a hand distractedly through her hair, barely seeing the curls of white clouds drifting across the azure sky. "If only I could escape back in time, to when my brother was still alive," she moaned. "He would watch over me. I was so happy then." Despair tendriled into every corner of her being. "Once he was gone, there was no escape. Every single man judged me inadequate. Every single man tallied my faults."

The voice at her side was low, without pressure. "Every man?"

She turned then, and was caught by those rich, deep eyes. Suddenly it was as if the whirlpool which had swirled before her vision has cleared and she could see what lay before her. Richard's gaze was resonant with longing and pride, with gentleness and determination. Shock struck her that she had not seen it before, that she had been so blind. Then he drew her in against him, and she went willingly into his arms. He tenderly kissed her, and a wave of insurmountable joy swept through her. Feelings and emotions she had never dreamt of burst into being. She nestled into his arms, simply being held by him, and there was nothing else on earth she could possibly desire.

It was a long while before he raised his head to gaze tenderly down at her. "Oh, Elizabeth," he groaned hoarsely, gently running a hand along her cheek.

Elizabeth found her eyes going to his lips, flushing at the amazing sensations they had brought forth within her. "Even your kisses do not bring pain," she found herself whispering in amazement.

His eyes sharpened in unbelieving surprise at that. "How in the world could -"

But she did not care. She twined a hand into his thick hair, he groaned in response, and his mouth was moving down against hers again, drawing out her pleasure.

At last he broke the contact with a ragged breath. "You bewitch me, Elizabeth." He lay back against the grass, his lungs drawing in long breaths.

She lay against that sturdy chest, his heart sounding strong and steady beneath her, and for the first time in a long, long while, she found peace.

***

The clouds began to tinge with maroon and tangerine, and yet she could not bring herself to rise, to quit this marvelous world she had found to wrap around herself. "I do not want to head back yet," she found herself saying, nestled in against his broad chest.

His hand was tenderly stroking her hair, and he chuckled low. "I would not recommend we stay out here in the meadow for the night," he countered evenly. He was quiet for a moment, then he added more softly, "My childhood home is a short distance away. It is exceedingly humble, but if you would like to see it, I could show you where I grew up."

"Absolutely!" cried Elizabeth in delight, drawing up to her feet. "I would adore seeing where you played as a child."

Richard came up more slowly, his face shadowed. "It is a small, one room cottage," he cautioned. "You might find it -"

"I would find it delightful," interrupted Elizabeth with a smile. "A large keep with a sadistic father is nothing to be proud of. I am sure your home was an Eden for you."

Richard smiled at that, nodding quietly. "It was indeed."

He gathered up both horses' reins, and then took Elizabeth's right hand in his left. Together they began walking up over the rise toward the east.

Elizabeth shimmered in the warmth of his grasp, the nearness of him, and it was a seductive siren's call to her as she moved. She brushed against him, drawing his eyes to her, and she caught his gaze with the full desire in her own. His step checked for a moment, and he groaned, forcing himself to look ahead, to keep in motion.

"You are indeed bewitching," he murmured under his breath. "You make it challenging for a man to behave honorably."

Elizabeth had a sense that, if any man was up to that challenge, it was Richard.

They crested a rise, and she gasped at the beauty of what lay before them. The tiny smudge of a keep lay in the far distance, but below them, nestled into a hollow, was the most beautiful cottage she had ever seen. A thick rosemary hedge edged it on all four sides, and she breathed in its rich scent, delighting in it, feeling it thrill through every part of her. The roof was well tended and secure, and the shutters were freshly painted and clean. A small stable stood to the far side.

"I will put away the horses," offered Richard gruffly, drawing himself with reluctance away from her side. He gave a gentle tug to the pair of horses as he moved them along toward the out-building.

Elizabeth moved her way down into the gap in the hedge, running her hands through the fragrant needles of rosemary, releasing their rich scent. Rosemary for remembrance. She breathed in deeply, absorbed in the amazing power of the aroma, tingling as it filled her.

God, she wanted Richard. For once she was safe, her worries were released, and a soul-filling desire and contentment had -

A strong hand latched onto her right wrist, fingers pressing into her flesh, spinning her around. She was being kissed, pushed up against the cottage wall, and she went willingly.

Wiry fingers burned into her forearm, sending searing pain down its length.

Tough lips forced her mouth open, and her lips bruised beneath the fierce onslaught which would not stop.

A muscular arm wrapped tight around her waist, cutting her breathing to desperate gasps.

She fought against him, at first gently, then in a panic. The pain intensified on her wrist, the sense of attack grew stronger, and fear and fury rose in a mixing cyclone within her. She struggled in earnest, and his strong arms pinioned her in place, forced her to accept -

"God's Blood, let her go or I will kill you where you stand!" snarled Richard, his voice rich with fury.

She was suddenly released. She half stumbled backwards, spinning her head in confusion to look at where the voice had come from.

Richard had his hand on his hilt, staring with focused attention before her. She drew her gaze back around -

Corwin stood there, proud, assured, running his eyes down her length with pleased satisfaction. "I had forgotten how delightful your feistiness was, my dearest," he smiled to her, his moss-green eyes coming back to meet hers. Then, almost dismissively, his gaze moved back to look at Richard.

"Thank you, dear brother, for bringing my fiancée into my arms again," he added. "I am sure I can handle her from here."

Chapter 11

Elizabeth stared in shock at the two men before her. She could see the resemblance now, the sturdy broadness of their shoulders, the leanness of their forms. And yet even traits which seemed the same at first glance were unique. Corwin's moss-green eyes were cold marbles, taking in the scene with sharp delight. Richard's were warm, deep, widening with growing understanding.

Richard slowly shook his head. "So you are *Corwin*?" he asked his brother. "You took our father's name when you left here?"

Corwin scoffed, his eyes hard. "That man should have given us far more than a name," he countered. "We were the elder pair! What did we receive besides a token payment, an amount even a faithful servant would have turned up his nose at? A name was the least that man could provide."

Elizabeth's world tumbled and whirled in chaos. "Wait … what is your name then?"

Richard held the man with his eyes. "His name is *Forwin*, and he is my younger brother."

His brother smiled wryly. "It is Corwin now," he corrected. "You will find that many things have changed." He stepped forward to grasp Elizabeth firmly by the arm. She winced against the pressure, his fingers digging deeply into the bruises he had created only a few moments ago.

"Get your hands off me," she snapped, ripping her arm loose. "You abandoned me six months ago, and now you think you can stroll back into my life?"

Corwin shook his head, tsk tsking her. "You get confused so easily," he offered in a dismissive voice. "I never left you."

Outrage bubbled up within her, and her face flushed with fury. "I was lying in the mud in front of five hundred people," she cut out, her voice tight. "You turned your back on me! You left me there to be thrown in the fetid dungeons!"

Corwin shook his head, sighing. "You knew your father would be furious if you lost. That was your own fault, for goading him with your feeble performance," he pointed out as if she were a toddling infant. "Once that began, his anger had to run its course. I made sure one of us could talk reason to him once he had cooled down. Which I did. You note that he has now decided to reinstate you as heir because -"

"If you had a hand in that, it is only because you want to get your hands on the keep and dowry," shot back Elizabeth, blood throbbing in her veins. Her hand twitched toward the hilt of her sword. "You let me rot in that hell hole for -"

Corwin made a dismissive gesture with his hand. "It was only a few weeks," he countered. "You are strong; you could have lasted far longer than that. Your father went through his typical blustering and screaming, and then everything would have gone back to normal. You are the one who fouled everything up, as usual, by going and running off -"

"You are damn right I ran off," interrupted Elizabeth, taking a step forward to glare at him. "There was no way I was going to remain anywhere near that man. And, now that I am free, there is no way I would return."

Corwin shrugged his shoulders. "So all that your brother held dear, you are simply going to let the bandits invade and destroy? I hardly think your beloved Jeffrey would be proud of that decision."

Elizabeth's stomach twisted. A seed of uncertainty lodged in her mind.

Corwin's eyes narrowed, and his hand shot forward, grabbing a hold of her left wrist, twisting it hard. She bit back a cry as he raised her hand up.

His voice grew harsh. "And where is the ring I gave you?"

A zing of fear thrilled through her body and she pushed it away angrily. He had no right to do this to her, to make any accusations or challenges. She ripped her arm away again, bringing her hands to her neck, removing the chain in one long draw.

"Here is your ring," she growled. "Have it back, with pleasure."

A low grin spread across his face as his eyes went between the golden circle and the cleft of her bosom. "Ah, a much better place for it to have rested," he murmured, his face flushing with desire. "I heartily approve."

"I only carried it because I wanted to give it back to you personally," she snapped. "Not because it held any meaning to me."

"Ah, but clearly it *did* have meaning," he countered. "You have carried it on your body all this time." His eyes grew wolfish. "And in such an intimate manner, too."

"I simply did not want it seen by others," corrected Elizabeth sharply.

His eyes moved possessively to hers. "Our *private* connection."

Richard's voice came quietly into the mix, and Elizabeth started at it, almost having forgotten he was watching the exchange, was witnessing her reunion with her ex-fiancé.

"Can I see that for a moment?" he asked evenly, holding out his hand.

Corwin's eyes narrowed, but Elizabeth handed over the ring without hesitation, plunking it into Richard's outstretched hand. Richard turned it over in his fingers for a long moment, then his eyes swept up to meet Corwin's with a hard gaze.

"This is our father's signet ring. The one that went missing after his death."

There was the smallest glimmer of hesitation in Corwin's face before his arrogance flooded back, his voice rising. "And well it should be," he retorted. "We deserved far more than one ring. It belonged with his firstborn sons."

"I vouched for you," continued Richard, his eyes holding his brother's. "When the others claimed you had been the thief, I backed you up and swore that you had not been involved."

"Yes, finally, you did something to defend your own flesh and blood," agreed Corwin, his lips thinning in anger. "And then you promptly went to support those whelps at their keep!"

"You were invited as well," reminded Richard.

Corwin spat on the ground. "That keep should have been ours," he growled. "To watch those puppies play lord in it, to see them lying in our beds, eating our food, was unsupportable. I had grander ambitions for my life. I was going to live my own life under my own terms."

Richard's voice was cool with challenge. "And so you courted a woman under a false name, and proposed to her with a stolen ring?"

The situation suddenly became too much for Elizabeth to handle. She needed to get away, to think. She turned from both men, striding toward the stables, grabbing her saddle off the bench and tossing it onto her roan's back. In a moment the men were beside her, staring at her.

Corwin's voice was sharp. "And just where do you think you are going?"

"I am returning to the nunnery," snapped Elizabeth.

Richard took her bridle from the peg, handed it to her. "I will ride with you."

Corwin scoffed, turning to Elizabeth. "Have you become so weak," he prodded her, "that you need a wet nurse to travel a mere few miles?"

Elizabeth's anger flared, and she tugged the bit into place before rounding on both men. "I will return home *alone*," she snapped, "I think I have had just about enough of this whole situation." She swung up onto her horse, gave a pull at the reins, and in a moment she was streaming across the countryside, her hair flying behind her, the wind whipping across her face.

The tears began to flow, a wetness covered her cheeks, and she struggled to pull the blanket of anger over her shoulders, to bury herself in its comforting embrace. Despite her most urgent efforts, the emotions slipped away from her at every tug, resisted her every attempt to draw them around in their familiar smothering.

She had no idea why the only sensations which drifted around her hollow core were tendrils of desolation.

Chapter 12

Elizabeth blinked in frustration as the faint glow of dawn gilded the windowsill. She had tossed and turned all night, and she doubted sleep had made even a hesitant visit to her exhausted mind. Her back ached in throbbing shards, and stress pulled tightly along her shoulder blades. Simmering fury lingered just beneath the surface of every thread of thought that pummeled her.

She let out a long sigh, then pushed herself to stand. She had dealt with sleepless nights for long enough to know how to fight through them. Her bruised arms throbbed. She groaned as every seam of her dress fought with her attempts to put it on. The belt buckle proved an equal challenge, and finally she convinced her sword and dagger to fit into their proper locations.

She ran a hand absently through her hair. There had to be a solution; she could not go on for long like this. She would talk with Richard. Somehow in the past he had been able to find the narrow path through the brambles, to find a quiet pool of calm seas amidst a tempest-tossed ocean. He would help her make sense of her current maelstrom.

She padded her way down the hall and around the narrow staircase, pressing open the keep's door with a weary shove. Her eyes swung down to the ring -

Her feet ground to a halt. Two men stood there. One was steady, gazing at her with quiet support. The other paced, prowled, his eyes swinging up to hold hers with a grin of dark triumph.

God's Teeth.

She blew out her breath, then strode down the steps, coming over to stand before the two men. "I want to talk with Richard, alone," she stated, her shoulders tensing.

Corwin laughed shortly. "No you do not," he countered in a sharp voice.

Elizabeth swung her head to look at him with rising fury. "What?"

Corwin's eyes swept her with a knowing look. "I know exactly what you want to do," he countered.

"And just what is it that I *want* to do?"

"As I recall," he mused, the corners of his mouth turning up in pleasure, "the last time I saw you, you were being slammed face down into the mud by your father in front of hundreds of people. You were blooded, bruised, and degraded." He chuckled. "And then I walked away from you."

"Yes, you did," snapped Elizabeth, hurt and anger roiling within her. His cold marble eyes were before her now, just as they had been that day. Hot fury filled every ounce of her being with a tense power.

He drew his sword easily, then, and held it out to one side. His eyes glistened with amusement. "Well, come teach me a lesson."

Richard's voice came low from behind her, rich with warning.

"Elizabeth, I do not think that -"

She barely turned, holding up a hand to him, waving him off. "This is between him and me," she snarled, maintaining a tenuous hold on the waves of hatred which threatened to swamp her. "You stay out of this."

There was no response, and her head snapped around. She saw the concern, tension, and protectiveness in his eyes. It needled her that he thought she was not up to this.

"He was *my fiancé*," she snapped. "This is personal, and I will handle it. You need to stay out."

When he again did not reply, her emotion spiked, and her eyes held his with fierce anger.

"Swear it!"

He hesitated, then nodded reluctantly, stepping back over the ring of hay bales. Elizabeth saw a quick movement at his side, and Michelle was there beside him, her face tight and scared.

She would show them both.

She spun back to face Corwin, drawing her own sword, the world narrowing down to just the two of them. She had sparred with him countless times, knew his moves, and she had the advantage now. She was filled with fury, imbued with righteous anger, and she would make him pay for what he had done.

With a cry she swept her sword high over her head, cleaving it down toward his bicep. She would mark him, scar him, carve into his skin a memento to remind him daily of the many wrongs he had inflicted on her.

He dodged to the left, whipped his sword around at her waist, and his block sent her arms ringing. She snarled, twisting the blade around toward his ankle, and he danced back, then forward quickly, laughing as he swung, and she barely evaded the whistling tip.

He flashed a sharp smile, delight dancing in his eyes. "*That* is my Elizabeth!"

She was not his.

She lunged into an opening, but then it was not there, and his blade was circling to her left, the flat of it coming hard against her bicep. The force of the blow shook her, nearly knocking the wind out of her. The length of her arm throbbed and she knew that another painful bruise was soon to follow.

Damn the man.

She lifted the hilt high, whipping the tip around, aiming for his shoulder blade, but he blocked, rotated, and she barely escaped the spinning edge. She lunged, lunged again, twisted against him, and his laughter spurred the anger within her, made her press that much harder to land the blow -

WHAM. The flat of his blade came down hard on the exact same spot on her arm. This time it sent a ringing, searing pain shooting along the length, and she staggered. She shook her head, fighting off the urgent signals from her arm, willing herself to continue.

He leered at her, his eyes bright with satisfaction. "You missed me, admit it."

She growled, reseating the hilt in her hand, and then she was driving hard, aiming for his waist, looking to hurt him, to drive a scar across his midsection. She needed to wipe that grin off his face, to make him pay. She thrust, dodged, ducked under the spinning swing, came up low, twisted around -

His blade whistled along the length of her thigh, and the tip carved along the flesh, leaving a sharp, stinging line which merged into wetness.

He gave a bark of disapproval. "You are slowing," he taunted her. "Was that brother of mine not pushing you hard enough? It is a good thing I am back in your life."

Elizabeth was exhausted, and her body throbbed with pain, but through sheer force of will she brought her sword high, diving at him with every ounce of anger she could muster. She swept down and across, pouring everything she had into the blow, seeking to hurt him … to hurt him …

SLAM. His boot lashed out at the edge of her kneecap, and her leg crumpled beneath her. She slammed hard onto the ground, crying out as her injured thigh struck the earth, feeling nothing but pain and frustration and exhaustion. She struggled to catch her breath.

Corwin smiled down at her. "And there, my dear brother, is how a woman should look when you are done with her for the day," he mused with pleasure. "Exhausted, out of breath, and on her knees." He gave her one last glance, then rolled his shoulders. "A delightful morning, I must say. Well, then, I will leave you to heal up. I know you will be looking forward to tomorrow."

He sheathed his sword and turned to stride over to the stables. Richard instantly moved to place himself between Elizabeth and Corwin. He remained there, tense, until Corwin emerged on his horse and, with an ironic salute, turned to ride out through the gates.

In an instant Richard and Michelle were on either side of Elizabeth, taking her arms. She groaned with pain as they helped her to her feet, walking her over to one of the hay bales.

Michelle's voice was shaky and tinged with fear. "Are you all right?"

There was a movement, and Richard's hand dropped to his hilt, his eyes hard. Claire stood there with mugs of mead in one hand, a basket of bread in the other. Her eyes went down the bruises on Elizabeth's body and she spun toward Richard, her eyes blazing with fury.

Elizabeth drove herself to speak, wading through the waves of pain. "It was not him," she defended in a groan. "It was Corwin."

Claire's stance did not gentle. "So you stood by while another man did this to her?" she challenged him.

Richard's face went tight, and again Elizabeth drew a breath, fought down the spinning of nausea that began to whirl around her. "I made him swear to let me handle it," she ground out. "It was between me and my fiancé."

"Your *ex*-fiancé," corrected Claire with a snap, "and apparently for good reason."

"He needed to be taught a lesson," snarled Elizabeth, taking one of the mugs from Claire, downing half of it in one long draw. Her leg throbbed with pain, and she kneaded it, trying to lessen the ache. Her hand came up red.

Richard was kneeling at her side in an instant. "Claire, please fetch some medical supplies," he requested in a low voice.

Claire nodded, making a motion to Michelle, and in a moment the two were trotting back toward the keep.

Richard wiped away the blood with the fabric of her dress, examining the wound. His voice was hoarse. "Why did you do it?"

"I was furious with him," she responded wearily. "I wanted to hurt him."

His eyes moved up to meet hers. "And because you were acting from anger, your blows were wild. Your blocks were only half set. You left yourself wide open to his attacks."

"I wanted to hurt him," she insisted. "I knew it would make me feel better to attack him."

He drew a hand up to her cheek, smoothing his fingers against her in a tender motion. "And do you feel better?"

She dropped her head. "No," she admitted. "I feel exhausted, and drained, but the fury is still in there, but just too worn out to take action."

He paused for a long moment, and when he spoke again, his voice was gentle. "Could it be that you also felt like you should be punished, for causing him to leave you?"

Her first reaction was to flare with anger, but he was so steady at her side, his voice was so tender, that she took in a deep breath, rolling the idea around in her head. She found, to her surprise, that a part of her resonated with the thought, latched onto it.

"Maybe," she conceded after a moment. "If I had not lost the tournament, my father would not have been furious with me. Corwin would not have been driven away from me. If I had just won -"

Richard went still at her side. "So you feel you had a part in the suffering you went through?"

She found herself nodding. "I failed, and I brought it on myself."

He tenderly raised her head so her eyes met his. His gaze was gentle and warm.

"If Michelle fought in a sparring match, and she did not win, would you cover her body with bruises and scars?"

Elizabeth's protective nature flared into heat. "Never," she ground out. "I would not hurt a hair on that girl's head."

Richard's eyes held hers, and a long moment passed. She found herself immersed in confusion. "But I ..." she began, then stopped.

His voice was a whisper. "Do you not deserve the same care that Michelle does?"

She looked down at her hands. It seemed an eternity before she put the thoughts to words. "I do not know."

He groaned softly, then drew her into an embrace. She sighed at the sturdiness of his chest against her, the strength in the arms that wrapped around her. At long last she was safe, tended to, protected.

His voice was a murmur in her ear. "I think you do."

A wave of warmth swept through her, pushing away the pain and exhaustion. She let herself relax against him, melt into him, give herself over to his watchful eye.

There was a movement, and Claire and Michelle were beside them. Claire glanced at Richard, then over to Elizabeth. "Perhaps we should do this down in the infirmary, where you will have more privacy."

Elizabeth looked at her, baffled. "For sparring injuries? I just patch those up in the ring when the match is over, and go on with life."

"But your leg ..." continued Claire, pointing at Elizabeth's tunic.

Elizabeth scoffed, hauling the fabric up to mid-thigh, laying it around the long gash. Claire and Michelle drew in breath at the full length of the wound, but Richard was kneeling at her side, holding a hand out for a clean rag, and began methodically working his way down its length, cleaning out any dirt or grime.

"I know this hurts, but we have to keep this safe from infection," he commented in a low voice.

Elizabeth was gripping the hay bale with both hands, focusing on her breath, fighting through the waves of pain. "Yes, yes," she ground back. "As if I have not been through this a hundred times."

"That is quite clear," returned Richard, his voice rough. "Your leg is criss-crossed with scars. I cannot believe even Forwin ... I mean Corwin ... could be responsible for this many." He paused for a moment to look at a twisting wound which ran just over her kneecap. "This one, for example, looks to be quite old."

Elizabeth glanced down, wincing slightly at the memory. "That was soon after Jeffrey was slain," she agreed. "My father did that to me, when I failed to retreat from a swing quickly enough. It had me in bed for three days, which made him even more furious."

Richard shook his head, his lips tight with emotion, and then he took the bandage from Claire and began gently wrapping it around her thigh, laying the fabric evenly over the wound. Soon he had the ends tucked in place. He gave a long look down her leg, at the myriad of wounds and injuries, then gently pulled the fabric back down over it.

His eyes came back to hold hers. "Any other cuts that we should know about?"

She shook her head, wincing at the pain which throbbed in her arm. "The rest are bruises, and they just have to go through their cycle of colors. I will be a living work of art for a few days, and then I will be as good as new again."

Richard handed over the mug of mead, and she drew down a fresh, long draw of it. "Ah, that helps too," she murmured with a half-smile.

Richard held her gaze for a long moment, then drew up to his feet. "These two women can care for you," he stated, his voice steeling. "I need to be heading out."

Anger flared through Elizabeth, and she shot to her feet. She winced as her leg nearly buckled beneath her. His arm was holding her in an instant, helping her to lower back to a seated position.

"This is my fight," she insisted once she had regained her breath. "I will not have you interfering."

"He is my brother," responded Richard tensely, "And I care for you."

Warmth surged through her again, but she held it off. "This situation is mine to deal with," she reiterated, her voice holding absolute certainty. "He was *my* fiancé. This was *my* relationship."

He held her eyes for a moment, then he pursed his lips and nodded. "For now, I will let you take your chosen course," he agreed. "Do not expect me to maintain this restraint forever, though."

"I will handle it," vowed Elizabeth, her eyes darkening. Once she regained her strength, she would take control of the situation.

Richard nodded, then turned, heading toward the stables. In a few minutes he was out in the courtyard, mounted, his eyes sweeping across the trio. And then he was turning, moving through the main gates, and out into the countryside.

Chapter 13

Elizabeth groaned as the light streamed across her face. Clearly she had overslept, judging by the strength of the golden glow filling her room. The bruise on her arm was swollen and throbbing, and when she prodded it cautiously with a finger, she winced at the burst of pain that followed. The line of fire along her thigh was not much better.

She took in a deep breath, then forced herself to roll to a standing position. Coddling her injuries had never done her much good in the past. She carefully drew her dress over her body, being cautious as she slid her arm through the sleeve. In a moment she was making her way down the stairs and out into the courtyard.

Corwin was pacing in the ring like a corralled wolf, Richard was watching him with tense, focused attention, and Michelle was sitting in a corner, her knees tight against her chest, her arms wrapped closely around them. All three pair of eyes swung up at her approach, and it was Corwin who strode toward her, his eyes sharp.

"Have you gotten lazy as well?" he snapped. "If your father was here, he would whip your derelict hide for lounging in bed like that."

"My father is *not* here," responded Elizabeth shortly. "And I do not answer to *you*."

"Apparently you answer to nobody," shot back Corwin. "I suppose the idea of responsibility got left behind with your vows."

"And what is that supposed to mean?" growled Elizabeth.

He held up his hand with the gold signet ring on it. "You vowed to accept me as your lord and master. Do you think you can just back out because the whim hits you?"

"You are the one who left me!" shouted Elizabeth in outrage.

He spread his arms wide. "I am right here," he pointed out. "You are the one turning your back on your promises."

Anger spiraled within her, and she struggled to rein in her emotions. "I am done talking. I am not going back to that keep."

He arched an eyebrow. "So now not only are you failing in your responsibilities to me, but you are abandoning those you owe your brother?"

Her world slowed down. "What did you say?" she ground out, turning to face him full on.

"Your brother, Jeffrey, the dead one," he prodded her mercilessly. "Your paragon, your knight in shining armor. The one you caused to be sent away and *slain*."

Anger whirled and billowed within her, hot crimson in color, the bright heat of steam, filling her with energy and power and a thirst for vengeance. She drew her sword from its scabbard, holding it high.

Richard's voice was hoarse and strained. "Elizabeth, I beg of you – "

She waved him off without looking, pointing over the hay bales. "Out of the ring. Now. Or I swear to God I will have you banned from the nunnery." She didn't turn, maintaining her focus on the man before her. His green eyes sparkled with amusement, the cold orbs seemingly carved from stone.

"There is my girl," he purred in a rasp, drawing his own sword.

His smile sliced into her soul; his dismissive laughter ripped her apart. That he could make light of Jeffrey's death ...

She lunged toward his right hip, aiming to chip a chunk off of it, and he rolled, blocking, tossing the tip of her sword high and right. She swiveled instantly, coming down at that sweet juncture of neck and collarbone, and he ducked beneath her, turning, whipping the blade. She saw its path, but her wearied body would not heed the urgent signals her mind sent.

WHAM. The blade contacted the fresh bruise and an anguished cry filled the air. It was a full second before Elizabeth realized it was her own, as she gasped for breath, struggled to keep a hand on her sword, and staggered back.

Corwin looked down at her dismissively. "Your brother would be very disappointed in you," he mused, shaking his head.

Elizabeth forced herself to regroup, to set in motion, to lunge at him, seeking to skewer his right breast, his left hip, his upper thigh. In each stroke he was there, blocking her, tossing her sword away, his eyes dancing with laughter.

SLAM. His sword slapped hard against her thigh, and she could feel the skin beneath the bandages pull apart, feel the wet soaking of blood drawing into the fabric. The jagged pain barely got through the exhaustion and fury and throbbing from the rest of her body.

A smile played on his lips. "Are you ready to concede I am right?"

Elizabeth gave her head a firm shake, then staggered, almost undone by the wave of nausea that followed. She forced herself to remain focused on his eyes, on the movement of his feet, on the tilt of his shoulders. She needed to hurt him. She needed to take him down, to make him suffer, to get him on his knees before her.

She dove in, twisting, slicing, turning, screaming, and he blocked high left, deflected her low right. Then his left arm slammed hard against her collarbone, nearly reaching her throat. She flew back hard on the ground, her sword skittering from her hand, staring up at the blank azure of the sky high overhead.

He was staring down at her, his face rich with disdain. "Maybe your father was right," he mused after a moment. "Maybe you are not even remotely capable of handling the keep's defenses. Your brother deserved far better in a sibling."

He gave his head a shake, then turned, striding off toward the stables.

Elizabeth sensed Richard moving in to protect her, sensed Michelle's worried gaze, but the words echoed in her mind, spinning in circles with the throbbing pain and rolling waves of nausea.

She was not worthy ...

There were hoofbeats, and arms pulling her up, and the scratchy roughness of hay beneath her legs, and yet it all seemed far away. A mug of mead was pressed into her hand, and she took down a pull. Gentle hands were working at her leg, removing the old bandage, cleaning her wound, and she felt the pain, mingled in with all the other fires and throbs, but they all seemed distant to her now. There were some murmurs, and some movement, and then a quiet settled down around her.

A few minutes passed, and she drew herself up, forcing herself to focus on the world around her. Claire and Michelle were gone. Only Richard sat by her side, his eyes shadowed.

"Tell me about Jeffrey."

Elizabeth closed her eyes against the pain. "He was the most wonderful man that could be," she stated, her voice hoarse, "and he was sent away because of me. It was because of me that he was in that French inn. It was because of me that he died."

Richard's voice was gentle. "Why did he die?"

"Because I forced him to be sent away," moaned Elizabeth in agony.

A pair of strong hands enfolded hers, and she looked up into his deep eyes.

"No." He waited a moment, then repeated. *"Why did he die?"*

Elizabeth hesitated, giving the question some thought. She had always blamed herself. It never occurred to her to look beyond that.

"Six bandits attacked in the night, seeking to rape the widow and her young daughter. My brother was lodging there. He took them all on. He held them off and killed every man. But his wounds were serious, and it was only a few days before he passed away."

"So who was responsible for his death?" Richard continued, his eyes tender on hers.

Her throat closed up. "The ... the bandits were?"

"The bandits were," affirmed Richard, his grip holding hers with warmth. "If the bandits had not arrived, seeking to harm others, your brother would have continued his journey safely." His eyes searched hers. "Or would you have wanted him to let them do their deed without any hindrance?"

She shook her head fiercely, regretting it when the world spun around her for a moment. She took in a deep breath to stabilize herself. "He was a man of honor," she stated firmly when the ground came to rest. "I am incredibly proud of what he did. Apparently those bandits had hurt many others in the area, and he brought them to a final halt."

"Then your brother left a magnificent legacy, and we should be respectful of his actions."

"I do respect what he did," agreed Elizabeth. "But why did he have to die?"

The corner of Richard's mouth turned up gently, and he tenderly stroked the side of her face. "Many wise people have asked that same question over the centuries," he pointed out. "There are no easy answers. We cannot choose how we die, or when. We can only choose how we live. Your brother made that choice, and his actions speak of the highest nobility of character."

Elizabeth's eyes welled. "I miss him so much," she whispered, and then Richard was pulling her in against him, holding her against his broad chest, and the tears spilled down in cascades. Her body shook with sobs. The aches, pain, and exhaustion all combined to release every last hold she had on her self-control.

She sat there for what seemed like hours, the sun sliding across the sky, Richard's arms around her, the smell of dry straw and dust and leather drifting all around.

Finally, Richard hoisted her up in his arms, and she did not resist or say a word. He walked slowly across the courtyard, bringing her up the stairs and around to her room. He laid her gently on her mat, brushing her hair back away from her face.

"You rest now," he advised her, his smile tender. "Tomorrow we will figure out a solution. One that does not rely on anger, or fury, but on what makes sense for you, to live the life you want going forward."

She found herself nodding, trusting in him to discover that path through the mists and fogs. He leant over and tenderly kissed her on the forehead. The warmth radiated through her entire body, easing the stress out of her aching muscles.

With that release, exhaustion cascaded over her, and in a moment she was fast asleep.

Chapter 14

Elizabeth blinked herself awake in the pre-dawn light, a sense of calm wrapped around her like an inner blanket, the gentle imprint of Richard's lips against her forehead echoing as a sensation of tender warmth that she had not known since her brother left her a decade ago. She lay for a long moment, relishing the serenity, letting it soak into her flesh. She rolled to her feet, her resolve kindling and firming. She would take on whatever the day presented, and she would pause before acting, to do what she knew was right. She would not let Corwin manipulate her into impulsive and self-destructive actions.

She dressed, brushed out her hair, and limped down the long spiral staircase toward the front door. She laid her hand on the sturdy wood for a moment, drawing in a deep breath. She knew she could do this. All it involved was taking a moment to gather herself before acting.

She pushed open the door, swept her eyes along to the ring – and stopped short. Richard stood there, alone, his hand resting easily on his sword hilt, his eyes holding hers, his dark hair ruffled by the gentle dawn breeze. Her breath caught. Here she had been girding herself for combat and the problem had melted away on its own! She almost floated down the stairs, she was so full of joy, and her face was beaming by the time she stood before him.

"Oh, Richard, I -"

His eyes flashed to look over at the stables, and Elizabeth automatically turned her own gaze to match. Her heart fell. Corwin was striding out of the darkness toward them, his eyes bright with satisfaction, a cruel smile tilting the corner of his mouth.

Elizabeth drew in a long, deep breath. She could do this. The man was nothing to her now. He was in the past, and she was moving forward with her life. Nothing he could do or say could reach her.

"I will be walking with Richard this morning," she informed him coolly. "You are welcome to wait here in the ring if you so desire."

Corwin's mouth curled up into a wolfish grin. "As long as that sweet Michelle sits in my lap to keep me company," he agreed with a rich laugh. "Those kisses of hers in the stable were quite thorough enough to whet my appetite for more."

It was as if the world slowed down to a halt around Elizabeth, as if the dust motes in the streaming sunshine hung suspended, as if the robin's warbling stalled mid-stream. Her eyes widened in shocked horror, her hand going to her hilt of its own accord.

He had drawn Michelle into his web of treachery. Innocent Michelle, sweet Michelle who had already shouldered so much in life. And it was all her fault that this was happening. It was her responsibility that the man's taint was affecting every corner of her world, every person she held dear.

She could hear the metal rasp as her sword drew clear of the sheath, saw Corwin's eyes brighten in delight, hear the dusty crunch as her foot settled more firmly into the dirt of the ring floor. She could hear …

But, wait. There was no call of her name from behind her, no pleading for her to stop, and at first she was filled with a fresh fury. Was Richard going to interfere? Was he going to step in and take over for her, as if her wishes did not matter?

No, there was no sense of movement, and it hit her in a flash which staggered her. He knew. He understood that she needed to handle this on her own. If he stepped in she would always be in Corwin's grip, always be susceptible to his next trick, his next assault. She had to reach the point, in her own mind, to withstand him on her own.

And suddenly she was there.

She was standing within the moment, apart from fury and pain and a craving for acceptance. She was fully aware of the manipulative gleam in Corwin's eyes. She could see in sharp relief the deliberate machinations which he'd laid out in order to force her down the path of his choosing.

But now she could select, for herself, where the next foot would fall.

She slowly, carefully, with focused attention, uncurled her fingers from her hilt, let the sword settle back into its sheath, and held his eyes with a steady look. Then she turned her gaze up to the curtain wall where Simon and his men stood watching, concern in their eyes. She raised her hand, giving them a short calling hand signal. They moved quickly down the steps, coming down to ring around Corwin. Simon stood immediately at his right.

She was surprised at how calm her voice was. "Please escort this man from the nunnery's grounds," she instructed Simon. "I am afraid Corwin is no longer welcome within our walls."

Simon did not hesitate. He tilted his head toward one of his men, and the guard sprinted toward the stables. The rest remained in their circle, their eyes focused on Corwin.

Corwin's smile widened. "So you cannot fight your own battles any more, my pet?" he prodded her. "You need to rely on those stronger than you?"

"I rely on my friends," responded Elizabeth, and somehow her anger eased, the heat which flooded her veins cooled. It almost seemed that his words were losing their ability to wound.

His eyes grew sharp. "Your father relies on you to defend the keep. So do all of its inhabitants. Are you going to abandon them to be raped and slaughtered when the murdering bandits swarm in?"

A tickle of anger flirted at the edges of Elizabeth's awareness, but she drew in a long, deep breath, and let it out again. "That is between my father and me," she informed him. "There is no reason for you to be involved in that."

"And your brother?" shot out Corwin, his voice becoming harsh. "Shall he have died in vain, all due to your female weaknesses?"

The young soldier was walking toward them, leading Corwin's horse, and Elizabeth made a motion with her hand. "I think it is time for you to leave now."

A wave of fury passed through Corwin's face, and then it was under tight control again, and he smirked. "You will miss me," he prodded her. "You will wither in the feeble heat of what my brother offers; you will miss the fierce power of my presence. It may be an hour, or perhaps a day, but you will crave the feel of my hand on your body. None else can bring you that release of emotion and fury."

He flashed a triumphant smile, and then he vaulted onto his horse. He pulled the reins from the guard's hand, turning and thundering out through the gates.

"Close them, and bar them," instructed Elizabeth, a flare of fear coursing through her at his unexpectedly easy departure.

Simon waved a hand, and his men moved quickly to the large gates, pressing them shut, sliding the long, heavy bar into position. He led his crew up on the wall, watching Corwin ride off into the distance.

At last Simon turned to nod down at her. "He is gone."

It was done. She would have said it was impossible only a few days ago, to break from his powerful spell, to resist the insinuations and webs he wove around her. And yet, here she was, and simply by taking that pause, and choosing her own course -

She turned, and Richard was there watching her, his face taut with concern, his shoulders tense with stress and worry. She wondered how hard it had been for him to remain there, to know that she could have easily walked into a third fight, been beaten, or injured, or worse.

"Oh, Richard," she moaned, and then they were in each other's arms. He murmured her name against her ear, holding her tight, pressing his lips against her forehead, her cheek.

At last he pulled gently apart from her. "You know how to test a man to his very limits," he groaned. "If you had drawn against him again, I do not know that I could have held back."

"And yet, all I had to do was stop and consider," she whispered, her voice tinged with awe. "That one moment, and suddenly I could see my way clear through the fog of fury and reaction."

There was a noise from the stables, and Michelle's small face peeked out from the darkness. "Is he gone?"

Corwin's boasts roiled back into Elizabeth's mind in a flash. She held open her arms, and a thin, shaking streak came flying into them, crying, and Elizabeth held her close. Richard wrapped them both with his strength.

Michelle buried her face against Elizabeth's chest. "I did not know what to do," she sobbed. "I did not want to fight him; he was only kissing me, and who knew what else he might do if enraged. I did not want to tell you, not with how he hurt you already. I just wanted him to leave. I just wanted him to go away."

Elizabeth looked down at the waif. "You mean you would not want me to hurt him for what he did?"

Michelle shook her head steadfastly. "That would not undo his actions. I only wanted him gone, so he could not hurt anybody here any longer."

Elizabeth gave her a warm hug. "Then your wish has been granted, for he is now banned from the nunnery grounds. You are safe here."

The wide smile on the child's face was more than she could have asked for in return. A glow of satisfaction spread through her, far stronger than she had ever felt in one of her furious fights, far more profound than disassembling a straw dummy had ever felt.

She turned to Richard in surprise, saw the nod of understanding. Then they were all hugging, laughing, and the sun shone down in golden streams.

Chapter 15

Elizabeth stood for a long moment in the entry hall before the main door to the keep. She stared at it, wondering what waited in the courtyard. She trusted the men on the wall, trusted them to keep Corwin out, and yet his manipulative schemes had surmounted so many hurdles in the past. She steeled herself to be strong, to withstand whatever new assault he planned to launch at her.

She pressed the door open, stepping out into the sunshine – and stopped. Richard waited at the center of the ring, his eyes sure, steady. Michelle sat on a bale of hay, her legs crossed at the ankles, a wide smile at her face. The doors to the curtain wall were firmly shut and barred. No other sign of movement stirred from within the courtyard.

Relief swept over her, and it was all she could do to rein in her stride, to walk with slow, measured steps down the front stairs of the keep, to make her way over to the ring of hay bales, to draw to a stop before Richard, gazing up at him in contentment.

The corners of his mouth quirked up into a smile. "Good morning," he greeted.

"A very good morning," she agreed.

Sunlight dappled the cobblestone, easing gently between her shoulder blades. A gentle autumn wind danced along the edge of the wall, sending a swirl of leaves into the air.

His voice was rich with curiosity. "So, what would you like to do?"

Her mind leapt to a thousand options. She would like to fold herself tenderly into his arms. She would like to press her lips against his, at first softly, and then with growing passion, leaning against his length, feeling his arms come up around her body …

A low voice called down from above the gate, its timbre tight. "We have a visitor," informed Simon.

The colors drained from her world, and in a moment she was sprinting toward the stairs, taking them two at a time, coming up alongside him to gaze out at the coastal road.

She knew the black horse, knew the arrogant rider who urged him along the path, and a cold darkness had settled into her heart long before he pulled in hard before the gate. Corwin gave a sweeping bow, looking up at her.

"My dearest fiancée, you look ravishing as always," he greeted. "The ocean air seems to agree with you."

Richard tensed at her side, and her throat grew tight. "Spit it out," she ordered. "What do you want?"

His mouth quirked into a smile. "Your wish is my command," he agreed with another flourish. "My darling siblings are ready to sign an agreement with this nunnery, to act as its patron. All that is required is that you and Claire come to dinner tonight to sign the contract."

Elizabeth's mouth pressed into a line. "You hardly need me present for that," she pointed out.

Corwin gave a gentle shrug. "And yet that is what they requested," he responded. "Are you saying you refuse?"

Elizabeth drew in a breath. It would be just like him to arrange something like this. Surely there was another way to get around -

His voice cut smoothly into her turmoil. "Oh, and there has also been a messenger for you," he added.

Tense anger drew her shoulders together. "What, from my father?" she snapped.

He shook his head. "No, this message comes from the pen of Father Godfrey," he murmured, his eyes dancing with delight. "He claims it is quite urgent."

Elizabeth leaned against the wall, panic thumping at her chest. That the sweet old man would write to her; something must truly be dire for him to take that step.

"What did he say?" she asked, willing the shake to leave her voice.

Corwin shrugged again, his smile growing. "I am a man of honor; I would not open your correspondence," he stated. "My brothers hold the message for you and would gladly place it into your hands tonight."

"I will be there," shot out Elizabeth. Corwin gave a flourishing bow, then he kicked hard into his steed's flank's, wheeling him, sending him at a hard gallop back the way he had come.

Elizabeth watched him go, darkness drawing down around her, blurring out the rolling blue and streaming green which lay before her.

Richard's voice was gentle at her side. "Who is Father Godfrey?"

Elizabeth wrapped her arms around her waist. "He was my one friend at my father's keep; the only man who had the best interests of its inhabitants in his heart," she muttered, her eyes still on the distant horizon where Corwin had vanished. How had the man done it? He had come up with the one thing which would lure her through the doors, would draw her back into his web.

"I will be there, at your side," murmured Richard. She wanted so much to turn, to press against his chest, to feel his sturdy arms come up around her and shelter her. She resisted with all her might. She would have to face this challenge with her own strength. She would overcome it, surmount it, and come out whole on the other side.

A long moment passed, then Richard gave her a bow. "I should head home: I need to make sure this offer is all it seems," he muttered half to himself. "I will return later tonight, to escort you to the dinner." His eyes drew to latch onto hers with steady regard. "Please, wait for me. Do not head off alone with him."

Her resistance flared at that, as if she could not handle that man on her own. She drew in a deep breath, finally nodding in agreement.

"In return," she prodded, "you will let me handle Corwin in my own way tonight. The last thing I need is for you trying to jump in between us."

His face was still; she could see the tension draw between his shoulders. After a moment he let out a breath and nodded. "If that is your wish."

He put out a hand to tenderly draw it against her cheek, then turned, heading down the steps. In a few minutes, the doors were being pulled open and he was thundering through the gates, following along the path where his brother had gone a short while before.

* * *

Elizabeth sat nervously on her horse, smoothing down the violet dress, her eyes on the coastal road before them. The keep gates were closed sturdily behind her, and she knew that Simon and the full force of the guard lined the wall, watching over her. Claire sat serenely by her side, her face a mask of calm. The crimson sun eased slowly down toward the horizon, sending streaks of color dancing across the clouds.

There – a pair of horses was coming toward them at a trot, side by side. The men seemed similar in so many ways, but to Elizabeth they could not have been more different. Corwin's arrogance was clear in every sharp movement, in the tight way he dragged on the horse's reins as they drew close. And Richard ...

Richard's gaze was on her, sure, steady, reassuring.

Corwin's eyes drew down her in delight, his grin growing ever wider as they took in her outfit. "Why, my dearest future wife, you have worn your engagement dress to meet my family! How wonderful!"

Richard's gaze sharpened in surprise, and she blushed. "It is simply the one nice dress I had with me," she snapped to Corwin, nudging her horse into motion. "We should get on our way."

"Of course," he agreed, falling in instantly at her left side. "And can I say you look absolutely lovely in that shade. My mother adored the color, you know. It was the blanket of columbines which decorated her world every spring. It is why I chose it for you."

Richard's eyes moved back to her dress, and her face became more crimson.

Corwin's voice wheedled into her brain. "But surely you recognize the fragrance of that flower," he continued. "Our mother taught us to make oil for our leather gear from an early age, and columbine and rosemary were key components of the recipe." His eyes brightened. "You would have smelled that every time I drove you into the dirt or brought my elbow into your throat."

Realization hit her, and she turned to look at Richard. It had been the familiar smell when he had drawn her in, had held her when she cried. It was the fragrant mixture of columbine and rosemary which had seemed such a natural combination with the leather.

Corwin chuckled. "Or perhaps your encounters with my brother were so feeble that you never made that connection," he mused. "I doubt the man ever put you on the ground."

Richard tensed beside her, and her anger shot out, hot with steel. "When Richard and I were on the ground together," she found herself snapping, "it was because my arms were wrapped around him and we were lost in passion."

A sharp spark flared in Corwin's eyes, and his hand came up half-way toward a hearty slap before he reined himself in. His voice had a growl in it when he spoke. "Are you telling me that, while engaged to me, you have spread your legs to another man?"

Richard's hand dropped to his hilt, and Elizabeth tossed her hair back. "First off, I am not engaged to you," she corrected Corwin. "You broke that off when you abandoned me face-down in the mud and left me to rot in my father's prison."

Corwin began to argue, but she talked over him. "And secondly, I have not spread my legs to anybody. We have only kissed."

Corwin's eyes brightened at that, and he sat back in smug satisfaction. "Of course he did not. My dear, honorable brother would never take such an action. That is why I shall be the victor," he grinned.

Elizabeth turned her eyes ahead, to where Claire rode before them, ignoring him. The party moved on in silence, a tense fury seeming to build with every step of the horses' hooves. Elizabeth felt as if they were a building storm, growing with every step, preparing to crash down on the keep which grew ever larger before them.

They were riding beneath the entry gates, walking through the courtyard festooned with yellow banners, moving up the staircase, and Corwin and Richard remained steadily at her side, even as they drew up to the head table and sat down before the twins. It was Claire who moved around to the other side, taking the vacant seat between them.

Corwin smiled with delight as he eased into his seat. "And here we have her, my dear brothers," he greeted, "just as I had promised. Does she not look lovely? Her father had this dress made for our engagement." He drew his eyes to look possessively at her. "She even had the fabric dyed in my favorite color."

Elizabeth ignored him, her eyes moving to the two men before her. "I believe you have a message for me?"

Ron blinked at the suddenness of her request, but nodded, drawing forth a scroll from beneath the table. "Yes, but surely it can wait -"

She reached across the table, snapping it from his hands, settling back to examine the parchment. Yes, this was Father Godfrey's seal; she knew the mark well. The scroll seemed untouched.

Servants came pouring mead into their flagons, setting out wooden platters of bread and cheese. She toyed with the edge of the seal, half considering putting off its opening until later, when there were not so many eyes watching her. After a moment she gave up, digging her fingernail beneath the wax, prying it off the textured vellum. She would never last the dinner wondering what news it held for her.

The tiny, scrawled letters trailed across the paper, and her heart went out to the elderly hand that had held the quill pen. The man must be nearing seventy by now, and life had not been easy on him. He had needed to stand up to her father often, insisting on more alms for the poor, on better protection for the villages nearest the menacing presence of bandits. He had been one of the few willing to stand up to her father, one of the few not driven away by her father's storming rages.

Her eyes took in the meaning of the words, and her hand moved to her chest. It could not be true. Surely what he was saying ...

She found herself whispering, "I have to go home."

Corwin's eyes blazed with triumph. "Of course you do. At last you are seeing reason and taking some responsibility for your actions," he crowed. "It took the scratchings of a doddering old fool for you to realize that?"

Richard turned to her, his face concerned. "What has happened?"

Her eyes drew in the message again, her shoulders sagging. "My father is near death; he will not last the month. If he dies, and I am not there to take control, Father Godfrey fears that my cousin Umfrey might storm in."

Corwin burst out laughing in delight. "Oh, that would make a pretty picture," he toasted, downing half his glass. "Here you are worried about bandits causing harm to the area. Umfrey could lay waste to your lands far more thoroughly than those bandits could ever dream of!"

Richard looked at her in concern, and she nodded. "Umfrey has his own lands far to the west, and he loathes my father with a passion. He would be quite thrilled to pillage everything of value from my land and burn the rest to the ground out of sheer spite, solely because my father adored it so."

Corwin ripped a piece of bread off the loaf, stuffing it into his mouth. It was a moment before he could speak. "So, when are we off?"

Elizabeth rounded on him, fury filling her. She had no idea how he had orchestrated this, but somehow everything seemed to be going exactly as he had wished, drawing her along in its inexorable flow.

"I will not be going anywhere with you," she shot out.

He waved his hands expansively. "The road is a free road; I may go where I wish," he pointed out. "And, besides, I swore to your father that I would see you home safely. I will stand by that promise and ensure the deed is done."

"Fine," she snapped, "I cannot stop you from riding the same stretch of dirt. However, I do not need to talk with you or look at you should you happen to be within eyesight."

He shrugged. "If you feel that looking at me or talking with me is far too tempting until we reach your family home then I will respect your frailty." A grin spread on his face. "After all, we would not want to end up in a Yorkshire Dales wedding, now would we? You are far too noble for that."

Claire blushed crimson, looking down at her trencher. Corwin chuckled, giving a half bow to her. "My pardons, sweet nun," he added. "I think you would agree that your dear friend should be properly married at the steps of a church, by a man of the cloth. She should be spared the old traditions of gaining a husband by spreading her legs wide."

Elizabeth put her goblet down hard on the table. "I will not be marrying you either way, Corwin," she insisted. "Either the old way or the new. You will never have me before a church, and you certainly will never have me in your bed."

Corwin's eyes twinkled. "Your feistiness is what I love about you," he grinned, leaning back in his chair and looking over her with a long draw. "You came eagerly enough into my arms back at the cottage."

"I thought you were Richard!" she snapped in outrage, storming to her feet. "I have had just about enough of this."

Corwin's eyes flicked to Claire. "And you will abandon your friend so quickly, when she has not done what she set out to do? You do seem to lack a sense of honor, after all."

Elizabeth looked down, impotent fury building with her, and then she slowly lowered herself back into her seat. He was right, of course. She was letting herself be drawn into his web. She knew better than that.

His voice came in a teasing lilt. "That is a good girl," he chuckled.

She raised her glass to her lips, taking down the cider in a long draw, willing herself to stay silent.

Claire's voice eased into the silence. "Ah, here comes the main dish. Roast goose – one of my favorites!"

The trenchers were laid out, the platters of meat, cubed turnips, and diced apples presented, and Elizabeth focused deliberately on the meal. She had lost all appetite, but she forced herself to down a few pieces.

Claire deftly took control of the conversation, talking animatedly to the twins, and slowly Elizabeth's shoulders unknotted, her fury ebbed. It mattered not if Corwin rode with her back home. She would need to head out first thing in the morning. If she simply reversed the trek she had just made, it would take another two weeks.

She sighed, poking at the meat before her. She had just gotten through the hellish ride here, and she was already being forced to turn around and go back again. It was just like her father to do this to her.

Claire was holding up her glass, and Elizabeth realized they were offering a toast. A rolled-up scroll was in her other hand, and she was smiling contentedly. Elizabeth brought her glass up with the others, a small amount of calm easing through her. At least one good thing had come out of all of this. She had been able to help her friend.

Claire placed the glass back on the table, then rose slowly. "And with that, I think we should be off," she offered regretfully to the table. "Elizabeth has received bad news, after all, and I should get her back to the nunnery to rest. I thank you for the meal."

Ron and John leapt to their feet as one. "But we had musicians prepared, and dancing!" called out Ron.

Elizabeth was already pushing her chair back. "Perhaps another time," she offered, her tone indicating that she found this quite unlikely. "As Claire has said, I really should be getting home."

Richard was offering his hand, and she took it, the strength and warmth infusing her as powerfully as any tonic she might take. She looked up into his eyes and saw the tension which lay behind them. It occurred to her suddenly that he had bit his tongue throughout the heated argument, not interfering with her interactions with Corwin. She could see the effort of will it had taken him, the pain he had endured by keeping silent.

"Thank you," she whispered, moving a hand to run it through his thick hair.

His eyes held her steadily, the moss-green warm and tender. "I would give my life for you," he murmured. "If what you require instead is for my soul to be flayed for a few hours each night, I will persevere."

"Oh, Richard," she sighed, and then she was pressed up against him, her lips finding his, and his arms came up around her, holding her tightly against him. His kiss was strong, and deep, and she became lost in the pleasure, holding nothing back from him.

There was a deep clearing of a throat to her other side, and Corwin's voice was tight with annoyance. "Surely my older brother can do better than that," he commented snidely. "That barely is the beginning of how a kiss could feel; the feeling of power that is released. You remember, Elizabeth, like you experienced in front of the cottage."

A ripple of tension ran through Richard's shoulders, and he let the kiss linger for another tantalizing moment before pulling back slightly, looking down into her eyes. His gaze was steady, sure, and she drew strength from it.

Her eyes never left his. "Come, my dear, let us head back to the nunnery," she murmured to him. "We have a long trek in front of us in the morning, and we both need some rest." The corners of his mouth eased slightly, and he nodded at her, then at his brothers, before tucking her hand into his arm and escorting her from the room.

They saddled their steeds side by side, a servant taking care of Claire's horse, and in a moment they were mounting and walking through the main courtyard. There was a clatter of hooves as Corwin came trotting up to join them.

"A good host sees his friends safely home," he commented, his eyes moving between the three. "Shall we be off?"

Elizabeth did not reply, pulling in more closely alongside Richard, and he smiled at her, moving in the moonlight beneath the main arches. Claire remained before them, and the group made its way through the quiet night, the dirt path wending its way through grassy meadows.

Corwin's voice interrupted the soft hoot of an owl in the distance. "When we get home, Elizabeth, you probably want me to do the talking with your father. He may be moving toward a reconciliation, but he is still fairly annoyed with your running away like that. He and I are good friends. I am sure with some effort I can smooth things over."

A stab of annoyance lanced into Elizabeth's shoulder, and she shook it off with effort. She turned to look at Richard, on her right. "When we arrive at my family home we should first seek out Father Godfrey and find out exactly what has been happening," she informed him smoothly. "We can discover how ill my father is and what must be done."

He nodded in agreement. "That makes sense. Get all the facts in hand before acting."

Corwin scoffed. "As if that doddering old fool really knows what is going on around him," he pointed out. "Where was he when your brother was being sent off to die? Did he ever take any action to protect you from your father? I am the one who stepped in and began to make real changes."

Elizabeth's emotions roiled. He was right, in a way. Father Godfrey had many good traits, but he had never tried to interfere with her father's harsh rule.

She took in a deep breath. This was how Corwin worked – taking pieces of truth and weaving them into his machinations. She had to build her resistance to it.

She looked over at Richard and he nodded quietly. "Words can be as jagged as a rusty sword's blade," he murmured. "But neither cause injury if properly deflected."

Elizabeth gave him a ghost of a smile. "Or avoided all together," she returned.

Corwin's voice was tight. "You know all about avoidance," he snapped. "You avoided your marriage vows, you avoided your duty to protect your home from attack, and you avoided your father's orders."

It came to Elizabeth's mind suddenly, as clear as a ringing church bell, as brilliant as the morning sun streaming into her practice ring.

She could avoid engaging in Corwin's verbal jousts as well.

There was no commandment which made her answer. There was no real reason to listen to what he said. She knew the words would be poisoned, hurtful, and meant to manipulate her. All she had to do is let them flow off of her, shed them from her body like a well placed deflection moved a sword out of harm's way. She would turn, pivot, and the skewers would drift harmlessly past her.

She gazed up at Richard, and he gave her an encouraging nod, a smile coming to his lips.

Corwin's voice became sharper. "What, afraid to even discuss it now, are you? Has your time away from me turned you coward?"

Elizabeth's voice came out in a gentle murmur, and her eyes were only for Richard. "You know," she suggested, "this ride could end up being fairly tedious, to deal with all the noise and chaos. Besides, winter is coming on. Maybe we should wait for the spring. That would give us several months to spend time together, in the security of the nunnery, just you and me. What do you think?"

Corwin's tone was tight with outrage. "But you and I must return to your father's side!"

Richard's eyes twinkled. "If it is your wish to remain in the quiet of the nunnery, spending our days together in peace, then I will absolutely support you in that."

Elizabeth found she could barely hold in a relieved laugh. "Peace and quiet does sound quite appealing to me right now," she grinned.

There was a muffled snort at her other side, but incredibly Corwin remained utterly silent for the rest of the ride back to the nunnery's gates.

Chapter 16

Michelle's eyes were brimming with tears as she stood with Elizabeth in the center of the courtyard, the faintest hints of morning light barely edging through the dense, dark grey clouds which drifted overhead.

The girl's voice was shaky with sadness. "But why do I have to stay behind?" she pleaded. "I can be a help. You saw how good I was on our way here. I can lead the horses and gather firewood. I promise I will not be any trouble at all."

Elizabeth ran a hand fondly down her short hair, pulling Michelle in close. "You could not be any trouble," she assured her, "and it is because you are so talented that your place is here by Claire's side. You know how much she has come to depend on you already. She says you are her right hand woman and absolutely indispensable."

"I am?" asked the girl, looking up with glittering eyes.

Claire's voice was rich and soothing. "Absolutely," she agreed. "With the new funds provided by the twins, we can now afford a stronger guard presence to keep us safe. Who will help me get all those men settled, learn how things work here?" Her mouth tweaked up into a smile. "And more guards will naturally mean more injuries, more illnesses. How could I lose my best nurse just as we head into the coldest months of the year?"

Elizabeth dropped down to one knee at the girl's side. "And besides, Simon has been quite impressed with your swordplay these past days. He asked me specifically if he could watch over your training while I was away. He has always wanted an apt pupil to teach his techniques to."

"He said that?" squeaked Michelle, her eyes tracking up to the wall of the gate. Simon was standing over the main doors, and he gave a wave, watching over the trio of women with a steady eye.

Michelle wiped her eyes with her sleeve. "I suppose, if it means so much to everyone, that I shall stay and do my part."

"That is my girl," praised Elizabeth, pressing a kiss to her forehead. "It is only because I know you will be here, keeping an eye on everything, that I feel willing to head back home."

"I will not let you down," promised Michelle, her eyes shining.

Elizabeth tousled her hair fondly. "I know you will not."

Simon's voice called out across the crisp morning air. "Two riders approaching."

Claire pulled Elizabeth into a hug, holding her for a while. "You stay safe," she whispered in her ear before pulling back.

Elizabeth smiled comfortingly at her friend. "I will be fine," she assured her. She turned as Susan brought over her horse, and together they all walked toward the closed main gates.

Simon came down the steps with another guard, and with a heave they pulled back the heavy wooden bar. They latched their hands through the leather loops on the doors and pulled hard, swinging the gate open for her.

Elizabeth moved through the stone arch into the quickening breezes as Corwin and Richard drew up to the gates side by side. Both men dismounted easily, moving to stand before her.

Corwin's voice was bright with energy. "About time we got you back home," he stated. "Your vacation was just enough to make your father's heart grow fonder. Any longer and he might have forgotten about you completely."

Simon looked steadily at Richard. "You take care of her," he instructed in a hoarse voice. "See that she makes it there safely."

Corwin scoffed. "I am her intended, and I am right here," he pointed out. "If anybody is keeping an eye on this woman, it will be me."

Richard ignored him, his eyes steadily on Simon's, nodding. "I take my responsibility very seriously," he agreed. "She will be safe."

Simon gave him one last look, then turned to Elizabeth, drawing her in to a warm hug. "You be careful," he murmured. "Winter is coming, and bandits can get desperate."

Elizabeth's mouth turned up in a half smile. "Well do I know it," she responded, pulling back. "I have lived with that threat all my life. I know how to handle it."

She smiled fondly at Claire and Michelle, then she climbed up onto her mount and took the leather reins surely in her hands. Despite all her misgivings, it felt good to be in the saddle, good to be turning her horse's head and pointing him toward the far off mountains. As much as she had enjoyed seeing the ocean, enjoyed the skittering shore birds and tangy salt air, a part of her did long for the high mountains, for the craggy rocks of her homeland.

If her father would have to be there too, she would just have to learn how to deal with him.

With a gentle nudge she set her steed into motion, and Richard and Corwin closed in on either side.

* * *

The rain held off for a half hour at most before it descended from the sky, first in gentle patters, then in steadily increasing sheets until the road before them had become a muddy stream. Elizabeth welcomed the storm. While the steady onslaught of water chilled her, dancing its way down her spine, it also meant that Corwin's mouth was mercifully kept shut. He would have been hard pressed to keep up his steady assault through the loud drumming of water on dirt. They rode with their hoods up, the trio moving inexorably side by side toward the west.

They stopped briefly for a quick meal by the raging tumult of a stream which was overflowing its banks, then pressed on to get as far as they could before the deep grey eased into a darker night. Finally, they were drawing up to a collection of run-down buildings which seemed vaguely familiar to her. As they came to the stables, she realized that it was Hyde's inn. A smile came to her lips. She'd like to see how it was doing under new management. She turned her horse's head, and in a moment the three of them were brushing down their steeds and settling them into their stalls.

A quick sprint across the open courtyard and they were in the main dining area, the same fire blazing in the hearth, apparently the same elderly man snoozing in a chair before it. She chuckled. Some things never did seem to change. There were footsteps, and she turned …

Her mouth dropped open. Hyde's pudgy face was flushed with ale, his eyes drank in her form from the ground up, and when they reached her face he started back in surprise. "And what do *you* want?" he snapped.

Richard's voice was a low growl. "I thought you were hauled in for justice."

Hyde's eyes flickered to Corwin, just for a moment, and outrage streamed through Elizabeth. She rounded on him. "You had something to do with this swine walking free?"

His eyes were stone cold. "And just what exactly was there to go on?" he snapped. "The ramblings of an orphan girl who dressed like a scavenger? And you, did he actually touch you?"

Elizabeth's face flared with heat. "No, but he -"

Corwin's sneer filled her vision. "He what, he hurt your delicate sensibilities? And you think yourself worthy of defending a keep in the mountains?"

Hyde's high voice burst into their argument. "I run a respectable establishment here!" he insisted. "I want you all out!"

Elizabeth's hand flashed to the hilt of her sword, and Richard was before her in an instant, his hand going to her arm. "I will take care of this later," he vowed. "We should move on, and not give him the satisfaction."

Elizabeth knew he was right, but it was a long moment before she could nod, could unwrap the tense fingers from around the hilt and turn. She yanked open the door, stared at the pounding rain which lay beyond, and stormed out into it. She drew to a halt half-way into the courtyard, closing her eyes for a moment, letting the thundering water wash her clean of the filth she felt coating every pore of her skin.

A rushing of feet raced past her on the left, but to the right a steady pair moved to stand beside her. Long moments passed as the cold rain pelted her body, draining away the slime and disgust.

A call shook her from the stables. "What, are you daft, woman? Get in and get your horse ready."

She blinked open her eyes, looking up at Richard. He nodded, and in a moment the two moved in, side by side, to prepare their horses.

The night had become pitch dark as they headed out again. They had barely gone a half mile before Richard slid from his horse, moved to the front, and took Elizabeth's and his reins in his hands, leading the two steeds through the mud with careful attention. Elizabeth could hear Corwin cursing at his steed from the other side, but thankfully much of his ill-tempered rant was lost in the dense storm. Time moved at a crawl as her cloak became even more saturated, pulling down on her shoulders. It seemed an eternity before the lights of the next inn drew into view, before they moved into the relief of the stables, wiping off the weary steeds and getting them settled.

She did not even bother to quicken her pace as she crossed the courtyard to the inn's front door, already as waterlogged as was possible on this long night. She pushed her way within, waiting for the two men before turning to close the door behind her. She shook off the drenched cloak, ignoring the large puddle that immediately began to form beneath it, and turned.

And stopped.

It was the inn. It was where she had first seen Richard on a night which seemed both so long ago and just a heartbeat away. He had been sitting there, at that empty table, with the two rambunctious children on either side of him. She had seen his moss-green eyes and had been lost ...

Corwin pushed past her, heading over to the table, and in a moment her feet were in motion, following him. She sat down at the chair in the center back, the chair Richard had been sitting in, and he settled in at her right. In a second, a pair of buxom shapes had moved over to stare down at them.

The redhead spoke up first. "Why, here is a sight for sore eyes. Corwin, Richard, it has been many years since we saw the two of you in here together. Finally put the hatchet in those old quarrels, have we?"

Richard nodded in greeting to her. "Anna, it has been a while. How is your father's leather shop doing?"

She shrugged. "Same as always, enough to keep us fed, but not enough to cover his gambling debts."

The blonde leant forward, her eyes gleaming. "Will you be needing any extra care tonight, Corwin?"

Corwin's eyes ran down her form with interest, then he reined himself back and glanced over at Elizabeth. "Mathilde, my darling, let me introduce you to the woman who will be my wife. This is Elizabeth."

Elizabeth's eyes flashed with ire, but before she could speak Mathilde was drawing her into a boisterous hug. "You are a lucky girl," she shouted out. "This man is one of the most generous I have ever met." She turned and called to the room. "Corwin is getting himself hitched! Ales all around!"

A hearty cheer went up around the room and Elizabeth shook her head. It was not even worth arguing about. Soon enough they would be gone and well rid of this place.

The women were back in a moment, setting down mugs of ale and bowls of stew. Calls came from all sides as mugs were distributed, and Elizabeth's cheeks flamed more brightly at each shout.

Richard's voice was gentle in her ear. "They are toasting your strength and value," he pointed out to her. "Take pride in that."

She downed half her ale. They were toasting free alcohol being deposited on their table, and not much more.

She focused on the stew before her, her body slowly warming back up as it dried out in the close quarters of the room.

There was a movement above them, and the blonde was back, her grin wide. With a quick flop she had sprawled herself across Richard's lap. "I suppose you are the free one of the evening, then," she purred.

Richard's look was gentle but firm. "You have many other opportunities here tonight, Mathilde," he advised her. "You had best try your luck elsewhere."

She stood with a pout. "You are never interested," she huffed. She turned to stalk across the room toward a pair of farmers.

Corwin's eyes followed her as she went. "You should have given her a go," he advised his brother. "She has this amazing thing she does with her hips."

Elizabeth had had quite enough of this. She downed the rest of her ale in one gulp. "I am heading to bed," she snapped.

Richard waved a hand, and Anna was back at their table in a moment. Richard fished some coins out from a pouch and handed them to her. "We shall need two rooms for the night."

Her eyes went to Corwin and Elizabeth. "One for the lovebirds, I assume?"

Corwin's enthusiastic "Yes!" was overridden by Elizabeth's outraged "No!" and the waitress smiled in amusement. "I will bring the two keys," she assured Richard, and in a moment she had returned, depositing them on the table. "I will leave this for you three to sort out," she advised with a wink before moving on.

Elizabeth pounced on a key, bringing it to her chest. "I am sleeping *alone*," she snapped to Corwin.

He shrugged, spreading his arms wide. "If you want to be cold and lonely, all the better. It means by the time we reach your father's keep that you will be desperate for my touch," he grinned. "You certainly came into my arms quickly enough by the cottage. You must have really missed me."

"I thought you were Richard," she snarled.

"So you say," he returned, his eyes twinkling.

Elizabeth pressed her lips together. She would not be drawn in again. She rose to her feet, and both men moved with her.

Tension streamed down her back. "I can make it to my room just fine on my own," she insisted.

Richard's voice was calm. "Of course you can. Good night," he offered.

She looked up into his eyes, and for a moment the chaos of the day faded away. His gaze was smooth, serene, and steady. She stepped forward toward him, laying her hands gently on his hips, and his arms came up around her as she pressed into him, as she touched his lips for a kiss, first tenderly, then growing in passion.

There was an outraged shout next to them, and Mathilde was standing there, her hands on her hips, looking between Corwin and Richard in shock. "I have heard of siblings sharing things, but this is ridiculous!"

Elizabeth smiled, placing one last kiss on Richard's lips, then winked at Mathilde and walked down the hall to her room.

Chapter 17

Elizabeth pulled her hood closer against the rain, weariness dragging at her very bones. It was only five days into their journey and already it felt as if her joints were permanently soaked. The days grew colder with each passing step, the inns' fires barely heating her up again before it was time for another trip out into the deluge.

She would almost be ready to deal with Corwin's acrid tongue and hostile commentary in exchange for a day or two of merely-gloomy weather. She would not even hope for sun – that might be asking too much. Just a cessation of the watery onslaught was all she hoped for.

There was a rushing noise ahead, and her heart sank. As if the day could not get any more drenched. Ahead of them the road moved toward a ford which, in drier times, was probably quite easy to pass. In the current state of affairs it was a raging river, the water tumbling and cascading, the far bank barely visible in the late evening gloom.

She pulled to a halt at the near edge, looking out over the churning water. At her sides the two men also reined in, their hoods sweeping left and right down the length. The marshy fields around them undulated, easing into dense forest fairly quickly on either side. There was no sign of a bridge or another path.

Richard glanced behind him, back the way they had come. "I believe there was a turn-off to the north about two miles ago," he commented.

Corwin scoffed, his eyes bright with disbelief. "For this tiny trickle? I think your time with the duo dunces has softened your head. There's no reason to retreat from this."

Elizabeth shook her head. "I am not chancing that torrent," she stated firmly. "Even if the steed could swim across -"

"*Even if,*" mimicked Corwin, his voice harsh. "What are you, twelve years old?"

Steel shot up Elizabeth's spine. "I am willing to face odds that are reasonable," she snapped. "This is simply ridiculous. I will not -"

His sword was out in a flash, it glittered in a sweeping arc, and the flat of the blade landed hard against her steed's rump with an echoing SLAM.

Her horse reared up in a wild panic, she flung herself forward to keep her seat, and in an instant the steed was lunging full bore into the raging river.

"Richard!" she screamed, pressing herself hard against her horse's neck, squeezing her thighs against his flank, willing herself to stay atop the powerful beast. His chest heaved as he pushed hard through the current and was instantly swept downstream. His breath came out in long whoofs as he struggled to keep his head above the churning water.

"Hang in there," she urged him, sweeping her head around in the chaos. The water roiled, the fog rolled, and steadily but surely the horse inched toward the other bank, trees and rocks racing by as they moved.

BUMP. A medium-sized branch bounced off her right leg, sliding past her horse's rump and swirling away into the gloomy mist. She shook off the surprise. Thank the Lord that it had only been -

Her eyes tracked to the right, and she stopped, all thought freezing in place in her brain. A massive willow tree was sweeping down the river toward them, its roots bare and outstretched toward the sky, its many branches swirling and grasping like the myriad arms of a monstrous octopus.

There was nowhere to go. Her horse was barely holding his own against the river. She took in a deep breath as the dark shape thundered toward her, and then -

SLAM.

* * *

An ocean's worth of water filled Elizabeth's lungs, and she sprawled face-first in the mud, coughing as hard as she could, desperately wheezing in breaths of air between the hacks. A strong hand pounded on her back, holding her firmly against a broad chest, and she could not think past the spewing of liquid, the desperate inhales, the raging sound of rushing river which bellowed around her.

Finally she could breathe in without panic, could cough out only on the third inhale, then every fifth, and then she fell back limp against him, completely spent, her mind blank.

He sat there for a long time, holding her close, his own breath slowing from desperate heaves to a sturdier pace. He folded her in against himself, cradling her with his body, tenderly stroking her hair, murmuring against her ear.

She finally turned to look up at him, and his eyes were haggard with relief, his gaze scanning over her face as if seeing her for the first time after long years of absence. His lips came down to meet hers, and her heart warmed with exquisite joy as they met, as she felt the love and tenderness which eased from the contact.

At last he pulled back slightly to look her over. "How hurt are you?" he asked hoarsely.

It was hard to see in the near twilight, but Elizabeth looked herself over. She was aching all over, her clothing was ripped in several places, and a shivering began to steal over her, slowly at first, and then more strenuously as she sat. She could not tell if she was injured, but flexings of her fingers and toes told her that at least all her major limbs were still functional.

She nodded tenuously at him, and he drew her carefully to her feet. "We have to get you to an inn," he stated firmly. To her relief their two steeds waited nearby, drenched to the bone but seemingly unhurt. "Can you ride?"

"I believe so," she agreed, moving toward her steed. "What happened to Corwin?"

His eyes darkened. "I do not know, and I do not care," he growled, helping her to mount, then quickly gaining his own seat. "Let us get you to a warm fire before we worry about his worthless hide."

They pressed on through the rain along the dark road, Richard close at her side, the path barely visible before them. Elizabeth was relieved when the lights of a village appeared just around a bend in the trees. Within minutes they were unsaddling the exhausted horses in a warm stable, laying out their food, and crossing through the sturdy door of a well-kept inn.

A hearty shout welcomed them, and Elizabeth staggered to a stop as Corwin, grinning widely, came toward them, a key in one hand, a large, grey-brown towel in the other. "There you are! You will be happy to know that everything is prepared for you. Warm food, a dry room, and even a fresh change of clothes if you want them.

This serving girl here seems to be exactly your proportions, and -"

Elizabeth's hand dropped to the hilt of her sword, and she took a staggering step toward him. Richard was between them in a minute, snatching the key out of Corwin's hand, turning to grab Elizabeth with the other as she half stumbled against him.

The waitress, her ebony curls bouncing, smiled at the couple. "These are ya friends, huh?" she laughed to Corwin, nudging him in the hip. She turned to the two. "She's in the second door on the right," she called after them as they moved toward the rooms. "Just yell if ya need anything."

Richard didn't slow in his movements, and Elizabeth was grateful for his support as he drew her in against him, fumbled with the lock for a minute, then pushed open the door. The room was as basic as they came – a straw mat, a stool, a tiny table barely large enough for a mug of mead. He kicked the door closed with his foot as she tumbled forward, and he helped to ease her down onto the bed.

Her shivering grew, and he cursed as he knelt next to her and began stripping off her sodden cloak, the water-logged tunic, and the chemise beneath. Elizabeth was beyond caring about issues of privacy or modesty. She lay back against the mat, the shivering growing, as Richard removed every last strip of clothing from her.

He drew the blankets close around her, then strode to the door, shouting out back toward the main room. "I need more blankets, and a jug of mead," he yelled out to nobody in particular. He left the door open a crack while he moved back to the bed, tossing his own cloak in a corner, kneeling down against Elizabeth and rubbing her limbs through the cloth.

"Come on now, hang in there," he murmured to her, his voice tense. There was a movement behind him, and the dark-haired woman scurried in, blankets over one arm, a pottery jug in the other. He grabbed the blankets without a word, draping them over Elizabeth, and she put the mead down next to the bed.

"He didn't say she were sick," muttered the serving girl, her eyes looking doubtfully over the figure huddled in the bed.

"Stew, and bandages," he ordered, his eyes not leaving Elizabeth's form.

She nodded, and as she hurried from the room another form eased in.

"If you baby her, she will only languish," Corwin insisted with a shrug, barely glancing at the form on the bed. "She needs to toughen up."

Richard was on his feet in a heartbeat, his hand at his hilt, his eyes cold marbles. "Leave now, or prepare to draw," he growled, his shoulders carved from stone.

Corwin put his hands up, stepping back. "Touchy, are we? The woman will clearly live. It was only a dousing."

The serving girl eased past him, carrying a bowl of stew, a roll of bandages tucked under elbow. Richard took both from her. In a moment he had closed the door behind them, dropping the bar firmly into place. Then he had eased to his knees by Elizabeth's side, first picking up the jug of mead. He raised it to her lips, and she took a shuddering drink, the warm liquid tracing a path down her insides. She closed her eyes in relief. At long last she was beginning to warm, the shudders were beginning to slow and drain from her body. She lay back against the mat, exhausted, as Richard carefully began to spoon up the rich stew. She could do no more than open her lips as it drew near, wait patiently for him to deposit it into her mouth, and work to swallow.

Finally she was full, the shivering ceased, and she could not hold her eyes open a moment longer. Richard had layered a mound of blankets over her and a warmth was slowly stealing over her from within. His hand gently stroked the hair away from her face, and she nuzzled into it. He had collapsed to sit at her side, and she curled up toward him, resting her hand in his, all else fading.

* * *

Elizabeth drifted into awareness, every part of her body aching. Her mind searched to latch onto what had happened. Had her father taken over a sparring practice again? She experimentally stretched with each finger, then each toe, testing to see what might be broken. Finally, convinced that she was fairly intact, she tentatively opened her eyes.

The room was unfamiliar. The late morning sun streamed in through the lone window, drawing her eyes to the worn walls, the scuff marks on the door. Her eyes traced around …

Richard was collapsed, exhausted, at her side. His leather gear was still damp against him, and his cloak lay flung in a corner.

She reached out to draw in the jug of mead which sat near the foot of her bed, then moved to sit up beside him. Carefully she brushed the hair from his face.

He sprang awake instantly, his hand coming down to trap hers, then relaxing back when he realized who it was. She raised the mug, and he nodded, leaning back as she poured some down his throat. Color rose to his face, and the tension in his face eased slightly.

His voice was hoarse when he spoke. "How are you feeling?"

The hint of a smile played on her face. "Nothing seems to be broken," she returned. "How are you doing?"

He shrugged that off, turning to look at her, drinking her in as if she had been gone for months. "You had a number of serious gashes; they should be looked at," he cautioned her.

She began peeling off the blankets in curiosity, and he turned in an instant, looking at the far wall. "You are not dressed," he quickly informed her. His voice was tight. "It was necessary to check -"

She scoffed at his prudery. "If you had not, and missed a serious wound, I could have bled out. And then where would I be?" She threw off the last of the covers, then sat up, stretching her feet out before her. She wriggled her toes.

Ten functional toes. Check.

His voice was rough, his back stiff. "How do the wounds look?"

"Toes are all right," she reported merrily, sliding her attention to her calves. A few scratches, but no major damage.

"Toes?" he asked in confusion.

She shrugged her shoulders, sliding her attention up to her knees. "How do you do your injury check? Surely you have some sort of a system?"

He shook his head in disbelief, and her eyes moved up to her thighs. Here is where it got interesting, apparently. A dingy white bandage was wrapped thoroughly around her right thigh. She poked at it experimentally. "So what is under this?"

He half-turned before catching himself. "Your leg? A sharp branch must have caught you when you got sucked under the tree."

Her eyes lit up with interest. "Really? I want to see." She began unwrapping the bandage with careful pulls.

"I am not sure that is the best idea," he insisted, again beginning to turn before stopping.

"Oh for goodness sake," she sighed, and leant forward, grabbing at a fresh chemise that lay at the end of her bed. She tugged it on over her arms, easing the bandage on her right arm through one sleeve, wincing at the pain in her left side. She would get to those soon enough. At last she had it over her and down to the top of the bandage. "You can look now," she informed him.

He turned at that, his eyes going to the myriad of scratches and bruises scattered along both legs, and his eyes hardened for a moment, then gentled as he moved to help her with the unwinding.

The gash was raw, crimson, crusted with dried blood and pus. It traced from the top of her kneecap, turning to slide along her inner thigh in a jagged groove, coming to stop just below her groin. About half way up the length it crossed the thinner mark made by Corwin's blade, which looked like a kitten's scratch in comparison.

Her eyes went wide as she carefully examined each end, at how the injury had barely missed her kneecap, at how it drew up just in time to avoid the major blood vessels at the top of her inner leg.

"By the grace of God," she murmured, drawing a finger along its length. "I could easily have been crippled, or bled out in minutes."

Richard was still at her side. "Well do I know it," he agreed hoarsely. "I could not sleep all night, with that very image in my mind."

He reached behind him, picking up a fresh bandage roll, then moved to the table and brought over the bowl of water sitting there. He wiped attentively along the wound's length, clearing away any loose debris that he could, careful not to disturb the crust of blood which had formed. That done, he gently wrapped the fresh bandage along the wound, tucking the last end in place.

A quirk of a smile teased the corner of Elizabeth's lips. "Turn around again, then," she instructed Richard, nudging him.

He dutifully turned to look at the wall, and she raised her chemise up, examining her stomach and back with careful attention. A massive bruise was turning purple-violet on her left side, but no ribs seemed to be broken. Her chest was merely welted and cut. She dropped the chemise back down to cover her body, then called out merrily to Richard.

"The torso seems to be all right. You can turn while I do the arms."

He helped her to pull her left sleeve back to the shoulder, and she looked down its length with meticulous attention, flexing her fingers, bending her elbow at every angle possible. "This arm is my life," she murmured, prodding at the bicep with her fingers. "Of any part of me, I am thankful it made it through unscathed."

Breathing a sigh of relief, she pulled down the sleeve. She next turned to her right arm. Richard sat alongside her to help ease the sleeve up over the bandage which encased her upper arm.

She eyed it with curiosity. "Is it any worse than the leg? Clearly I can move my fingers and elbow, so it could not be too horrific."

He gave a wry grin. "You certainly have a lenient way of judging injuries," he murmured. "I would say about the same severity."

"Then I am fortunate," she proclaimed, beginning the unwrapping effort. When the last bits of cloth had been pried away from the skin, she agreed with his assessment. Once again the deep gouge had barely missed her elbow, had cut its way along the tender flesh beneath her arm and ended a hair's breadth away from the life-ending area beneath the armpit, the one she had been trained to protect at all costs in a sword fight.

She held her arm up above her as he cleaned the area and wrapped it with fresh bandages. Then she turned to face him.

"I find it challenging to examine my own head," she admitted with a smile. "Anything to report there?"

She bent her head forward to him, and there was a long moment before he leant in against her, his breath warm on her neck. She found herself relaxing against him, drinking in his strength.

"You are making it challenging for me to focus," he murmured, his hands carefully working their way along her neck, up her skull.

She turned in his arms, bringing her eyes up to meet his, and she was caught by the desire she saw shining in them. "Maybe the touch of your healing hands is just what I need to mend properly," she teased, leaning forward slightly to brush her cheek against his.

He groaned, almost leant in, then pulled back, rocking back on his heels. "I will bring you safely to your father's," he ground out, letting out a deep breath. "Your injuries need time to mend, and you need time to plan out your next step."

She shrugged with a smile. "These scrapes will not hold me back," she insisted, drawing to her feet easily, looking around for something to put on over her chemise. A pale violet dress lay in one corner, and she moved toward it, drawing it on over the white under-dress.

"One of the women staying here had a spare dress with her, and I bought it from her," explained Richard as she settled it into place. "The clothes you were wearing were shredded, and the pack with the purple dress and your other gear was swept downstream when you were ripped from your horse's back."

"This will do quite fine," agreed Elizabeth, giving her left arm an experimental swing. "It is tight enough not to get in the way, and loose enough to offer free range of motion."

He gave a low chuckle at that. "Is that how you judge your clothing, by your ability to sword-fight in it?"

She glanced up. "Surely you consider it as well?" she pointed out.

He nodded, and was lost in her gaze for a long moment. Then he gave a small shake and looked around the room. "We can stay as long as you need, but if you are ready it might be best to head out. There is only one inn within the day's ride, and if we do not make it there we will have to sleep in the rain."

She rolled her shoulders, noted where the aches were, then nodded. "I seem good to go," she agreed. He unbarred the door, and together they headed out to the stables. Thankfully the rain seemed to be easing off. The day was chilly, but only a light scattering of drops drifted from the sky.

Elizabeth moved into the stables – and pulled to a hard stop. Corwin was standing there, his eyes sweeping around to look at her, disdain in them. "About time," he snapped. "Is he making you soft? There was nothing even broken!"

Richard took a step forward, his shoulders tense. "You nearly killed her," he snarled.

Corwin's face held disgust. "The woman is standing; her limbs are moving fine. You act as if she is a toddler," he returned. His eyes swept to pin Elizabeth's. "And what is that dress you are wearing? Why not put on the engagement dress, as we will be at your home in a few days?"

Richard's voice snapped back at him. "That was in the pack, which was lost downstream, as she nearly was."

Corwin's eyes sharpened in displeasure. "You lost the engagement dress?" he asked, his eyes drilling into Elizabeth.

Richard's hand dropped to the hilt of his sword. "I will not allow you to risk her life again," he stated coldly. "You will ride out of earshot of us from this point forward. If we can hear your voice, if you are within thirty feet of us, I will turn her right around and we will return to the nunnery for the winter. She will be safely within those walls until spring."

Elizabeth would not have believed it if she had not been staring into Corwin's eyes in growing fury – but for an instant there was a flicker of fear, a nervousness that she would not have thought possible. Then his arrogance had returned, and he was scoffing openly.

"Your father is dying," he laughed to Elizabeth. "Your honor would not allow you to retreat now."

Elizabeth took a step forward, coming to Richard's side, twining her fingers into his. "Absolutely I would go with Richard," she stated calmly, amazed at how the anger ebbed, how a rich sense of evenness descended over her as she spoke. "My father was an abusive tyrant. It would give me the greatest of pleasure to think of him dying alone."

Corwin opened his mouth – then to her surprise he closed it again. It had never occurred to her that she might be able to counter his arguments. He had seemed so strong, so right, so able to twist her words to fit his own needs. And yet here he was, drawing new measure of her.

"It might do you some good to miss me for a while," he cut out at last. "I saw how you greeted me at the cottage after an absence. You need some reminding of what it is like to be without me."

His horse was already saddled, and in a moment he had pulled out of the stables, leaving them behind in silence. Elizabeth almost could not believe it. She looked over at Richard, who gave her hand a gentle squeeze. Then they were working side by side, preparing their horses, riding them out into the late fall chill.

Corwin shadowed them, and she could see his scowl even at a distance, but the day went by in quiet calm as they moved along the road, ever closer to her home. The landscapes were beginning to become more mountainous, the ground more rugged, and her shoulders eased. It was good to be coming home. Despite all the painful memories, it still felt right to watch the heights climb, see the beginning of the snowcaps she loved so much.

It seemed only the blink of an eye before dusk was settling across the landscape, before they were pulling into a stable and settling their horses into stalls. Corwin came in a few minutes later, and Elizabeth could see the effort it took him to ease his scowl, to present a look of superior strength. He took the lead as the three pushed into the busy inn.

Elizabeth eased wearily down into her chair, and Richard looked over in concern. "How are your injuries doing?"

Elizabeth ran a hand carefully along the wound at her thigh, the leg throbbing more steadily now. "I am glad we are resting for the night," she admitted. "I will need a solid sleep to be ready for tomorrow."

Corwin's voice was sharp. "There are still four more days ahead of us," he commented, waving for ales. "Time for you to stop acting like an infant, and just handle the pain."

Elizabeth bit back the response which sprang to her lips. She could certainly not control Corwin, but she could control her responses to him.

The ales were served out, and in a moment stews followed. Richard leaned over and murmured something into the waitress's ear, and she nodded, her eyes moving momentarily to Elizabeth.

Richard took a draw of his ale, looking around the noisy room. "When she has time later, she will come by with fresh bandages for you," he explained. "We need to keep those wounds clean."

Corwin let out a laugh. "She is not a fainting flower," he sneered at his brother. "She has taken far worse than this in the past."

Richard's face went still, but he took Elizabeth's hand in his, giving it a squeeze before returning to his stew, taking in another drink of ale.

Elizabeth finished off her stew, weariness dragging at her shoulders. It had been a long day, and the injuries had worn at her more than she cared to admit. Richard took one look at her face and stood, helping her to stand alongside him.

Corwin leant back in his seat. "I will get the girl to bring along the bandages," he offered. Elizabeth gave him a nod, then together she and Richard made their way to her room.

He eased her down onto her mat, and she lay her head back onto the pillow, twining her hand into his. Exhaustion settled into every limb. "I think I will just sleep like this; I am sure the wounds are fine," she sighed, curling up on her side, pulling his arm in against her. Her eyelids were heavier than she could have imagined. "Stay here with me," she murmured.

There was a sigh, and his hand stroked gently against her hair. "I think it best if I return to my room," he answered softly.

She relished the strength of his fingers, the warmth of his body where it touched her. "I care little about what the innkeeper might say," she muttered.

"It is not -"

There was a hammering at the door, and his hand withdrew in an instant, dropping to rest on the hilt of his blade. She knew she should be scrambling for her own sword, leaping to her feet, but it was all she could bring herself to do to struggle to a seated position as he strode to the door and stood against it.

"Who is there?" he called out, his voice sharp.

The voice was muffled by the thick door. "It is the inn-keep. Open up immediately."

Richard glanced back at Elizabeth for a moment, then unbarred and opened the door half way. "What is this about?"

The inn-keep was a swarthy man, short, stout, his flame-red hair askew. His eyes were crackling with heat, and his cheeks burned crimson. "Out. Both of you. Immediately."

Elizabeth pushed herself to her feet, wincing as her thigh almost refused to hold her weight. Richard was at her side in an instant, putting his arm around her. "What is this about?" he called back to the surly man. "Surely you can see this woman is injured."

"I do not care. Get out. Get out, or I will throw you out," he snarled.

Richard reached down with his free hand to grab her scabbard and belt, then tossed the two cloaks over his shoulder. He slowly, carefully helped Elizabeth down the hallway and out into the common room.

Most of the candles were out now, and the main light came from the fireplace at one end of the room. The tables and chairs sat empty in the dark night. All but one. A young girl, perhaps thirteen, sat sniffling. When they passed her, she raised her head to look at them, tears streaming from her eyes.

Elizabeth staggered to a halt. The girl's eye was swollen and closing, the lids nearly glued shut by the pressure. A large bruised area was rising around cheek.

"What in the world -"

The inn-keep strode forward, raising his hand. "Out!" he snapped.

Richard put a hand up in appeasement, the other firmly around Elizabeth, and in a moment they were out in the deep chill of the dark night, making their way through torchlight to the stables.

Corwin looked up with a shake of the head as they came into the open area at the center of the building. "Can you believe how touchy they are in these parts," he scoffed. "Clearly if the girl had just -"

Elizabeth stared at him, mouth open. "You were responsible for doing that to that young girl?"

Corwin's eyes narrowed. "She was a servant! And can you believe she -"

Elizabeth took a step toward him, her heart hammering in her chest. "She was barely thirteen!" she cried. "She was half your size! How could anything she did be worth that kind of reaction from a grown man?"

He shook his head as if she were daft. "How could a woman with your past even make such a statement?" he retorted. "How old were you when you caused your brother to be sent to his death?"

Elizabeth's world slowed to stillness. For the first time she saw the scene from another vantage. Her father, burly, strong, a seasoned warrior, came storming into the keep's courtyard. She was toned, yes, but still young, so young, with a thin body not yet filled out with a woman's curves. Her father had picked up the quarter staff, had swung it high, and had brought it down …

"How could he have done it?" she found herself whispering, and Richard's arm was sturdy around her, holding her up.

Corwin's voice was harsh, the cawing of a crow. "Are you trying to claim you did not deserve the punishment you received?" he scoffed.

Elizabeth's response was the faintest of threads. "No child deserves to be beaten," she stammered, the reality of it growing from a kindle, flaming more strongly within her.

Corwin's eyes glowed as he stared at her. "As the Bible says, 'He that spareth his rod hateth his son' – and that applies to daughters too," he snapped. "And once you are my wife, you will discover that discipline applies equally in marital relations."

Elizabeth's voice grew strong and cold. "I shall *never* be your wife," she snapped, her eyes holding his.

Corwin took a menacing step toward her. "We shall see what your father says about that," he growled.

Richard dropped the cloaks and belt on the ground, stepping strongly between the two, his eyes on Corwin. "You have caused enough damage to Elizabeth to last a lifetime," he ground out. "I expand my previous order. It seems that not even 'out of earshot' can keep you from creating harm. If you are even seen by us for the rest of this trip – even a glimpse – then we will both turn around and return to Claire and Michelle. I will see Elizabeth safely within those walls, and those gates will never open to your call."

Corwin waved a hand back in the direction of the inn. "She was just a girl!" he snapped. "All this angst over a little girl?"

Elizabeth's voice was cold. "Just a *girl*," she snarled.

Corwin took another step forward. "But this is -"

Richard snapped his head to look at Corwin. "That is it; back we go," he stated, turning to gather up the cloaks. "If we press hard, we can be safely there by -"

"Fine, brother," snarled Corwin, falling back a pace. "I will leave you alone as you take Elizabeth home to her father. I am sick of seeing your face anyway." His gaze turned to lay on Elizabeth, heavy with disdain. "I will press on ahead and prepare things with your father. He will want to hear what has been going on, and how to handle you."

"Give him my regards," responded Elizabeth flatly.

Corwin's eyes swung back to hold Richard's, and the green marbles took on a menacing sparkle. "See that you treat your charge with honor," he growled. "If you lay one hand on my wife, if she comes to me in a less than pure state, then you will answer not only to me, but to her father as well." He held his gaze, then turned and mounted in one smooth motion. He wheeled his mount, then pressed out past them into the ebony night.

Elizabeth stared out after him. As she stood there her leg began to throb with fresh pain. She winced, lowering her hand to rub against the wound.

Richard looked at her in concern. "I could go back in, try to reason with the inn-keep."

She shook her head, straightening up again. "They have been through enough for one night," she murmured. "Let us press on a few miles. I am sure we can find somewhere to hole up." She glanced out through the open doors. "At least the rain has stopped. With a good fire we should be able to hold off the chill."

In a few moments they had saddled up their steeds and were heading out side by side. Elizabeth was past exhausted, but she pressed her lips together and held in the moans. Her side ached, her arm felt as if fiery rats were gnawing it, and her leg shuddered with her steed's every step.

It seemed like hours before Richard pointed out a hollow on one side of the road, nestled under an elderly oak with spreading branches. A fallen trunk and ring of stones showed that it had served other travelers in the past. He dismounted and led both horses down into the nook, then eased her off her steed. It was all she could do to remain standing until he lay both cloaks down against the trunk and helped her down into the cocoon. He wrapped the layers against her and then began gathering up sticks to make a fire.

In a short while a sturdy heat was blazing within the rings, but Elizabeth still fought off a coldness within her core; she began shivering against it. Richard knelt at her side in concern. He offered a skin of mead, and she drank from it gladly, but still the darkness pressed down on her from all sides, sapping her strength.

His face creased with concern and hesitation. At last he lifted off the cloaks and eased himself in behind her, drawing the cloaks down around them both, wrapping his arms around her.

All at once her shivering ceased; warmth eased through her, spreading into every limb, stretching tendrils into every part of her. She nestled back against him, and he gave a soft groan, his arms wrapping more tightly around her, his lips nuzzling down against her neck.

She sighed in contentment. "This is more like it," she mused, her eyes blissfully shut, as she fit herself more perfectly to his strength, to his warmth.

The pains and aches of the world drifted away, and she was lost to the night.

Chapter 18

Elizabeth drifted awake, a most delightful lassitude filling her body. She could sense, remotely, the throbbing of her leg, the edged pain in her arm, the chill of the air beyond their cloaks.

None of that mattered.

She rotated within Richard's arms, relishing the warmth of his body against her. She turned up to look up at him in the dancing, golden morning light.

"Good morning," she murmured, brushing her lips against his.

He groaned, pressing his lips against hers for a long moment. At last, with a sigh, he pulled back. He drew up to one knee, looking down at her.

"How are your injuries doing?" he asked, his eyes going to her arm, then her thigh.

She sat up, giving her arm an experimental shake, then wriggling her leg in the air. "Mending," she offered with a smile.

He stood, drawing her up, then turned to begin breaking camp. He gathered up the cloaks and poured the pot of water over the remains of the campfire's embers.

She watched him for a minute, her eyes creasing. His motions were already becoming as familiar to her as her own stride.

"Did you get any sleep?" she asked suddenly, taking in the lag in his step, the infinitesimally slower way in which he snugged up his steed's saddle.

His eyes swung to meet her, surprised, then, with a long exhale, he shook his head. "Not a wink," he admitted.

Elizabeth flushed with guilt. It was one thing for her to enjoy the sensations of his body against hers, but it was quite another to drive him to survive without any rest. "I am sorry," she murmured.

His mouth rose in a half smile. "Tonight we will find a proper inn, and I shall catch up," he stated. "I can survive a night without rest, not to worry."

In a moment they were mounted and riding through the misty dawn. Her breath came out in soft, shimmering clouds of pearl-white, and the mountains rose before her with each passing step.

A comforting sensation began to wrap itself around her. Home. She was going home. With all its pains and aches and traumas, it still had the power to call to her.

The day scrolled by in tranquil quiet. They saw few people along the way; the quiet villages they passed were tucked in against the coming winter, the barn doors closed, the shutters sealed tight. Richard was a steady presence by her side, his eyes alert, but Elizabeth could see the fatigue in his shoulders.

She was glad when the sun began easing toward the horizon and they entered the stables alongside their chosen inn for the evening. Together they tucked the horses into their stalls and pressed open the door to the dining area.

The room was sparsely populated; only a few tables were occupied with local farmers or passing merchants. A buxom woman in a mustard-colored dress came bustling up to them with a regretful frown. "You are welcome to stew and ale, but I am afraid we are full up for the night," she apologized. "I might suggest ..."

Richard was shrugging off his cloak and turned to look at her. She started, gazing at his eyes, then back at

Elizabeth. "Oh, my pardon," she corrected herself. "Two of the rooms are reserved for you, I believe. You are Elizabeth and Richard?"

Richard glanced warily at Elizabeth before responding. "We have rooms reserved?"

The woman nodded with a relieved smile, running a hand through light brown curls. "Yes indeed, your brother was through here earlier. It is all arranged and paid for. Now, if you will come have a seat?"

Elizabeth moved at Richard's side, taking a seat at a round oak table, and in a moment the stew and ale were laid out. Elizabeth watched the woman go, then turned to gaze at Richard.

"What do you think?" she asked with curiosity. "Could he be up to something?"

Richard's eyes were creased with thought. "My brother is always up to something," he mused. "But it could be that he simply is trying to get back into your good graces before you arrive home. He wants to give you the impression of being the one who cares for you."

Elizabeth scoffed, downing a long draw of her ale. "His tossing money at me does not impress me," she ground out, "especially since the money he is spending is undoubtedly part of the dowry my father gave him."

Richard's eyes dropped to his bowl, and he began taking in bites of stew, not speaking.

She put her hand over his, and his eyes came up to hold hers. Her voice was warm and sure. "I do not care what my father chooses, or what Corwin chooses," she stated in a low voice. "I will make my own decision in life about the path I follow."

His gaze stayed on her for a long minute, then at last he nodded. "I am just exhausted," he stated. "It will be good to get some rest, once I see you safely to your room."

Her mouth quirked up into a smile. "Well then, let us eat and be on our way there."

A few minutes later they were scraping their bowls clean and finishing off the drink. Richard waved for the inn-keep, and she was over in a minute. "Ready for sleep already? If you will just follow me."

They rose and went after her up two flights of stairs, ending up at a small hallway in the attic, flanked by a pair of doors. "This is our safest floor," the woman stated with pride. "Just as requested." She pushed open the door to the left. "And here is your room, miss."

The bedroom was cozy and neat. The shutters were closed against the night chill and a mound of quilted blankets waited on the mattress in one corner.

The woman nodded in satisfaction. "You should be quite comfortable here." She turned to face Richard. "And your bed, sir, is on the ground floor, as requested, facing the stables so you can keep an eye on the steeds."

Elizabeth spun in surprise, her eyes seeking to the room across the hall. "But there is that room there -"

The inn-keep nodded warmly. "I am right there," she agreed congenially. "Anything you need, any time at night, just knock. I will be keeping an eye out for your every wish."

Elizabeth flushed, looking down. Corwin had indeed thought of everything. She glanced up at Richard's face, and sighed. The man was indeed exhausted. Perhaps this was for the best.

"Good night," she offered, and already the loneliness was drawing out the warmth. He had not even left her threshold and she was missing him.

"Sleep well," he returned, his eyes gentle. "You will be safe, and I am content." He pulled the door shut, and she could hear him waiting outside until she moved to slide the bar in place. Then a pair of footsteps was receding down the flights of stairs, fading until a silence settled over the empty night.

Elizabeth moved to the lone candle on the table. She cupped her hand behind it, then blew it out. She unbuckled her belt, dropping her sword and dagger by the side of bed, then climbed under the covers fully clothed.

The blankets were warm, and the room all she could hope for, and yet an emptiness pulled at her, echoed in her ears. She missed Richard's warm body behind her, his sturdy arms wrapped around her in a protective embrace. She drew in deep, long breaths, striving to will herself to release her longing, to settle down to sleep. Yet every part of her was filled with a deep-seated craving, a soul-wrenching desire. Every creak of the aging building caused her heart to leap with the wild thought that he was coming up to join her.

The night passed at a crawl, her mind unable to rest, her body wanting him with every breath.

Chapter 19

Elizabeth knew dawn was finally coming as the slatted shadows on the floor began to resolve with more clearly defined edges. Wearily she pushed the blankets away, drawing on her belt with a sigh, running her hands through her hair before sliding the bar free and heading slowly down the creaking stairs.

Richard was sitting at a table by the window, staring out into the growing gold of dawn. He turned at her approach, rising with a smile, then his brows creased as he took a step toward her.

"Did you get a wink of sleep?" he asked, offering a hand to her and bringing her to sit beside him.

She shook her head with a sigh. "I tried my best," she grumbled, "but …" She shook her head.

His gaze softened. "I know," he murmured. "Only a few more days before we are at your father's and everything becomes resolved. You are shouldering a lot right now."

Elizabeth looked down at his hands, twining her own into them. "It is not my father which occupies my thoughts," she suggested, and her eyes drew up to hold his.

His gaze shot to hers, his eyes widened slightly, and it was a long moment before his breath released. His fingers rippled into hers more fully, drawing her in.

A figure bustled over toward them. "Your bill is fully settled," offered the woman with warmth. "Would you like anything before you head out? Mead? Some bread?"

Elizabeth rose, shaking her head. "We must be on our way," she responded. "I want to get this trip over with as quickly as possible."

In a moment she and Richard were saddled and riding through the crisp chill. She stayed close by his side, drinking in his presence, making up for the long night she had been apart from him. She reached out a hand for him, and he smiled as he adjusted his reins and took it, their horses ambling side by side. Despite the grey day's chill a warmth grew within her, easing into every corner of her being, shimmering in a golden light.

They broke for lunch and she sat against him. His arm came up around her, sheltering her within its crook. She was hard pressed to draw apart from him when it was time to get back on the road, and her thigh nearly touched his as they set back in motion down the road.

The sun was barely easing toward the hills when she began seeking out the next inn, watching for its approach. They entered the outskirts of the village, wended their way past the blacksmith and rough-hewn church, then finally came to a stop within the quiet stables. He helped her slide down from her steed, her injuries throbbing with fresh pain, and she barely protested as he took over the care of her steed. In a few minutes he had finished and was escorting her into the well-lit room.

All eyes swung to stare at them as they drew to a stop within the door, and she could not put a finger on the emotion they held. It was interest, surely, but coupled with something else. The thin, reedy inn-keep glanced at Richard sideways before showing them to a corner in the back recesses of the room, slapping down a pair of bowls and mugs before skittering nervously away.

Elizabeth was too tired for this. She dropped her eyes, doggedly downing the stew which was fairly overcooked and dry. At her side Richard was eating more slowly, his gaze carefully scanning out over the room, making note of each eye which met his or slid uneasily to the side.

She downed the rest of her ale, and a waitress bubbled up to the table with a smile. "Well, there, would you like …" her gaze moved to catch Richard's and she stopped, falling a step back, looking at his eyes. "I mean …" she flustered, glancing between the two.

Elizabeth surged to her feet, glaring around the room. "I have no idea what Corwin has done now," she muttered under her breath to Richard, "But I will not stay within these walls tonight."

Richard looked as if he agreed wholeheartedly, but his gaze turned to hers in concern. "You are exhausted," he pointed out.

She gave a rough shake of her head, reaching into her pouch and tossing down a few coins. "All the more reason to be somewhere safer," she pointed out.

He nodded at that, and in a few moments they were working side by side in the stables, remounting their horses, and moving out into the ebony blackness.

After a few miles, Elizabeth could barely hold her eyes open. Richard stayed close at her side, and as soon as a grassy area opened up on the left he guided them toward it. He laid out his cloak and settled her onto it. He hobbled the horses, then prepared a small fire while she shivered, curled up in a small ball.

He eased down behind her, drawing his own cloak up over them both, and she sighed, settling into his nooks as if they had always belonged together.

Her voice was weary. "I am sorry if I keep you up again," she murmured, drawing his arms in against her.

"You just rest," he returned soothingly, and in a moment she had fallen sound asleep.

* * *

Elizabeth blinked her eyes open, looking out at the delicate tracery of hoarfrost which lay over the meadows before her. It was as if an ice-winged fairy had danced across the tops of each strand, laying a delicate weaving of snowflakes there to delight her. Richard's arm was warm beneath her head, and she gave a gentle pull to his hand, wrapping it more securely around her waist. He moved instinctively, nestling her in closer, moving his lips against her neck for a soft kiss.

"Good morning," she murmured.

His voice was throaty. "Good morning," he agreed against her ear.

She rotated within his embrace, turning to look up at him. "Did you at least get a little sleep this night?"

He nodded with a half smile, his eyes gazing down into hers. "It seems exhaustion does bring some benefits," he murmured.

She was caught by his gaze, the gentle melding of fondness and strength and protective concern, and then he was separating himself from her, drawing to his feet, holding a hand down to her. She took it, amazed as always at how easily he lifted her weight, at how his muscles barely flexed as he brought her up to standing. And then he was saddling the horses, gathering their cloaks, and getting them on their way.

* * *

The sun was barely easing its way down when Elizabeth began to rein in at the small village, looking at the small, run-down inn with curiosity. Richard drew alongside her, his eyebrows raising. "I thought we would be moving on another few miles, where the larger inn was located?"

Elizabeth's mouth drew up into a smile. "I am sure Corwin thought that as well," she pointed out. "We may actually be safe here for the night."

Richard nodded. "That would be a nice change," he agreed.

They pushed their way into the main room, and the heavyset woman barely glanced over at them as she wiped off a table. "Sit anywhere you like, ducks," she called out, "I imagine you want ale and stew?"

Elizabeth sighed in relief. "Yes, thank you," she agreed, weaving through the half-filled room to take a seat by the fire. "At last," she added, leaning over to speak more softly to Richard. "I just needed to start thinking like him."

The corners of his mouth quirked up into a grin. "Just do not do that for too long," he warned. "It might start to take hold of your soul."

She shook her head. "Believe me, that could never happen," she promised. The food and drink were set down before them, and she clinked her mug against his before taking in a long, grateful drink.

The night passed uneventfully; a young flaxen-haired man with a well-worn lute took a seat opposite them and sang songs to the room, his tunes telling of love and war, of trial and victory. Elizabeth leant against Richard, his arm came up around her, and she could not imagine a more delightful ending to the day.

At last, the evening drew to a close and the room began to empty. Richard waved the inn-keep over, murmuring quietly in her ear. She was back in a moment, dropping off two iron keys on the table. "Last two rooms on the left," she indicated with a nod, gathering up their remaining items.

Elizabeth knew it was necessary, and yet her heart fell as they made their way down the darkened hallway. He unlocked the last door, pressing it open and looking around. The small room had a shuttered window, a mat against the left wall, and a small fireplace to the right. He nodded, then took her hand, drawing her back down the hall.

She watched with curious interest as he opened his own room. The fireplace was on the left in his room, the bed tucked in the corner aside it. A low table was on the right wall.

He strode forward, tugging the table under the window, then hauling the bed over to the right wall, laying it up alongside it. Then he was heading back toward her room now, and she was close at his side, intrigued by his actions.

He moved to her mat, sliding it slightly along the wall, then standing back and gazing at it, satisfied. "There, they are exactly opposite each other," he stated, turning to look at her.

Her eyes widened as she realized what he had done. "Only the thin wall separates them," she murmured. "You will be right there at my side."

He ran a hand through her hair, gazing down at her, his voice thickening. "Maybe this way we can both get a solid night's sleep," he commented roughly.

She reached up, pressing her lips gently against his at first, then drawing her arms up against his back. He resisted for a long moment, then groaned, his own arms drawing her hard against him, deepening his kiss until she lost all sense of time. At last he drew back, his breath coming in long draws.

"You push a man to his very limits," he growled, drinking her in with his eyes.

Craving deluged every part of her; she wanted his hands on her shoulders, her arms, on her hips and waist. "I would pull you past every wall between us," she growled, drawing him in again.

She could feel the tension stretch within him, the ultimate effort he put in to draw back from her, to hold her at arm's length. "Elizabeth, please - do not do this," he pleaded, his voice tight.

Her heart pounded in her chest; she wanted him with every cell in her body. "Do you care so much what my father thinks?" she ground out in anguish.

He shook his head, utterly baffled. "Your father? That man is the last person on my mind," he countered, his eyes growing more serious. "It is you I think of, your life that spreads out before you."

He took her hands in his, his gaze full on her. "My mother was the sweetest woman I have ever known, but many in our village treated her with scorn and disrespect. It was the little things; the way they said her name, the way they slid their eyes when they walked past her on the path." His eyes were somber as they held hers. "I would never in a thousand years put you in that position," he insisted.

Elizabeth saw the pain in his eyes, and her heart dropped for the childhood he had gone through, the hurt of seeing his mother mistreated.

"I had not realized," she murmured.

His hand traced gently along her cheek. "It is not an easy life, the life of an unmarried woman who is not pure; the life of a child of such a union. I spent half my childhood saving my brother from fights he had become embroiled in. Surely many were his own fault, but many others were brought onto him simply because of the circumstances of his birth."

His eyes looked away for a moment. "Children were harsh, but even adults would made snide comments, would treat us as if we were barely worth the mud we stood on. I can understand how it ate at my brother, how he felt the urge to lash out at the continual mistreatment."

His eyes drew back to hold hers. "I swore to myself at a young age to never put a child of my own in that position. Any child I bring into this world will come into a loving family, will be adored, respected, and treated with kindness. There will be no question about the legitimacy of their birth."

Elizabeth lowered her head, resting it against his chest, wrapping her arms around him tenderly. In a moment he had drawn her in, sighing against her, and she stood there for a long while. It had never occurred to her what he had gone through, that his restraint held so much importance to him.

Finally she looked up, smiling gently. "I will torment you no longer," she promised. "We will sleep on each side of this wall, and that will be enough."

"Thank you," he murmured, gently kissing her on the forehead. "Good night," he added, then he was moving through the door, closing it behind him.

She barred the door, then slipped out of her belt and dress. She lay down on her bed, pulling the covers to her shoulders, turning to face against the wall.

She heard a thunk from the other side, then some rustling, and then there were three soft taps from just in front of her chest.

She put her hand there for a long moment, then gave three answering taps. She could almost feel the warmth of his hand there, almost feel the watchful gaze of his eyes upon her. A sense of calm swelled through her, and she fell into a contented sleep.

* * *

Elizabeth smiled as they drew closer to the high walls of the keep. "I am sure Thomas will be delighted to host us for the evening," she told Richard, "and I am equally sure Corwin would have no idea of this change of plans. He would have thought we traveled further yesterday, and would be arriving home tonight. This will help to throw whatever devious intrigues he has off a bit, which can only be a help to us."

Richard eyed the men lining the walls of the keep. "And this Thomas is a friend of yours?"

She nodded calmly. "I stayed with him for several weeks after I escaped my father's grasp, when I was moving from place to place and deciding on what to do. He and his wife Malota were delightful hosts."

They drew up before the large gates, and a burly guard peered down at them for a moment before his face split into a broad grin. "Elizabeth, is that you? My arse still smarts from where you whapped me during our fight. Are you up for a rematch?"

"Of course," called out Elizabeth in delight. In a moment the gates were drawing open and they walked their steeds through the archway, coming to a halt in the open courtyard.

The main doors of the keep swung open, and a tall figure in a heavy, dark brown cloak came sweeping down toward them, his arms wide, his red hair flaming in the frosty dusk. "My dear, back again so soon?" Thomas called out, coming up to her and drawing her around in a warm hug. "Malota will be so delighted. She misses your engaging conversation. And who is this with -"

His eyes came around, latched onto the moss-green glow in Richard's, and his hand flew to his hilt in a flash. Elizabeth dodged between the two, holding her hands out to the side, drawing Thomas's attention.

"Thomas, this is Richard. He is Corwin's brother, and he is nothing like him," she hastily reported, creating a wall between them with her form.

Thomas's eyes creased with doubt as he looked Richard up and down, then at last he nodded, bringing his hand up off his hilt. He looked down at Elizabeth, his gaze gentling. "I would have hoped you had more than enough of Corwin by now," he murmured. "But I hear he is back at your father's keep, waiting on your return?"

Elizabeth sighed. "It is a long story. One I will gladly share over some warm food."

The corner of Thomas's mouth quirked up into a smile. "And a few glasses of my special cider, I wager?"

She burst into a laugh at that, tucking her arm into Richard's. Her eyes swept up to meet his. "You will see shortly one of the reasons this keep is my favorite place to visit," she grinned at him, and then the three of them were moving up into the warmth of the main hall.

Malota was just as delightful as she remembered, with her delicate blonde curls and engaging smile. Roast pheasant and warm bread were brought, the cider was poured, and soon Elizabeth was laying the entire story out for them, from start to finish, not holding back any details. She immensely enjoyed the company of her two friends and the fire behind them swept a comforting warmth around the evening.

The embers were fading into a bed of coals by the time she had finished. Malota sat back, round-eyed at the enormity of it all.

"But the man should be hanged – and then quartered!" she gasped, looking between the men at her side. "How can he still be free and loose?"

Richard's eyes were shadowed. "He has a way of twisting situations to fit his needs," he commented. "It is a skill he has built up over many years. He is able to wriggle out of the tightest spot, to somehow make the accuser feel as if they are the one at fault."

Thomas shook his head, draining down his mug, waving a hand to call for yet another refill. "I do not know that I like the idea of you walking back into that hornet's nest," he stated to Elizabeth with concern. "You barely made it out of there the last time. Who knows what your father might be prone to do if you place yourself under his control."

Elizabeth turned to look at Richard, and his eyes held tense worry. He put his hand over hers. "I will follow you wherever you lead," he vowed. "Still, we must be cautious. He will have the full might of his household guard around him. Once we are within his walls, we will be at an enormous disadvantage."

Elizabeth nodded. "And yet my father knows that he has created enmity with literally every neighbor around him. It would not take much to push them all into an assault on his doors, given what he has done to them over the long years. He would be cautious about doing anything too outrageous." She nodded in resolution. "I got the sense from Father Godfrey's message that my father only wants to talk with me. He is very sick, and he always did love his keep with a passion. He wants to make sure it remains in safe hands; that it does not fall to the bandits the moment he passes on."

Thomas's voice was cold. "I concur that the man is gravely ill; I am surprised he has hung on as long as he has," he agreed. "But never underestimate the craftiness of a dying man. He may feel he has little left to lose at this point."

Richard nodded at him. "We will be careful," he agreed.

Elizabeth gave a loud yawn, and Richard was standing at her side.

Thomas stood as well. "My dear, you have your usual room, up next to Malota. And Richard ..." He turned to the man before him. "There is a room on the lower level that I think will suit you well."

Elizabeth found herself speaking before she could rein herself in. "But I thought ..." She drew to a stuttering halt as Thomas swept a gaze to look at her, an eyebrow raised in curiosity.

"No, no, nothing like that," she hastily amended. "It is just, with all we have gone through, I find I sleep better knowing he is near."

Malota stepped forward to pat her on the arm. "Of course you do," she agreed warmly. "If I had been through what you had been, I would not want my Thomas more than five feet from me at all times." Her eyes swept to Thomas. "Surely having him on the same floor would not be *that* improper."

Thomas held Richard's eyes for a long moment. "Be sure you are worthy of the honor," he commented at last. "Elizabeth is very dear to me."

"She is precious to me as well," returned Richard in a serious tone, nodding.

Thomas waved at a servant, and in a moment they were ascending the stairs, moving to the room alongside her own.

He pushed the door open, and she saw that his bed was alongside the right wall; against where her own was in the next room. Her shoulders eased in relief. His eyes caught the movement, and he almost reached out toward her before reining himself in and simply nodding to her, his gaze holding so much more.

"Sleep well," he offered, his voice rich and resonant.

"And you," she returned, every part of her craving to step into his arms, to inhale, to have his rich scent of musk and rosemary and columbine wrap around her. It was with the greatest of efforts that she turned, moving with Malota down to her own room.

Malota's voice whispered in her ear. "He is indeed quite the gentleman," she murmured. "I think you finally may have found someone worthy to stand by your side."

Elizabeth's eyes glowed, and she gave her friend a warm hug. "I will see you in the morning," she offered, then turned and moved into her own room. She closed and barred the door, then moved to the side of the bed, shedding her belt and dress in one motion. She climbed into bed, curling up to face the wall, waiting a long moment. Then she put her knuckles to it, giving three short raps.

A heartbeat, and then three raps returned to her, strong and clear.

She pressed her palm against the place, a rich warmth spreading throughout her, and she closed her eyes.

Chapter 20

Elizabeth pulled her cloak more tightly around her shoulders, the gloom of dusk settling around her, barely noticing as the servants led the two horses away. She looked around her at the small cobblestone courtyard which had been her sparring field for so many years.

She knew each stone, each upturned lift, each sudden dip as if they were carved into her own hand. There was the stone with the deep grooves in it where she had fallen after her father shattered her thigh. Over there was the pair of stones with grain like wood where her wrist had been broken. Each stone had a story to tell, marking out her life in punishment and pain.

There was a movement from the keep stairs, and she smiled fondly. Father Godfrey was carefully making his way down the steps, his rickety frame navigating each movement with attention. She walked forward to take his hands as he reached the ground, then drew him into a fond hug.

His voice eased out of him, faint and raspy. "My dear child, it is good to see you again. I am thankful to Mother Mary that you have returned home without serious injury."

Richard's eyes moved to her thigh, but he pressed his lips together, saying nothing.

Elizabeth stepped back to stand beside Richard. "Father, it is due to this man that I come to you as whole as I am. Richard saved me from near disaster in a flooded river and much else, in addition."

Father Godfrey held out his hand, and Richard bent to kiss the ring there.

Father Godfrey's eyes sparkled for a moment. "Ah, yes. Corwin has been entertaining us with stories of what went on during your travels."

Elizabeth snapped her eyes up to meet his. "What has that man been saying?"

Father Godfrey's mouth quirked into a smile. "Not to worry, my lass. I know better than to believe his version of things. And most of the men here have had enough encounters with his tales to know the same." His brow furrowed. "But your Father, lass; he is very ill. You should come in to him at once."

Elizabeth glanced at Richard, then nodded. Together they moved with the frail, elderly man up the steps and toward the front doors.

She paused a moment, staring at the ancient oak doors, at the heavy ax marks which scarred them. She knew the stories well, of how her grandfather had held off a bandit attack in the dead of winter, how he had sacrificed two of his sons in poorly planned sallies before the victory could be claimed. She laid a hand against the scar, nodding her head as she always did, before pulling hard on the iron circle and hauling the door open.

The hall looked as it always had, but with Richard at her side she took in its dismal, grey gloom with even more critical eyes. The small windows barely let in any light, and few candles were lit to hold back the shadows. The scattering of tables were strewn with remnants of food, and the rushes beneath the chairs had not been replaced in weeks. The stone walls were bare of tapestry or decoration, and only a feeble fire guttered in the fireplace to the right. The head table, stretched out at the far end of the hall, was warped, had a crack tracing down its front, and sported innumerable stains.

Her face flushed with shame. "Welcome to my home," she muttered to Richard, looking away.

His hand gently turned her face back to his, and his eyes shone with support. "Where you are, there I will be," he vowed.

Her heart warmed, and she nodded, turning to move forward. As they approached, she could see a frail figure propped up in the large, central chair. It took a moment before she could discern that the man before her and the bear of a figure who had been her father, who had domineered over her life, were one and the same.

Father Godfrey had not been exaggerating. The man was surely clutching with every ounce of strength he had to his remaining threads of life. She shook her head in confusion, coming to a stop before the table.

"Father?"

He growled at her, the spite flared in his eyes, and it was all she could do not to take a step back. The father she had known glowed from within that desiccated frame, and she wondered that the skin did not burst from the heat which roiled within.

"Finally you come home," he coughed out, his eyes searing her. "Corwin was here days ago. You were always a disobedient child." His eyes snapped to the man at her side. "And who is this? An uninvited guest in my home?"

Elizabeth turned to indicate Richard. "Father, this man is Richard, brother to Corwin. It is thanks to his efforts that I have been safely escorted here."

Her father turned slightly to his right, and Corwin stepped out from behind the chair, taking his seat there. Elizabeth's spine stiffened. That was her chair; that was her position at her father's right. She pushed the feeling down with effort. Surely the last thing she cared about right now was where she ranked in her father's affection.

Her father grinned slightly, his eyes flashing. "Ah yes. I have heard all about this man, about his deeds," he sneered. Richard stiffened beside her, but said nothing.

Elizabeth's voice remained calm. "I am sure we can tell you alternate versions of those same stories," she indicated. "There are often two sides to a tale."

His brows came together in a harsh line. "I do not need to hear your version to know the truth," he snapped. His face flushed with heat. "Not when you ran off, you refused to do your duty, you turned your back on your vows …" A strong hacking spell took a hold of him, and it was several long moments before he was able to get his coughing under control.

Elizabeth looked back at Father Godfrey. "What is wrong with him? What does Doctor Tyrian have to say about this?"

"Here I am," called out a voice from the side of the hall. A middle-aged man with greying hair and a sparse beard moved into the hall, carrying a small jar. "I have brought your medicine, Lord Masci," he added, coming to a stop by the chair and holding out the container.

Her father snarled, but took the jar and tossed it back in one gulp. He grimaced, grabbing his mug of ale and washing it down. When he spoke again his voice was clearer, but still ringing with disdain.

"This lack-wit has no idea what is wrong with me," he snapped. "Nearly seven months now, the wasting has been afflicting me. First he thought it was 'the burning disease', picked up from one of these servant girl whores who clearly do not keep themselves clean. Then he was sure it was leprosy. Who knows, next he may blame the plague."

The doctor's face was pale. "My Lord, I am still researching your baffling symptoms," he insisted.

Her father picked up the jar and flung it at the wall, shattering it into a flurry of pieces. "Research faster," he snarled.

A young girl with blonde braids came scurrying into the room, dropping to her knees beside the broken bits of jar, gathering them up into a grimy cloth.

Her father waved at the chairs before him. "Come, sit down already. You are hurting my neck making me stare up at you like this." His eyes turned to the girl. "You there, get them ale and bread. Be quick about it."

The girl nodded and raced off toward the main door.

His eyes swung round to pin Richard. "I suppose you want some sort of reward. You want a boon for staying with Elizabeth while she lagged behind. It figures the girl's weakness would force Corwin to come ahead on his own to let me know what was going on."

Richard shook his head. "No, sir. I seek no reward."

Her father's eyes narrowed. "No man does something without wanting to get something out of it," he snapped. His eyes swung to stare at his daughter, and his face darkened. "Out with it, girl. Did he violate you?"

Outrage filled her chest at the way her father was treating her, but she reined it in with fierce effort. She just had to get through this one night, to figure out what was going on.

"He did not touch me," she huffed out.

"Good," he snapped. "You will be ready to marry Corwin two days hence."

Elizabeth's blood ran cold. She had expected this, but to hear it stated so firmly by the man who had run her life for so many years still had the power to send shivers through her.

"I shall not," she countered without hesitation.

His eyes raised up to meet hers, and the fire that blazed within them was the same flame that used to scald her before a hand thundered down at her head, before a sword spun toward her thigh. "I have said you shall, and that is final," he snarled.

Father Godfrey leant forward slightly, and all eyes drew to him. "In the eyes of the church, marriage is the most holy of sacraments," he wheezed out, fingering the gold cross at his chest. "It absolutely must be taken voluntarily. One cannot force an adult to be baptized; such an action would have no validity in the eyes of God. In the same way, a woman who is forced into a marriage is not a legitimate wife and will not receive the Lord's blessings."

Her father's eyes burned into hers. "Then we will just force her to see reason," he snapped. "The agreement was already settled on. The man was her choice, by God! And now she backs out, after she is paid for? The chit needs to learn her place."

Elizabeth was half out of her seat, but Father Godfrey put a frail arm on her shoulder and she stopped. "It is late," he wheezed, his eyes on her father. "You are very tired, my Lord. Let us discuss this in the morning when we have all had a good night's sleep."

Her father's glare faded slightly, and he nodded. In a moment Doctor Tyrian and Corwin had taken each of his arms, carefully helping the frail man up toward his quarters.

Elizabeth settled back down into her seat, taking a long draw on the ale, turning to look at the elderly priest. "I see his temper has not improved any," she commented with a half smile. "How have you been holding up?"

He shrugged, looking at her fondly. "I get by. We have a long history, he and I, and I do my best to act as intercessor between him and the others of the keep." His eyes grew shadowed. "I am only sorry I could not do more to keep you safe over the years."

She took another draw on the ale. "You would only have gotten yourself killed, if you had tried to get between him and me," she soothed him. "He had a strong belief that his children were his pawns, to be used and abused however he wished."

Richard's voice was low. "What do you intend to do?"

She twined her fingers into his own, resting her head on his shoulder for a moment. "I certainly will never marry Corwin," she promised him. "By the look of things, I do not know how much longer my father will last. I will try to make his few remaining days ones of peace, if I can." Her eyes went doubtfully to Father Godfrey's. "I do still hold out some tiny hope that, when he sees the end is near, he will repent and show even a small fondness for me."

Father Godfrey smiled comfortingly at her. "It has been known to happen, child," he reassured her. "It is why I sent the message to you. If there is any hope of him gentling, now would be the time." His eyes were warm on her. "You are a good daughter, to give him this one last chance at redemption."

Elizabeth shook her head doubtfully. "I am a fool," she answered, giving a long sigh.

Finally she looked around at the darkening hall. "Well, then, I suppose we should get to bed." She glanced at Father Godfrey. "Where will they be putting Richard?"

He looked down at the table for a moment. "In the barracks, with the other men," he admitted. "Your father claimed that no other room could be cleaned on such short notice."

Elizabeth's face flared with anger. "Of course he claimed that," she shot out.

"I will be fine," calmed Richard, his eyes on hers. "It matters not where I sleep. As long as we keep you safe, that is what is important."

Elizabeth nodded, but her heart fell. He had been close to her every night, had been just within reach. To think of him further away drained the warmth from her body.

He made an attempt at a smile. "Come now, show me where your room is," he offered. "I will see you there safely, and then I will get along to my own bed."

Father Godfrey got up with them. "I will see you both tomorrow morning," he offered. "Stay safe until then."

Elizabeth moved to the side of the hall, heading up the narrow spiral stairs to the upper floor, and to her surprise a sense of nervousness began tripping at her heart. Few people had seen her bedroom, had crossed its threshold. For some reason the idea of Richard being there with her caused flutterings in her stomach.

She glanced down to the end of the hall, to where the large, ornately carved door stood slightly ajar. Corwin and the doctor were apparently settling her father into bed. She turned and pressed her own door open to the tiny bedroom she had slept in since a small child.

The room was shrouded in darkness, with a lone candle flickering on the table by her bed and the barest of embers glowing at the hearth. The shutters were closed tight against the coming winter's chill. Dingy grey covers lay over her bed, and a trunk to one side held her few possessions. A wardrobe by the window contained her dresses. The stone walls were bare of decoration, and the floor, while swept, was badly in need of polish.

"Home sweet home," she offered wryly, waving a hand at it. "This is what I have."

His eyes swept the room and came back to hold hers. "It has a sturdy bar on the door?"

Her mouth quirked up into a grin. "That it does," she agreed.

He nodded. "Then it has everything it needs."

She took a step toward him, suddenly caught by the realization that he was going to leave her, abandon her for the night. "It does not have you," she whispered.

He took a half step forward, then there was a movement in the hallway. Corwin and Doctor Tyrian were there alongside him, their faces moving between the two.

Corwin's voice was tight. "Just saying good night to my wife, were we?"

Elizabeth's eyes flared, but she kept her voice even. "I am not even your fiancée," she corrected. "I am nothing to you."

His eyes blazed with heat. "That is far from true," he countered. "But we will discuss that tomorrow, when you are more yourself. Once you settle back into your old routine, you will remember your duties to your father." His eyes swept past hers to hold Richard's. "Come now, dear brother. Let us get you into your own bed, where you belong."

Richard's eyes moved to hold Elizabeth's, then glanced for a moment at the door. She nodded. He stepped back into the hallway, and in a moment she had closed the door on the trio, sliding the bar firmly in place. She waited as their footsteps faded down the hallway, disappearing into the customary creaks and groans of the keep at night.

Despair began to roll in at her as the all too familiar surroundings crawled into her spirit, infiltrated her soul. How many nights had she sobbed in here, alone, without a means of escape? How many mornings had she pleaded for some way to get away from the pain and suffering? And now she had returned, was back in the clutches of the two who had hurt her the most.

She drew in a deep breath, focusing her thoughts. Richard was here. With Richard by her side, she knew they could get through anything. Her father was frail; he only had a handful of days left. No matter what happened after that, he could no longer hurt her.

She turned to look around her small cell, at the lack of decoration, at the grimy bed with its cracked wooden headboard. There would be no knocking on the wall tonight, no reassuring touch keeping her company. He was far from reach, not even a token there to remind her of ...

Her hand dropped to her hip before she was aware of the action, and she moved forward to her bed, to kneel on it, facing her headboard. She had control over her own life. This was her room, and she was going to start taking charge of it also, as she was learning to do with so many things.

She imagined the headboard as a piece of leather, and began cutting the lines with her dagger, laying out the pattern. First there were the five star petals, creating the outer frame. Then the inner petals, more square in shape, offset. Then finally the center piece that held the flower together.

She sat back, admiring her handiwork. Her years of leatherworking had paid off – the columbine was perfect, carved into her headboard. As she pressed her hand against it, her heart warmed. Some part of Richard was here with her. She would be all right.

Contented, she laid her sword and dagger by her bed. She pulled off her dress to lay it on the trunk, then climbed beneath the heavy covers. In a moment she was drifting off to sleep.

Chapter 21

A gentle rapping at her door roused her from a sound sleep. She blinked wearily, turning over. Faint streams of sunlight came through her closed shutters; it was nearly mid-morning.

She cursed, a tremor of fear running through her as she rolled to a sitting position. Her father would be furious that she had missed the first half of morning practice. He would beat her mercilessly; he would ...

She froze, suddenly realizing that she was beyond his control now. She was no longer a child who would be abused and punished for slight infractions. She was an adult; she had come back on her own terms, and the man was near death.

It was almost too much to take in. The specter of danger that had hung over her for so many years was fading into the past. She could choose a new course now; she could redirect her path into one that brought her joy and peace.

The knocking came again, and her heart leapt. Was this Richard coming to bring her down to breakfast? She ran to the door with light feet, leaning against the crack. "Who is it?" she called out.

Doctor Tyrian's voice came gently through. "It is me, child. I heard you had injuries, and I thought I might look at them before you started your day."

Elizabeth slid aside the bolt, opening the door to the doctor. "No worse than you have seen countless other times," she assured him, stepping back into the room.

"You have probably set and re-set my limbs enough to know them as well as your own."

He nodded. "Probably true, and yet it is always wise to watch for infection," he warned. He turned and closed the door behind him, sliding the bar back into place. Then he moved next to the bed, setting his bag down beside him. "Come on, lass. You know the drill."

She climbed back into bed, dutifully pulling her chemise up to her upper thigh to show him the leg injury. Doctor Tyrian had been the one who birthed her, and he had helped her through more injuries than she could count. She was long past modesty with the man.

He unwrapped the bandages carefully, then knelt at her side to carefully probe at the long gash. "Did you tend to this yourself?" he asked as he worked. "This is healing quite nicely."

She shook her head. "Richard helped me with the wounds," she informed him. "He has some skill in that area."

"Apparently so," he agreed. "And you were quite lucky. Just a little more distance in either direction and you might not be sitting here today."

"No thanks to Corwin," she growled, remembering how he had used his sword on her horse, had driven her into the raging river.

The doctor's mouth quirked up slightly. "In Corwin's version of the story, it is Richard who caused you to have the injury."

"Richard?" cried Elizabeth in disbelief, half rising.

He patted her on the shoulder, chuckling. "Most here know better than to believe that man," he soothed her. His eyes shadowed slightly. "Your father, though, still seems to feel he has some good qualities."

"My father believes many things," growled Elizabeth.

"He is still Lord of this keep," mused the Doctor in a cautionary tone.

He gave himself a small shake, rummaging through his bag. "Here, drink this," he instructed her. "It will help to ease some of the aches you will feel as your thigh heals."

Elizabeth nodded dutifully, drinking down the liquid in a long draw. It was syrupy, with a heavy herbal flavor to it.

The doctor's eyes were moving to her arm. "And it is your right arm as well, I believe? Thank goodness it was not your left."

"I know," agreed Elizabeth, sitting back against the headboard and offering her arm. "I suppose it was a time where being left handed ended up being a good thing."

Her arm began to feel heavy, and she lowered it to lay against her chest. Doctor Tyrian's eyes flicked up to hers, then he began unwrapping the bandages slowly, taking his time.

"You know," murmured Elizabeth, a lassitude coming over her, "They thought that I killed the twins' mother solely because I was a left handed swordswoman. Apparently the entire region was out hunting for her." She gave a low laugh, closing her eyes. "Two left handed swordswomen in that one area of the world. What are the chances of that?"

"What indeed?" asked the Doctor's voice, and he seemed remote, drifting away, and then she was high in the mountains, surrounded by clouds, and the world ceased to exist.

* * *

There was a quick rapping at the door, and she wanted to make it stop, but her lids were just too heavy to open up. She tried to press herself up to sitting, but her arms were leaden, and her legs were splayed open in an unnatural way.

"Go away," she muttered, shaking her head wearily.

"There you are," sighed the Doctor with relief. She pried her eyes open and saw him glance at the door, then move to bring the covers back up over her, propping her up a bit more in bed. That done, he hurried to the door, sliding the bar back and opening it.

Corwin stepped into the gap, his gaze moving between the Doctor and Elizabeth, his brow furrowing when he saw she was awake. "I told you to let me in sooner," he snapped at the physician.

The Doctor looked down for a moment. "These things are tricky," he murmured. "She has a strong constitution; she awoke before I would have expected."

Corwin let out a low growl, then shook his head, dismissing it. "What is done is done," he snapped. "So, is she still pure?"

The fog burned from Elizabeth's mind in an instant, and she drew herself fully up to a seated position, drawing her knees up against her, staring at Corwin and the Doctor in shocked realization.

"You had him check my *virginity*?" she cried out in shock.

The doctor's face flushed. "It was your father's order, my dear, and a natural precaution to take before any marriage. He only thought, with the situations you have been in recently, that -"

"Situations?" yelled Elizabeth, fury turning her vision red. "Situations like Corwin nearly causing my death, nearly causing me to be both drowned in a raging river and ripped open by a gouging tree?"

There was the sound of running feet, and then Richard was striding into the room, glancing around in a quick scan. His shoulders eased when he found Elizabeth huddled in bed, then his eyes sharpened as they took in her fury.

"What is it?" he asked in a tense voice.

"Get them out," she ordered. "Get them both out!"

Corwin's voice was harsh. "I am your Lord and Master," he snapped. "You will submit to me."

Richard turned on him, his eyes flashing. "You are neither," he growled, "and you will obey the lady in her own house." He gave Corwin a shove, and the Doctor scurried out after him. In a moment Richard had closed the door and slid the bar firmly into place.

He was kneeling by her side, and she folded against him, the tears streaming down her face.

"I am here now," he murmured in her ear. "They had me off on a wild goose chase, but I realized quickly what they were up to and came back to make sure you were all right. I shall not fall for that again." He pulled back slightly. "What happened? Did they hurt you?"

She shook her head no, still hunched up. "The Doctor was alone with me, checking my injuries," she explained hesitantly. "But then he drugged me, and while I was unconscious he …" she found she could barely say it. "He checked that I was still intact."

His hand stilled in its soothing motion, and it was a long moment before he could speak. "While you were drugged? Without your permission?"

She nodded mutely. After a minute she took in a breath, looking away. "I know he is a doctor; I know he has tended to every wound my body could bear. But somehow the thought of what he did upsets me to my core."

He drew her in again, and his voice was iron. "As it should," he stated coldly. "He drugged you because he knew, if you were awake, that you would never consent to his actions. He did it completely against your will."

He lifted her face to his, and his gaze softened. "You did an honorable thing by coming back here, to give your father one last chance. You have done your duty. Whenever you are ready to leave, we can go. Even if it is to stay with Thomas, to be nearby but not under his control, that may be the better option."

She nodded slowly, her world slowly settling back into place. "Maybe you are right," she agreed. "If my father was willing to resort to this, who knows what else he might try." She thought back to the scene of her awaking, how Corwin had seemed to want to gain access to her unconscious and unprotected body. "And Corwin …"

Richard's eyes sharpened. "What did Corwin do?" he shot out, his shoulders tensing.

She smiled slightly, leaning up to press her lips tenderly against him. "Corwin did nothing," she reassured him. She knew if she said more that he would challenge his brother, would hinder their ability to simply leave and put the past behind them.

"Come, let us go down, make our farewells, and get clear of their influence."

He helped her to stand, and she moved to her wardrobe, sorting through her dresses. Richard turned around while she removed her old chemise and drew on a fresh one, then adding a violet dress over it. She smoothed it down in place, smiling at the color. It matched the fields of columbine which sprung up around the keep each spring.

Richard's voice was a startled whisper behind her. "What is this?"

She turned and saw he was staring at the columbine carving she had made in her head board. She moved to stand next to him, smiling. "I was lonely," she explained.

He stared at it for a long moment, then turned and drew her into a tender hug. "I missed you too," he murmured against her hair.

There was a rapping at the door, and both heads swiveled as one to stare at it. Richard strode over to stand beside the door. "Who is it?" he called out.

An elderly voice rasped through the crack. "It is Father Godfrey," he informed the pair.

Richard looked back at Elizabeth, and she nodded. He pulled the bar clear, drawing the door open.

The elderly priest took a few steps into the room. "My child, I heard what happened. You are all right?"

"Yes," she answered, coming to stand alongside Richard. "We will be going to stay with Thomas for a while," she continued. "I know you wanted me to be here, but -"

He was nodding before she finished. "I understand. It was but a vain hope of mine. I still remember your father as the sweet child he once was."

Elizabeth took one last glance around the room, then headed out, with Father Godfrey and Richard following close behind. They made their way down the main staircase and into the great hall. The tables were half filled with guards and staff, with servants moving to and fro serving the morning meal.

Her father's voice cut across the murmuring voices. "There she is at last, the lazy wench. A few years ago I would have beaten her for her weakness and taught her a lesson."

Elizabeth strode up to stand before the table, her eyes cold. "Yes, you would have," she answered. "And now you will not. Richard and I are taking our leave."

Corwin's gaze went between the two in shock. "You cannot leave," he snapped. "Your father is deathly ill."

"So he is," she agreed. "And I have come to see him. Based on his recent actions, he apparently has no interest in family reconciliation. There is no more to say."

Her father's voice was rich with fury. "You will marry Corwin, and that is final!"

A calm settled over Elizabeth's shoulders. "No, I will not," she told them smoothly.

Corwin's voice rose high. "You will marry me if it is the last thing you ever do!"

The front door yanked open, and a man came racing down the hallway, pulling to a stop before the head table. "There is a trio of bandits at the jousting field," he reported in a hurried rush. "I think they have one of our serving girls."

Corwin stood at once. "You five, with me," he ordered, his gaze raking a group of soldiers who stood to one side. He spun to glare at Elizabeth. "And you, weak one, you will stay here."

"Like hell I will!" she shot back, her heart pounding. Was it sweet Vera who had been caught up this time?

Corwin barely heard her. He spun around the edge of the table, racing toward the main door. Elizabeth and Richard fell in with him at once, grabbing their cloaks along the way, pulling them tight against the chill November wind.

They burst as a group into the stables. "Saddle our horses – now!" called out Corwin, and there was a flurry of activity as the stablemen got the horses ready for action. Elizabeth slid the bit over her own steed's head and was flying through the gates first, the rest of the men close on her heels.

Her heart pounded as they thundered around the side of the keep and toward the long fields which lay in the valley below. Undoubtedly the wolves' heads were in the stable building alongside the tournament area, where they could be sheltered from the wind. Which girl might they have in their clutches? Surely not Mary, the sweetest creature she had ever met ...

The stable doors were before her, and she was sliding from her steed, her sword out in her hand, racing to push them open, looking around quickly.

Richard was at her side in a moment, his eyes sweeping the room. Corwin strode past them both, calling out loudly, "Wolves' heads! Come out and face justice!" He moved quickly to one of the stalls, peering over the gate, then along to the next. He stopped suddenly, his eyes focusing on the shadows within. "Elizabeth," he called, his voice holding concern.

Elizabeth's heart pounded against her chest. Surely not sweet Sarah. Corwin was pushing the stall door carefully open, and she went past him with flying feet, her eyes searching for -

The bite of cold steel was at her neck and she froze in shock. Where had the bandit been hiding? She had seen not a soul, not even the trace of -

The arm pressed her back against a solid chest, and a scent came up from it, of rosemary and columbine. Her eyes flew open in shock.

"Corwin?"

He wheeled her around, and she saw Richard pressed in by the five guards, their swords against him. Corwin gave a twist of his knife against her neck. A warm trickle of blood danced down her throat.

His voice was bright with delight. "Drop it, dear brother," he ordered.

Richard hesitated a moment, his eyes on Elizabeth, then the sword clattered from his hand onto the ground. The guards were on him in an instant, drawing his hands behind his back, lashing them tightly with rope.

Elizabeth's throat closed up with panic. "Corwin, let him go," she pleaded. "You have me. You do not need him."

Corwin's voice was rich with pleasure. "Ah, but I do," he corrected her.

The guards tied a length of rope to the bonds at Richard's wrists, then tossed it up over a beam high overhead. They drew the spare end over to a hook in the wall, cinching the length tight until Richard's arms were high over his head, his feet on tip-toes.

Elizabeth's heart constricted in fear. "Corwin, no!"

The rope was secured, and Corwin handed Elizabeth off to a pair of guards who held knives against her neck and stomach. He strode toward Richard, his grin growing.

He called back over his shoulder to Elizabeth. "You had that straw dummy at the nunnery," he mused. "You knew the pleasure it brought you to hack at the limbs, to watch them slowly separate from the body, to finally fall free."

Elizabeth's legs weakened beneath her. "God, Corwin, please," she pleaded.

Corwin walked up to Richard, eyeing his brother. "All those years," he muttered. "All those years that you interfered with the things I wanted."

Richard's eyes shadowed as he looked down at his brother. "I only sought to protect you. Every action I took, it was for your safety."

"My safety?" sneered Corwin, his voice harsh. He moved up to his brother's side, staring at him for a long moment, then without warning he coiled his right arm back, launching it hard into Richard's side, rolling to follow through. Richard grunted in pain, his body swinging back from the blow, then settling into place again.

Elizabeth lurched forward against the men who held her, then was hauled back into place, the knives sharp against her.

Corwin's voice was tight. "I finally had that bully, Odo, down beneath my dagger. I could have castrated him and made up for the years of abuse. And you stopped me!"

Richard's voice was hoarse. "His father was the sheriff," he ground out. "If you had gone through with it -"

Corwin swung again, this time his fist landing on Richard's jaw, rocking him back. Elizabeth sagged, a moan escaping from her lips, as Richard swung, groaned, settled back into place.

Corwin's voice hammered at Richard. "And Isolda, that buxom wench who would never give me the time of day? Far too high and mighty for the likes of us? I had finally caught her alone by the river, after weeks of planning, and you show up and -"

Richard's voice shot out, tough with anger. "The girl was unwilling!"

Corwin's blow connected with his stomach, and he groaned, his body half twisting from the force of the punch. Corwin's voice was fierce with fury. "She would have learned her place," he growled. He glanced back over his shoulder, and a grin spread on his face. "As Elizabeth will learn her place," he added. "To submit to and obey her lord and master."

Richard's face went pale, and Corwin punched him again, drawing a shuddering moan.

Corwin's eyes moved back to hold Elizabeth's for a moment. "You know you can stop this at any time," he reminded her. "Just say the words and your darling man of honor will be safe."

Richard coughed to gain his breath. "Do not do it, Elizabeth," he rasped. "You cannot trust anything he says."

Corwin's fist rocked his head back. "Ah, dear brother," he corrected. "She can trust what my fists say. She will watch as your body is battered into oblivion, as you lose the use of your arms, your legs, and at last your breath."

Elizabeth could barely stay on her feet. "No …" she implored, her eyes held tight on Richard's moss-green ones. "I cannot allow you to be hurt in my name."

His gaze held hers in steady certainty. "This is just the pain of my body," he stated, and she could see the firm resolve which lay within him. "I will not see you wed to this monster."

Corwin's mouth quirked up. "You may be right at that, dearest brother," he commented, launching a fist into Richard's side. There was a cracking noise, and Richard gave a long, trembling exhale.

Corwin rounded to smile at Elizabeth. "I do think I might have broken something," he sneered at her.

Elizabeth sagged down against the men holding her, her eyes on Richard's.

Her voice was hoarse. "Corwin, stop. I swear to agree -"

Richard's cry cut through her vow. "No, Elizabeth," he urged. "A day of my pain is not worth a lifetime of yours. Do not do it."

Corwin turned, sending his fist into Richard's jaw again, cutting off his voice. "You were saying, my dear? It is about time we got you to the steps of your chapel, to see you properly wed by Father Godfrey, in a way befitting your noble station."

An odd memory tugged at Elizabeth's mind, at the words Corwin was saying. They were half of a whole; there was something important there.

Then Corwin was swinging again, landing hard on the same spot. Richard's groan was deeper, more ragged, and his eyes fluttered shut. All thought fled, and the words burst from her mouth. "Enough! I will marry!"

Corwin spun, his eyes bright with delight. "You will? Voluntarily?"

"Yes," she promised, her throat closing up. "I will. Today. Voluntarily."

His eyes traced up and down her form with hot interest. "And submit fully to your husband?"

Richard's groan came from the depths of his soul. "Elizabeth, no."

"Yes," she responded, all hope gone. There was aught she could do but to stand on the steps of the chapel, to stand before Father Godfrey, to have a proper wedding. The alternative was …

A thought sprung into her mind, and she looked down, closing her eyes, holding her face as still as a mouse before a snake. The alternative was a wedding in the old tradition, the vows given between man and woman, the joining of the two the ultimate symbol of their promise to each other. Such a joining had the power of consecration; it could not be undone, could not be overridden.

A plan began to form in her head, and she drew in a deep breath. Corwin was a master of machinations. He would be watching for a deception. She had to be as cautious as all her years of experience had taught her, had to trace the labyrinth with delicate attention, every foot-fall precisely placed.

She drew open her eyes, her gaze fully on Corwin.

"I will marry today," she vowed, standing tall, her voice growing stronger. "And I will proclaim loudly that this marriage is of my own free will. But first I demand three conditions."

Corwin moved to stand before her, his smile wide. "And what might those be?"

Elizabeth fought the urge to glance back at Richard. She had to hold this together, to maintain the front she was presenting, just for a short while longer. "First, you are to let Richard go. I want to see him ride from here with my own two eyes."

Corwin chuckled. "Of course," he agreed. Elizabeth could see in his cold marble eyes that he did not intend for Richard to get further than the horizon, but she bit back the knowledge. One step at a time.

"Second, I will choose for myself what horse Richard takes, and what supplies go with him. You will bring all of the horses in here for me to choose from, and you will leave us in here as long as we deem necessary to make that selection."

Corwin's eyes widened with appreciation. "You may yet be the woman worthy to sit by my side," he murmured, looking at her with new respect. "I will find this very interesting. Granted."

"And third," she stated, "once Richard has ridden away, you and all five of your lackeys will sit with me, outside the stables, not stirring, until the sun touches the horizon. Your horses will not be examined, not a man leaves my sight, until that time has passed."

Corwin's grin stretched ear to ear. "Ah, my dear, I may yet mold you into a proper wife," he praised. "I accept whole-heartedly. And when these terms are met, you swear you will be wed?"

She nodded, her eyes holding his with firm promise. "I vow it. I swear it on the death of my brother."

Corwin's eyes moved to his crew. "You heard my wife," he called to them. "Bring in the horses, and make it quick. I want to see how this game plays out."

There was a flurry of action around her. The three men went to and fro leading in all of the horses, settling each one into a stall. Corwin moved to stand before his brother. He leant forward and murmured into his ear. "You think, when you are fleeing from these lands, how my hands will teach this woman what it means to be properly ridden," he advised Richard. "You think, with every step your horse takes, how it is my whip now which drives Elizabeth."

Richard tensed, and Corwin gave him a solid pat on the jaw, his hand landing on the purpling bruise. Then he turned and gave a toss with his head to the two men who still held Elizabeth. The men stood back from her, moving over to stand at Corwin's side.

Elizabeth's voice was low as she spoke to Corwin. "As long as I need to prepare the horses," she reminded him.

Corwin's eyes scanned the row of stalls, and he laughed. "Yes, certainly, dear wife. Take as long as you wish to concoct your schemes. But remember, we stay put only until sundown. The longer you take in here, the closer that eventuality comes."

With a final grin he stepped through the main stable doors, closing them solidly behind him. Elizabeth ran forward, sliding the bar in place, then glanced around at the darkened hall. The other windows had all been long since sealed against the coming winter, and only glimmers of sunlight trickled through the higher windows in the loft. None could see inside.

Satisfied, she ran over to the hook on the wall, drawing her dagger with one smooth motion and slicing through the rope. Richard fell heavily to his knees. She was at his side in a moment, sawing through the bonds at his wrist. She sighed in relief as they came free, as his arms swept around to hold her close to him, his head nestled at her neck.

His voice came ragged and rough. "You cannot do this," he growled. "I will not allow you to give your life for mine."

She pulled back gently, her eyes holding his. "I have already sworn it," she reminded him. "On my brother's death, I have sworn to marry today."

He shook his head, his eyes steady on hers. "There is no way I will let yourself pledge to be under Corwin's control for the rest of your life."

The edges of her mouth tweaked up into a grin, and she moved to one side, grabbing up her cloak. "I never said I would marry *Corwin*," she pointed out. She moved to the back wall, to where a thick layer of hay lay spread before the wood face. She lay her cloak out on the hay, then knelt at it, using her dagger to scratch out the shape of a cross.

Richard staggered up behind her, looking between her and the wall. "I do not understand?"

She finished with the cross, then began working on a shape to its right. She began with the five star-shaped petals, then sketched in the inner white petals, more square in shape. "I only said I would be married today," she stated evenly, nodding in satisfaction with what she had created. She drew to her feet, turning to stand before him.

His eyes went to the symbols on the wall, then back to her, and suddenly they went wide with understanding. His breath caught for a long moment, and at last his hand moved to gently stroke her cheek, his gaze holding her with growing wonder.

"You are sure?"

She nodded, stepping to stand before him. "If you will have me," she whispered.

He was pulling her in against him, holding her close, and she could almost feel his arms tremble. "If I would have you," he repeated, his voice incredulous. "There has been nothing else I have hoped for, have prayed for, since we first met. Your honor, your strength; you are what I have waited for these long years and never hoped to find."

She nodded her head down at the ground before the symbols. "Then lay out your cloak," she indicated with a gentle smile.

He removed it in an instant, turning it over and laying the softer, inner lining face up, providing an extra buffer against the hay. She dropped her belt on the ground, then moved to kneel on the fabric. In a moment he had done the same, and they faced each other.

Her breath caught as she gazed up at him. His eyes were steady on her, and she knew with every cell in her body that this is what she wanted.

"Richard, I swear before God and all of nature that I here take you to be my husband, for now and for all time." She heard his intake of breath, felt his warmth wash over her with a steadying strength. "I will love you, honor you, respect you, and be loyal to you. I will stand by your side whatever the injury, and I will nurse you back to health whatever strikes us. I will take on all comers, defend our family against all who would hurt us, and go wherever life drives us. All that will matter is that you are there by my side."

Richard twined his hands into hers. His voice was hoarse. "Dearest Elizabeth, you are the most precious person in my life. I will honor you, love you, and be loyal to you. No other will share my bed or my heart. You will be the mother of my children and the light of my life. I

will stay by your side, defend you, protect you, and give
my last ounce of blood to keep you safe."

Elizabeth warmed with heat. She brought his hands up
to her lips for a kiss. "You are now my husband, and I love
you. Only death shall part us."

He brought her hands to his lips, his voice echoing her
pride. "You are now my wife, and I love you. Only death
shall part us."

He glanced down at her hands, and his brow creased
slightly. "I have no ring for you," he murmured.

She leant forward, placing a gentle kiss on his lips. "We
are in the old tradition now," she whispered into his ear,
brushing her lips against his cheek. "It is not a ring that I
want from you, my love."

Her eyes went up to his, and suddenly he was kissing
her hard, laying her back down against the cloak. She went
gladly, drawing him in, feeling the power of him against
her, the urgent need which was matched by her own. She
wanted to kiss every part of him, and her dress was off,
then his tunic, then the under-layers, and they twined,
naked, the shadows of the stable drawing around them like
a blanket. His hips rose over hers, and she wanted him …
wanted him …

He hesitated for a long moment, looking down at her.
"This will hurt for a moment, but not longer." His eyes
held hers. "I wish it would not -"

"Hurt me?" She smiled up at him, her hand moving to
the bandage at her thigh, the wrapping at her arm. "You
think I care aught for that one sharp moment of sensation,
when I can then share a lifetime of your warmth?"

He groaned, and then he was in motion, and the brief
pain was soon overwhelmed by a soaring, shuddering
ecstasy.

* * *

Elizabeth lay in his arms, her breath slowing, drawing into a more even pattern, the sturdiness of his body beneath her filling her with warmth. It was overwhelming that the touch of another could bring so much pleasure. She had known only pain over the years, had not imagined that such a thing existed.

She rolled over, pressing a gentle kiss against Richard's lips. "If I could, I would stay here all week with you," she murmured. "But as it is, we have a deadline. There are several hours left before sunset; more than enough time to get you safely away."

"I will not leave you," he stated, his hand moving to brush the hair from her face. "To think of you in the hands of that monster -"

She shook her head gently. "I am safe now," she pointed out. "I am now your lawful wife. I cannot be wed twice. You must get to Thomas, and from there to Charles, to James, and to the others. Raise an army of our neighbors, and return in force. Whatever Corwin has up his sleeve, he will not be able to stand against your strength."

"And what of you?" he asked, his eyes holding concern.

She smiled reassuringly at him. "Oh, my father will rage, and Corwin will threaten, and they will lock me in my room. But they would never permanently hurt me, not when my father is now so close to having the one thing he has always craved in life."

"And what is that?"

She moved her hand to her abdomen. "A grandson," she murmured.

His hand moved to tenderly rest over hers, his eyes drawing up to hold hers.

Her voice was low and gentle. "Your son will not be a bastard," she promised. "He will be loved, and praised, and his father and mother will always be there for him."

He was drawing her in again, and as much as she knew time was of the essence, she went willingly, opening herself fully to him.

* * *

The sun slid lower as she drew on her chemise, then the dress, buckling her belt in place with a sure tug. At her side Richard was doing the same, drawing up their cloaks and carrying them along to lay before the stalls.

"I will take my own steed," he decided at last. "While the others might be quicker, or have greater stamina, Fidelis has seen me through more battles than I can count. I would have no other."

She nodded in agreement, looking amongst the others. "I hate to harm any horse," she added after a moment. "And yet, undoubtedly these will be the creatures who are thundering after you in short order. To think one of them could carry the man who delivers your death blow …"

He shook his head. "We do no damage at all to any horse here, nor to the saddle, the bit, or any other aspect."

A shiver dashed through Elizabeth. "Surely Corwin would not be so honorable," she mused.

Richard nodded, turning to her. "Indeed he would not," he countered. "And so, the moment he is able to, he will begin searching the horses and gear for the signs of our sabotage. When he cannot find any, it will never occur to him that we are innocent. Instead, he will think we are too clever for him, that we hid the marks of our efforts with great skill. It will cause him to spend even more time searching out the tiniest clue, examining each horse for the smallest indication of what we have done. Every cough, every slight tug will send his mind racing." He smiled wryly. "By doing nothing at all, we do far more than one could imagine."

She smiled at that, and then they were going through the supplies, ensuring he had ample ale and cheese for the flight. He patted his steed fondly on the neck, drawing him out of the stall. He turned again to look down at Elizabeth. "We can still find another way," he offered, his gaze serious.

She shook her head. "This is the best way," she returned, leaning up to kiss him. He drew her in hard against him, pouring his love down into her, and at last they parted. She drew her cloak snugly against her body, then nodded. He moved to the bar, sliding it hard, then pressed the large doors open.

Corwin was standing there, staring at the doors with a smile. He gave a whistle, and in a moment his men came trotting to his side from the corners of the barn where they had been watching guard.

"There you are," he grinned, looking over the pair of them. "Done with all your arrangements are we? I am quite interested to see just what they involve. I enjoy puzzles. But for now, I believe it is time you are on your way, dear brother." He glanced at Elizabeth. "Say goodbye to my wife now. Think of how she will be pleasuring me in the years to come."

Richard stiffened, but he glanced down at Elizabeth, his eyes softening. "You take care," he offered, his voice warm.

"Safe travels," she returned, holding her cloak tightly against the chill.

Corwin's eyes scanned down the form of his brother, and his eyes sharpened. "What is this? Blood on your cloak?"

Elizabeth froze; there was indeed a bloodstain clearly evident on the side of the cloak, at Richard's hip. If Corwin were to guess ...

The man's eyes moved up to Richard's face, and then he gave a short laugh. "I see that you injure more easily than I would have thought, brother," he scoffed. "See that you do not fall on the road before night comes. It would be a shame to ruin the hunt in such a manner."

"I will not fall," agreed Richard, his voice a vow, his eyes moving to hold Elizabeth's.

Corwin made a sweeping gesture with his hand, and Richard gave her one last look before turning his horse's head and thundering hard from the jousting field. In moments his steed was lost in the woods beyond.

Corwin laughed, moving to stand alongside Elizabeth. "And there, my dear, is the last you will see of my brave brother, as he rides as quickly as he can away from you. Luckily for you, I am made of sturdier stock."

Elizabeth stared after Richard for a moment, sending her most fervent hopes with him. Then she dropped to a sitting position, giving a controlled wave with one hand. "And now we wait until sunset."

Corwin nodded in pleasant agreement, indicating to the men. One by one they settled down into a ring, drawing their cloaks close against the wintry chill. "And now we wait for the games to begin," he answered with a smile.

Chapter 22

Elizabeth looked around the darkened courtyard as the keep's inhabitants bustled into it, filling it with each passing minute, the ring of torches sending flickering shadows dancing. Dusk had fallen as they led the horses back from the jousting grounds; she had smiled with amusement as Corwin had steadfastly refused to let any be ridden. Now three of his men had galloped out hard on fresh mounts while the other two stayed close at her side. But his eyes had gone from wary to complacent pleasure as she had given him quiet compliance, as she had bowed to every request. She stood, as ordered, by the front steps of the small stone chapel, her cloak pulled tight, the two guards alert on either side of her.

Corwin's voice was warm with pleasure. "Ah, and here comes your father," he informed her, as a pair of burly men carrying a carved wooden chair walked through the main doors of the keep. He called out to them. "Right over here, at the place of honor." Her father's eyes blinked open blearily as he was settled down at the foot of the chapel stairs, facing up them.

Corwin turned to the elderly priest. "And you, Father Godfrey, you belong at the top of the stairs, of course," he added.

Father Godfrey's eyes moved with concern to hold Elizabeth's. "My child, are you sure you are making the right decision here?" he asked, his voice tight with worry. "There is no rush, after all."

She offered a reassuring smile to the wizened man. "I vowed I would marry today," she stated. "That vow is my word and my bond."

Corwin grinned with delight. "And she is nothing if not stubborn," he agreed. "I will see pig dung turn to gold ere I see her go back on her word."

He looked around as the flow of people into the square faded to a trickle, then stopped. "Good, good, is that everybody?" he called out. "I want there to be no question about what goes on this night."

He put out a hand to her, and she placed her own into it, moving to take a place at his side. Together they ascended the stairs, stopping at the second to last one, standing before the priest.

Father Godfrey glanced at Elizabeth with concern before looking out over the congregation.

"Marriage is a sacred institution, and it should not be entered into lightly," he intoned. "It is the most holy of vows. It is about a man and a woman pledging their lives to each other, promising to forsake all others. Both partners strive to be loyal, true, and to treat each other with the highest respect at all times."

He glanced nervously at Corwin. "There was no time to properly publish the banns, so this serves as the final request. I make it to all present. If any here knows any reason – any reason at all – that these two should not marry, it is your Christian duty to speak now and draw a halt to these proceedings."

He looked slowly around the filled courtyard, his eyes hopeful, but the only noise was the shuffling of feet and a low coughing. After a moment he nodded in resignation, drawing his eyes down to the two individuals standing before him.

"Corwin, you stand before us to take the hand of Elizabeth, only child of Lord Masci, in the bonds of matrimony. Do you swear to honor her and cherish her? For as the Ephesians say, 'Husbands, love your wives, just as Christ loved the church and gave himself up for her.' Will you treat her with gentleness and tenderness?"

Corwin let out a snort. "I believe that same passage states, 'Wives, submit to your husbands as to the Lord.' She had best submit to me, as is required." His eyes moved down her body, sharpening with interest. "Yes, I most definitely shall have her as my wife, and all that the bargain entails."

Father Godfrey pursed his lips unhappily at the response, but he nodded, turning to Elizabeth. His eyes softened.

His voice was low, almost pitched for her ears alone. "My dear Elizabeth," he offered, then gave a cough and increased his volume. "Elizabeth, you are here to join yourself as wife to Corwin. You will be respected by him, handled with kindness, as all good Christian wives should be. As the Proverbs say, 'a wife of noble character is her husband's crown'. The Proverbs also say, 'A wife of noble character who can find? She is worth far more than rubies.' You will be the glory and wealth of Corwin's life, and all around you shall see his true Christian behavior, and comment on it. On these terms, will you have him?"

Elizabeth smiled gently at Father Godfrey's concern, seeing all too clearly in his face how much he worried for her.

She turned to Corwin, his eyes shining with eager anticipation. She pitched her voice to carry loud and strong across the courtyard.

"I am sorry, but I am afraid it is completely impossible."

Corwin's eyes turned to green marbles. His voice was a low hiss. "What are you doing, my wife?"

Her voice was calm and clear. "I am afraid that I cannot marry you."

His hand shot out to grab her hard on the arm. "You swore a vow," he reminded her, his voice steely.

She turned to face out over the gathered group. "I did vow to marry today, and I have done so. This afternoon, in the jousting stables, Richard and I pledged our love to each other, in the sight of God and all of nature. We sealed our vow in the most powerful way a man and woman can."

Corwin's face burned crimson with rage. "You *what*?"

Her eyes flickered to Doctor Tyrian, who stood at her father's side. "The good doctor had me certified this morning as a girl innocent of man's touch," she reminded him calmly. "I think he will find that I am now a married woman." She smiled. "What I have given to Richard, no other man can ever have."

"You slut!" His hand lashed out, slammed into her face, and she was driven hard to her knees. She gave her head a shake, then carefully stood back to her feet, staring at him with fierce pride.

"No, not a slut," she informed him. "I am a lawfully married woman. I shared my wedding bed with my honorable husband. He is the only man, by law, who can touch me from this point forward."

Corwin rounded on Father Godfrey. "You are a priest," he snapped. "Make her undo her vow."

Father Godfrey held his gaze with innocent eyes. "Marriage is a sacred institution," he stated resolutely. "Once it is entered into, with both parties pledging themselves voluntarily to each other, then only death can part them."

"Death you say," growled Corwin, skewering Elizabeth with his gaze. "That is certainly a thought."

Elizabeth found breath returning to her. "Your plans have failed you," she informed Corwin, her shoulders easing, a distance forming between the chaos around her and her own soul. "Whatever machinations you have set into place here, you have failed. Richard will come to claim me as his own. My father will die, and Richard and I will rule as proper heirs to my father's holdings."

She was utterly unprepared for his savage response. He swung as if the fiery hells had driven him to madness. Elizabeth was slammed face first into the dark mud, and above her Corwin's shout carried to the far corners of the courtyard. "Put her in the dungeons!"

It was as if her old nightmares had come to life, as if she were back at the tournament, the crowd hushed, the disrespect seen by all. To her surprise, she felt only a welling of pride within her; a sense of deep satisfaction. She stood tall as Corwin's men dragged her to her feet; looked from her father to Corwin with fierce determination.

"Richard is coming for me," she told them, her voice strong. "If you try to hold his wife from him, woe be it on your heads."

Her father's hoarse rasp cut through the night with fury. "You ungrateful wench! You will rot in that flea-infested prison until you bend to my will!"

He gave a motion with his head, and the guards hauled her through the main keep doors, pushed her down the narrow staircase, and flung her into the dark cell. The door was slammed shut, and she could hear the lock turning. Then the guards moved back up the stairs, taking their torches with them. She was plunged into absolute darkness.

She moved back into a corner of the cell, sat down with her knees hugged to her chest, and settled in to wait.

* * *

Elizabeth blinked her eyes open. The room was still pitch dark, the musty scent infiltrating every pore of her body. She had no idea how much time had passed. Her stomach rumbled with hunger, and her mouth was dusty and dry.

She looked around with sightless eyes, trying to sense a slight glimmer of light in any direction. Several pairs of footsteps grew more distinct as they came down the stairs, and a soft glow moved with them, growing as they came toward the small, barred grate high in her door. She stayed where she was, her back pressed against the slimy stone, waiting.

Her father's voice growled through the grate. "You in there. Are you ready to admit that your time with Richard was the meaningless act of a harlot? Corwin will take you, tainted as you are, if we demonstrate that your time with Richard was not serious."

Elizabeth laughed out loud. "Is that your thought?" she called out. "That I would undo my marriage with a lie?" Her voice grew in strength. "Never. I will never dishonor Richard, nor what we have together."

"Then you will sit in there until Judgment Day," he snarled. The footsteps faded from earshot, leaving her again in pitch black.

* * *

The door slid open, some items were placed on the ground, and then the door was pulled shut again. She

waited until the feet moved into the distance before
making her way forward. It was a skin of ale, along with a
bowl of gruel, and she consumed both hungrily. It seemed,
at least, that she would not be starved to death in her cell.
Then she moved back to the dark corner to wait.

* * *

Her eyes pulled wearily open, not that it mattered
much. Perhaps four or five days had passed – it was hard
to tell any more. What had pulled her from her dark
dreams this time?

There were solid footsteps coming toward the door with
a bright torch. They stopped before the door, a key turned
in the lock, and it was pushed wide open. She squinted
against the light. Corwin stood there, his eyes drawing
down her form with a sneer.

"Not so high and mighty now," he scoffed, wrinkling
his nose against the smell. "You note that only my
personally chosen lackeys have been delivering your food,
to keep you from wriggling your way out like last time."

"I have no need to run," she returned calmly. "Richard
will be coming for me."

He took a step forward, his eyes blazing with anger.
"Your Richard has fled the region, the coward that he is,"
he shot out. "My men have searched every meadow and
hill. He cannot be found anywhere."

"I am sure he cannot," she agreed smoothly, her eyes
holding his. "And yet he will come for me."

Corwin was at her side in a heartbeat, dragging her hard
to her feet, glaring down at her. "You should have been
mine," he snarled. "The agreements were made. You had
no right to do anything but obey."

Elizabeth held his gaze with absolute peace of heart. "I am Richard's wife."

His hand flew out, and the slap threw her back against the wall. His voice shot out, harsh and cruel. "And how would Richard feel when he finds his wife has slept with another man? He would throw you out, abandon you, and then you would have no choice but to come crawling to me, begging for me to take you back."

Her eyes shot up to meet his, fierce heat shooting through her veins. "If you take me by force, not only could you create a bastard, but one brought about by the rape of a married woman." Her eyes drew down him in scorn. "You know what it was to grow up as a bastard of a loving couple. How much worse do you feel it would be for your first-born son to instead be the result of such violence? What types of slurs would follow him at every corner, would be shouted from every person he passed?"

Corwin's hand went up again, and she stood still, not flinching, her gaze holding his. He stared at her, his green eyes shimmering rocks, and then with an oath he turned, stalking from the room, slamming the door behind him and turning the key. In a moment, the room had faded into its silent blackness, the bottom of an eternally deep well.

* * *

Bright light flared against her closed eyelids; a pair of strong arms dragged her roughly to her feet. She struggled to force her eyes open against the salts which held them together. Her feet barely carried her up the long, spiral staircase. Candles flickered in the hall as she came up to the main floor. Apparently it was nighttime, and a cloudy one at that. No moon or stars interrupted the dark blackness of the sky. She groaned wearily. What cruel fate would have her time out of the cell be a mirror of her black captivity?

The men at her side pushed open the main door of the keep, half-carrying, half-dragging her across the dark courtyard. A line of soldiers manned the wall before her, the flames of their torches whipping in the night wind. Her guards moved her up the stairs to the top of the wall, and she stumbled to a halt beside a cloaked figure.

Corwin turned to glare at her, then looked out into the inky expanse beyond the curtain wall. His shout carried on the night winds. "You see? Here she is. Can we finally get on with this? These talks have gone on for quite long enough."

Elizabeth pressed up against the wall to look beyond its crenellations. To her surprise, flickering torches dotted the landscape, casting pools of light on formations of foot-soldiers, contingents of mounted riders, and even a battering ram. There were a good three hundred soldiers surrounding the keep. And at their front …

"Richard!" Her voice was hoarse with disuse, but it carried clearly into the night.

"Elizabeth!" he shouted, his eyes steady on hers, and she saw the relief and weariness in his face. "Are you all right? Are you hurt?"

"I am fine, now that you are here," she called out, drinking in his strength. She saw now that Thomas stood by his side, and James, and countless other men she had sparred with over the years. The men and their forces stretched for as far as she could see.

Her father's raspy voice came from her other side. "She is fine. So you can all leave now."

Richard shook his head. His tone brooked no option. "She is my wife. I will not leave without her."

Her father scoffed, giving a harsh bark. "The chit spread her legs for you for a brief tumble in a stable," he countered. "If every girl who did that ended up married to the blackguard who bedded her, our land would be populated with bigamists galore."

Richard's eyes became steely. "Either you hand over my wife, or we come in and get her ourselves."

Her father rounded on her, his thin frame tight with fury. "This is all your fault," he snarled. "If you did not behave like a whore, everything would have been resolved the way I wished."

Elizabeth's eyes shone. "I love Richard, and I am his wife," she shot back. "There is nothing you can do to change that."

His face filled with fury. "You dare defy me? You worthless slut!" He swung hard at her, his fist aiming for her chin.

Elizabeth reacted by instinct. She dropped down and left, her hands drawing up to protect her face, fully prepared for the flurry of blows she knew would follow.

Her father flailed as his fist whistled through open air. He half-turned, losing his balance, his arms throwing wide. He toppled. She leapt forward, but her hand swiped on empty space as he fell, shrieking, the three stories down toward the earth. His body hit the rocky ground at the base of the wall, and he lay still.

"Father!" she screamed, her eyes pinned on his still form. "Open the gates! Open the gates!"

Corwin grabbed her hard on the arm. "Are you insane?" He swung to look at the guards around him. "Keep those gates shut!"

She pulled herself free, all thoughts of her father. "He could be alive," she cried, turning to race down the stairs. "Open the gates!"

A flurry of men ran to her side; in a moment the heavy bar had been drawn back and the gates were pulled open. She raced to her father's side. Richard was there in the same instant; he carefully gathered the limp body up in his arms. Together they moved with him back into the courtyard. Thomas ran alongside to sweep a work table clear of its supplies, and they lay the body gently on its wooden surface.

Elizabeth leaned over his frail form, her heart pounding. "Father? Father?"

At long last his eyelids fluttered open weakly. "Grecia, my dearest sister, is that you?"

Elizabeth blinked in surprise. Her father had not mentioned his sister's name once in all the years he had raised her. Elizabeth knew of her, of course – how she and his other brothers had died during the brutal raid on the keep.

"No, Father, it is Elizabeth, your daughter," she gently corrected him.

His focus dimmed. "One must be strong to survive in this keep; one has to be as tough as forged iron to keep it safe." His gaze came back up to hold Elizabeth's face. "You have to be sharper than the longest icicle, able to tolerate the pain of a thousand wolf bites to keep the people within safe from harm."

"I know," she soothed him. "I will hold the keep."

His eyes held her for a long moment. "I know you will," he agreed, his eyes softening for a moment. And then they dimmed, and his breath eased out of his throat.

An arm came gently up around her, and she turned, sobbing, into Richard's sturdy chest, mourning the loss of a man who had seemed such a force of nature. Now his body lay there, frail, broken, a mere wisp of a man, and he was gone.

At long last she pulled back from Richard, her eyes joining with his, a feeling of awe growing over her. He was her husband. He would stand beside her, support her, and together they could make the keep a place of strength and safety.

There was a rippling movement of bodies around her, and she turned to see the people of the keep slowly lowering themselves to one knee, bowing their heads. She realized that they were acknowledging the couple as the new head of the keep. Thomas and the other supporters nodded their heads to her, their faces both somber and proud.

A sharp cry of outrage blistered through the stillness. "No!" screamed Corwin, looking around in disbelief. "This is not what was supposed to happen! The keep should be mine. Elizabeth should be mine, to do with as I will!"

Richard took a step before Elizabeth, shielding her with his body. "Your plans and schemes are done with, brother," he informed him, his voice tight. "It is time for you to leave."

"Leave? Leave my own keep?" cried Corwin in fury. "After all I have gone through to get my hands on this pile of rocks?"

Several of the keep guards took a step toward Corwin. He drew his sword in a flash, sweeping a glittering arc around him to keep them clear.

His voice was harsh. "Did your dear *wife* tell you what I did to her while she was in that prison? She is tainted now. Your precious honor will not allow you to keep her. I will take her off your hands – go on back to those twins you love babysitting so much."

Richard's head turned quickly to Elizabeth, his eyes rich with concern, and she shook her head. He looked back to Corwin, his eyes more serious. "Even if you had assaulted her, it would not change my feelings for her one grain. I love her with all my heart, and I will stand by her as long as I have life left to breathe."

Corwin raised his sword high over his head. "I can take care of that," he challenged.

Richard's hand flashed to the hilt of his sword, and Elizabeth drew in a deep breath, fighting the instinct to interfere with every ounce of her strength. This was Richard's fight; this was his relationship with his brother. He had stood back, all those times she had wrangled with Corwin as her fiancé. She could see now just much effort it had taken him.

A long moment passed, then Richard spoke. "I will not mar today with further senseless death," he growled. "You have made your mistakes in life. I again offer you the chance to leave and find a new path for yourself."

Rage billowed in Corwin's face as he realized Richard was not going to fight him. He took another step forward, his eyes black pits of shadow. "I killed Launa, our father's second wife!"

Richard shook his head slightly, and he stared at Corwin with growing focus. "You what?"

Corwin's face blossomed in satisfaction, and his voice echoed in the courtyard with pride. "Yes, that trollop who managed to lure our father away from our mother. I am the one who cut her down."

Richard's gaze held bafflement. "Why in the world would you do that?"

Corwin laughed with delight. "Why did I let her live as long as I did, you mean! It was only because father seemed to care for her, and I did not want to bring him any pain. But once he passed on, it was merely a matter of choosing the right circumstances. The imagining of the act was nearly as satisfying as actually plunging the sword into her chest."

Richard's voice grew harsh. "She was an innocent woman!"

Corwin's eyes sharpened. "Innocent? The schemer took our father away from the woman he loved! Then she promptly made a pair of sons to replace us." He shook his head. "To see her there sitting at our father's side, sharing his table, sharing his bed! It simply could not be tolerated."

Awareness brightened Richard's eyes. "And the left-handed female assassin?"

Corwin grinned. "A touch of genius, if I might say so myself. I could take out two rabbits with one trap. I got rid of the odious interloper, and I also set out a wide net to catch my wayward wife." He swelled with pride. "You note that I made sure the rumor listed her with ice-blue eyes. I would not want an overenthusiastic lynch mob to slay her before I got my hands on her. But I did need to find her quickly, of course."

"Of course?"

Corwin's eyes flicked to the dead body lying on the table, then he glanced around him, as if suddenly remembering they had a large audience hearing this interchange.

Richard's sword drew out of its sheath in a hiss. "You poisoned Elizabeth's father?" he ground out.

Corwin stepped forward eagerly, his sword held high, circling Richard. "And what if I did?" he countered. "The old fool was letting everything slip away from him. Someone had to take action."

The watchers drew back into a ring, giving the men space to move, and Thomas moved up alongside Elizabeth, his stance alert. Her sharp focus was on the two men before her. They were so similar, their eyes the same color, their sword skills clearly the product of similar training. And yet they were so different from one another. Her heart pounded as she thought of Corwin's willingness to stoop to any foul trickery.

It took every ounce of her self-control to hold in her breath, to step back. She could feel now what Richard had gone through these long weeks, to allow her to deal with Corwin on her own terms. It was his turn now. Corwin was his brother; he had a history with the man which far outweighed her own fractious one. If anyone had a right to take on Corwin and his deceptions, Richard was that man.

Richard circled his brother, his gaze somber. "I still offer you the right to a trial," he stated, his voice low. "You could have – "

Corwin drew his sword high and down, aiming to cleave Richard's arm from its socket, and Richard barely dodged back in time, avoiding the swipe, drawing his own sword forward in defense. He dove toward Corwin's leg, but Corwin leapt back, retreating to safety, and the men were circling again.

Corwin's voice was harsh. "You always relied on the system," he snarled. "A system which consigned us to the lowest rungs merely because of the way we were born."

Corwin lashed out again, the sweep of his sword as quick as an adder's fangs, and Richard evaded the whistling tip by mere inches.

Richard's eyes were steady on his brother's, filled with resignation and regret. "However we were born, we could always choose to act in the most honorable way possible," he reminded his younger sibling.

"We could take all we had coming," countered Corwin, dodging in again, and then they were in a maelstrom.

Elizabeth held her breath, barely able to follow the spinning blades, the flashing steel, the hammer-like blows and the twists and turns. The battle seemed to rage for hours; her heart pounded in her chest as if it would escape to join in the war.

Richard was in there, her beloved Richard. If he fell, she had no idea if she could survive.

A cascade of dust, the reverberation of swords, and suddenly the two men stepped apart, staring at each other.

Elizabeth could not breathe. If Richard fell ...

But it was Corwin who sighed, who staggered forward, who drew a hand shakily to his chest, and then who plunged toward the earth. Richard was there in an instant, at his side, easing him toward the ground, rolling him over onto his back.

Elizabeth ran to Richard's side, leaning against him in heartfelt relief. Together they stared down at Corwin, the blood now burbling up out of the wound in his chest as an erupting spring.

Corwin's eyes were sharp. "I deserved glory," he ground out. "After all I have gone through, I deserved ..."

Richard's voice was tight. "You deserve peace," he murmured.

Corwin's face eased at that, and then his eyes went glassy, and the spark faded from them.

Elizabeth turned to Richard, and his arms drew around her, pulling her close. The courtyard went quiet, with the two corpses lying on either side of them, and finally, for the first time in her life, her home was absolutely silent.

Chapter 23

Two years later

Elizabeth reached her arms out to the tiny, toddling form, her smile warm, the heat of the fire stretching toward them.

"Come on, Jeffrey, you can do it," she urged, her gaze caught on his moss-green eyes.

The child smiled with delight and eased himself up against the worn stone of the wall. He took one shaky step, then two. Then he was in motion, crossing the short distance across the hearth and falling into his mother's arms.

Richard's voice called out with pride from across the hall. "Did you see that! My son! He is walking!"

A cheer sounded around them, and Richard came up to draw them into a warm embrace, kissing her warmly on the cheek, stroking a hand fondly across their son's head.

Elizabeth returned his kiss, her soul becoming lost in the beauty of her life. Tapestries hung on the walls, decorated with purple columbines and beautiful landscapes. The dreary dirt of her father's reign had long since been replaced with fresh rushes and polished tables, with fragrant flowers and cascades of candles. Young Jeffrey had blessed their life with his smiling laughter, and she moved a hand to caress the growing bulge at her stomach. Soon, perhaps, a younger sister would be there at his side, to lend warmth and strength to his life.

Thomas stepped into the entryway, his eyes moving fondly to the young child between them. "Malota and young Thomas Junior are taking their nap," he commented with a smile. "But you might be interested to know that you have visitors."

Richard glanced up, his hand falling to his hilt.

Thomas shook his head gently. "They seem friendly enough," he advised his friend. "Foreign, though. I think they are from France."

Richard gathered up his wife and son, settling them behind the head table. It was a few minutes before there was a movement from the main doors, before a young man and woman came cautiously into the room.

Elizabeth looked over them in interest. They appeared to be in their early twenties, their style of dress clearly not of local wear. They were weary, too, as if they had come quite a distance. Still, they stood resolutely side by side, coming to kneel before her and her husband, then drawing themselves up to their feet.

The woman looked at her with a searching gaze. "You are Elizabeth?"

Elizabeth nodded in curiosity. "I am."

"I am Framberta," offered the woman, dropping a curtsy. "And this is Abram."

Elizabeth waited, her eyes drawing over the young couple.

The woman's mouth eased into a smile. "I was the daughter of the inn-keep at Rennes," she expanded. "Your brother, Jeffrey, saved my life."

Elizabeth's son smiled in delight at hearing his name, reaching his arms out to his father. Elizabeth took in the moss-green eyes, so like her brother's, and sighed in pleasure. Richard swept the child up in his arms, drawing him close, and Framberta nodded in understanding.

"I was only a child when the attack came," she continued, "but I am absolutely certain that we all would have died if it had not been for Jeffrey. He had no thought of his own safety. He stood strong, taking on the entire force of the bandits, and he created a wall between them and my family. It is solely due to his strength that I am here today."

Abram dropped his eyes, nodding. "God be praised," he added.

Framberta dropped a hand to her abdomen. "The moment Abram and I wed, I told him that we had to come here. I had to offer my thanks to your family for being here today. If it were not for your brother, I could not have the joy I do. I would not be bearing a son for my husband, and bringing our family to life. It is all due to your brother that I have this happiness."

Elizabeth's mouth quirked into a smile. "You know that it will be a son?" She had felt the same certainty that first day she had laid with Richard. She had known beyond any doubt that they had created a son, there in the fragrant hay of the stables, beneath their columbine.

Framberta nodded, a smile on her lips. "It will be a son," she agreed, "and we will name him Jeffrey."

Elizabeth opened her arms to the young Frenchwoman. "Then you shall be my sister," she welcomed, "and you can stay as long as you wish."

Framberta's eyes glistened. "I would like to hear more about the man who risked everything to keep me and my family safe," she murmured, her voice breaking.

She glanced behind her. "Maybe we could just take leave of our traveling companions?"

Elizabeth looked up. Indeed, she hadn't noticed the other three who had entered the room, so quietly had they moved. There was a young woman with long, brunette hair and two older men, all in dark blue tunics emblazoned with hawks. Each wore a sword at their side.

Framberta smiled. "Let me introduce Lucia and her two guards. They hail from the far north, near the Wall. They were returning from a funeral of a relative and kindly escorted us all this way."

Elizabeth waved them over. "Please, join us. Your generosity deserves equal treatment. You are welcome here as long as you wish to stay."

Lucia stepped forward, the guards maintaining their positions at her side. She gave a short bow. "I appreciate the offer, and we will indulge in a night's rest. But we must be off first thing in the morning. Winter is upon us and my father will be hard pressed by the bandits. I'm afraid they're getting worse with every passing year. As Captain of the Guard, it's my duty to be up on those walls."

Elizabeth looked over the young woman before her. "Congratulations on your position. Your father must have quite a high estimation of your skills to trust you with that responsibility."

One of the guards at her side nodded. "She earned it. She's the best archer in the land."

The other guard chuckled. "And not a slouch with that sword, either."

Lucia's eyes shadowed. "It will take more than one sword or one bow to keep our lands safe, if these tensions continue."

Elizabeth's hip hummed, and she looked down at the green-leather-hilt sword which hung at her side. Kay's words came back to her, from that distant meeting two long years ago.

Do not become too fond of Andetnes. When you have at last found contentment, there will be another whose fate balances on the point of a pin. You will know when it is right. And the sword will have a new mistress.

Elizabeth's throat closed up. For a moment she was beyond words. Her home was warm and comforting, the man she adored was at her side, and their precious child was smiling up at her with moss-green eyes.

Tears came to her eyes, and she knew that, at last, her world was absolutely right.

She smiled at Lucia. "Come, have a seat. Tell me all about your troubles. And I will see if I might be able to help, in some small way."

The Sword of Glastonbury series continues with Book 3, *Believing Your Eyes* –

http://www.amazon.com/Believing-Your-Eyes-Medieval-Romance-ebook/dp/B008RIBYTI/

If you enjoyed *Finding Peace*, please leave feedback on Amazon, Goodreads, and any other systems you use. Together we can help make a difference!

https://www.amazon.com/review/create-review?ie=UTF8&asin=B008FQZ8JY#

Be sure to sign up for my free newsletter! You'll get alerts of free books, discounts, and new releases. I run my own newsletter server – nobody else will ever see your email address. I promise!

http://www.lisashea.com/lisabase/subscribe.html

Join my online groups to get news of free giveaways, upcoming stories, and fascinating trivia!

Facebook
https://www.facebook.com/LisaSheaAuthor

Twitter
https://twitter.com/LisaSheaAuthor

Google+
https://plus.google.com/+LisaSheaAuthor/posts

GoodReads
https://www.goodreads.com/lisashea/

Blog
http://www.lisashea.com/lisabase/blog/

Be sure to download all of my FREE books! Each of these is completely free and available on Kindle.

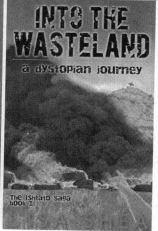

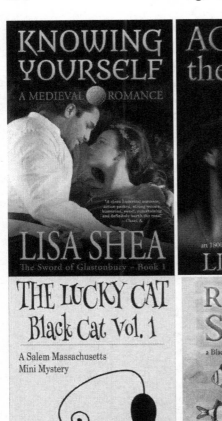

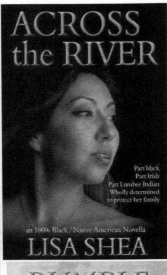

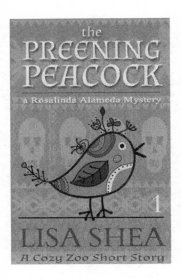

Medieval Dialogue

I've been fascinated by medieval languages since I was quite young. I grew up studying Spanish, English, and Latin, and loved the sound of reading Beowulf and the Canterbury Tales in their original languages. I adore the richness of medieval languages. How did medieval English people speak?

There are three aspects to this. The first is the difference between written records and spoken language. The second is the rich, multi-cultural aspect of medieval life. And the third is how to convey this to a modern-language audience.

Let's take the first. Sometimes modern people equate the way medieval folk would talk, hanging around a rustic tavern, with the way Chaucer wrote his famous *Canterbury Tales*. Something along the lines of this (note this is a modern translation, not the original Middle English version):

"Of weeping and wailing, care and other sorrow
I know enough, at eventide and morrow,"
The merchant said, "and so do many more
Of married folk, I think, who this deplore,
For well I know that it is so with me.
I have a wife, the worst one that can be;
For though the foul Fiend to her wedded were,
She'd overmatch him, this I dare to swear."

Sure, it seems elegant and rich. But did worn-down farmers sitting around a fireplace with mugs of ale really talk like this?

Do we think the London street-dwellers in the 1600s skulked down the dark alleys emoting like Shakespeare –

Two households, both alike in dignity

In fair Verona, where we lay our scene
From ancient grudge break to new mutiny
Where civil blood makes civil hands unclean.

And, in the 1920s in Vermont, did farmers really wander down their snowy lanes murmuring to their farming friends, a la Robert Frost:

Whose woods these are I think I know.
His house is in the village though;
He will not see me stopping here
To watch his woods fill up with snow.

As someone who lives in New England, I can pretty resolutely say "no" to that last one. And, given my research, I'm equally content saying "no" to the previous two. There is a big difference between poetry written with deliberate effort and the way "normal people" talked, flirted, cajoled, and laughed day in and day out. People simply did not talk in iambic pentameter. I'm a poet and even I don't talk in iambic pentameter :).

Modern people sometimes think of the medieval period in terms of the plays we see. We imagine actors on a stage, speaking in formal, stilted language, carefully moving from scene to scene. But medieval life wasn't like that. It was a rich cacophony of people struggling hard to survive amongst plagues and crusades, with strong pagan influences and the church trying to instill order. People fought off robbers and drove away wolves. They laughed and loved in multi-generational homes. It was a time of great flux.

England - A Melting Pot

England wasn't an isolated, walled-off island. It was continually experiencing influxes of new words and sounds. The Romans came and went. The Vikings came and went. The French invaded. Nearly all of the English men headed off to the Crusades, leaving behind women to gain strength and position. The men returned with even more languages. Pilgrims went to

Jerusalem. Merchants arrived from all over. This was a true melting pot.

So, in part because of this, Middle English was a rich, fascinating language. People in this time period had a wealth of contractions, nicknames, abbreviations, and combinations of words they used. Often people could speak multiple languages - their old English, the incoming Norman language, Latin from church, and random other words from tinkers, merchants, and pilgrims they encountered. Medieval people had all sorts of words for drinking, for fighting, for prostitutes, you name it. They had slang and shortcuts just like any other language does. After all, these are the people who turned "forecastle" (on a ship) to "foc's'le" and who pronounce the word "Worcester" as "Woostah."

But, here's the trick. With the medieval language being so rich, varied, intricate, and full of fascinating words, how can we bring that to life for a modern audience?

Centuries of Change

Let's start with a basic issue - most modern readers simply cannot understand authentic medieval dialogue. They don't have the grounding in Middle English, French, and Latin that would be required. Even the fairly straightforward, basic Chaucer works look like this:

And Saluces this noble contree highte.

Modern readers generally wouldn't know that "highte" meant "was called" as in "And Saluces this noble country was called."

This happens over and over again. Words change meaning. In the Middle Ages, if you *abandoned* your wife it means you subjugated her. You got her under your thumb. It didn't mean you left her - quite the opposite. Awful meant *awe-ful* - as in stunning and wonderful. It had a positive connotation. Fantastic wasn't great - it was a fantasy; something that didn't exist.

Nervous didn't mean worried or agitated - it meant strong and full of energy. Nice meant silly, and so on.

If a book was written with proper medieval words and meanings, first, even if the words are reasonably close to what we use now, modern readers would have to struggle with the spelling -

By that the Maunciple hadde his tale al ended,
The sonne fro the south lyne was descended
So lowe, that he nas nat to my sighte
Degrees nyne and twenty as in highte.

But, again, that is just the tip of the issue with medieval language. The word "bracelet" didn't exist until the 1400s. Necklace wasn't a word until 1590. The word "hug" wasn't around until the mid-1500s. We also didn't have the words tragedy, crisis, area, explain, fact, illicit, rogue, or even disagree! Shakespeare invented the words "baseless" and "dwindle" in the 1600s. Staircase is from 1620. A story written solely with words that existed in the year 1200 - and that still retain their modern meaning so modern readers could understand them - would be fairly basic.

(Speaking of which, the word "basic" didn't exist until the mid 1800s.)

Conversely, some words we might think of as thoroughly modern, like "puke", were also used in Shakespeare's time. "Booze" traces back to the 1500s. And these are just the proofs we have. While "shiner" for a black eye can be traced definitively to the 1700s, it could easily have been used for centuries before then and we just don't happen to have a letter or newspaper article which mentions it.

It's fair to say that people in medieval days did get black eyes and had a wealth of interesting terms for that situation. After all, it could be a rough life back then. Was one of the terms used "shiner"? Maybe, maybe not. Out of the ten fun phrases they used, probably nine of them would make zero sense to a modern reading audience. So authors strive to find phrases that provide meaning to a modern audience without being too *l33t* and techno-speak. It doesn't make sense to completely avoid the word "bracelet" simply because it technically didn't exist in the 1200s. Surely people in the 1200s had several words for "bracelet" and we are simply using the word modern readers understand. Similarly, people in medieval times hugged! They just called that action something else.

Medieval people loved playing with words. They called their kids "dillydowns" and "mitings" (little mites). They called sweethearts "my sweeting" and "my honey. They loved snapping out insults, from "dunce" to "idiot" to "pig filth" and "maggot pie." And, again, these are just the ones that happened to get recorded.

Medieval people loved contractions. There's a phrase "ne woot," meaning *knows not*. They'd simply say "noot". They did this with all sorts of words.

So writing in modern English should have this same sort of loose, fun sense to the writing. It's important to remember that even the kings, in this era, were rough fighters. They were out with soldiers, crossing multiple countries, and experiencing a range of languages. They weren't necessarily concerned about speaking in iambic pentameter. They were more concerned about breaking down their enemy's walls to plunder what lay within and then drinking themselves under the table to celebrate.

So, certainly, treasure the poetry and prose of the time. As a poet, I appreciate that immensely. But also keep in mind that people did not talk in poetry. They did not speak in fantasy-speak of *Lord of the Rings* or *Game of Thrones*. They talked and laughed, flirted and cursed, gossiped and cajoled in a rich, multi-lingual, contraction-filled, sobriquet-laden dialogue which mirrors how we talk in modern times.

About Medieval Life

When many of us think of medieval times, we bring to mind a drab reality-documentary image. We imagine people scrounging around in the mud, eating dirt. The people were under five feet tall and barely survived to age thirty. These poor, unfortunate souls had rotted teeth and never bathed.

Then you have the opposite, Hollywood Technicolor extreme. In the romantic version of medieval times, men were always strong and chivalrous. Women were dainty and sat around staring out the window all day, waiting for their knight to come riding in. Everybody wore purple robes or green tights.

The truth, of course, lies somewhere in the middle.

Living in Medieval Times

The years in the early medieval ages held a warm, pleasant climate. Crops grew exceedingly well, and there was plenty of food. As a result, their average height was on par with modern times. It's amazing how much nutrition influences our health!

The abundance of food also had an effect on the longevity of people. Chaucer (born 1340) lived to be 60. Petrarch (born 1304) died a day shy of 70. Eleanor of Aquitaine (born 1122) was 82 when she died. People could and did lead long lives. The average age of someone who survived childhood was 65.

What about their living conditions? The Romans adored baths and set up many in Britain. When they left, the natives could not keep them going, and it is true they then bathed less. However, by the Middle Ages, with the crusades and interaction with the Muslims, there was a renewed interest both in hygiene and medicine. Returning soldiers and those who took pilgrimages brought back with them an interest in regular bathing and cleanliness. This spread across the culture.

While people during other periods of English history ate poorly, often due to war conditions or climatic changes, the middle ages were a time of relative bounty. Villagers would grow fresh fruit and vegetables behind their homes, and had an array of herbs for seasoning. The local baker would bake bread for the village - most homes did not hold an oven, only an open fire. Villagers had easy access to fish, chicken, geese, and eggs. Pork was enjoyed at special meals like Easter.

Upper classes of course had a much wider range of foods - all game animals (rabbits, deer, and so on) belonged to them. The wealthy ate peacocks, veal, lamb, and even bear. Meals for all classes could be flavorful and well enjoyed.

Medieval Relationships

Some movies present a skewed version of life in the Middle Ages. They make it seem that women were meek, mild, and obediently did whatever their father or husband commanded.

This was *far* from the truth!

Medieval times were times of immense change. Men were off at the Crusades, leaving the women to run things. Christianity was trying to get a foothold, but many areas of Britain were still primarily pagan, with all the Goddess worship and female empowerment which had been tradition for centuries. The vast majority of brewers were female. Most innkeepers were female. Women's knowledge about herbs, health, and food was respected. Healthy women were treasured as the key to a child-rich partnership.

Medieval life was heavily focused on fertility. Farm animals had to be fertile in order to create meat to feed the family. Women had to be fertile to create helpers for the farm and household. Celebration after celebration in medieval times focused on fertility. These people weren't shy about the topic. They watched their horses, cows, and dogs continually engage in these activities. Their festivals focused on the topic with bawdy delight. Their songs lusted about it.

The church tried, again and again, to squelch this behavior so that all aspects of relationships could be regulated by the church. However, half of all medieval couples were together outside of a church marriage and, for those sanctified by the church, a large proportion were "sealing the deal" for a couple already pregnant.

This was the way the medieval people looked at it: they needed to know their partner could create children. This was a key consideration for a relationship.

The Medieval period was far from an era of Victorian prudity. Quite the opposite. People of this era celebrated fertility, felt it was wholly natural, and even felt it was unhealthy for a man or woman to go for too long without sex. The celibacy would block critical flows of the body.

It was considered natural that a male noble might take on mistresses and that unmarried couples might seek out partners. It was the same as someone needing food if they were hungry. It was a bodily function which had to be tended to for the health of the person.

So where does marriage fit in with this mindset?

Medieval Marriage

In medieval times, marriage was primarily about inheritance. It was almost separate from sexuality. Sexuality was an important part of bodily health, like eating well and getting enough exercise. Marriage, on the other hand, was about ensuring one's lands and chattel were cared for from generation to generation. Sex, within a marriage, was focused on creating family-line children to then tend to that wealth.

For this reason, wealthy families would put immense energy into arranging optimal marriages for their children. This was about the transfer of land far more than a love match. Parents wanted to ensure their land went to a family worthy of ownership - one with the resources to defend it from attack. It was not only their own family members they were concerned with. Each block of land had on it both free men and serfs. These people all depended on the nobles – with their skill, connections, and soldiers – to keep them safe from bandits and harm.

That being said, both the woman and man would be consulted about the match. Their input was a critical aspect of the decision. Choices were often made with intricate selection processes. Keep in mind that the woman and her suitors would have been raised from birth to think of this process as natural. They would participate in that choice-making with an eye as to how it would secure the stability of their future family.

Yes, villagers sometimes married for love. Even a few nobles would run off and follow their hearts. Even so, they would have first seriously considered the potentially catastrophic risks which could result from their actions.

Here is a modern example. Imagine you took over the family business which employed a hundred loyal workers. Those workers depend on your careful guidance of the company to ensure the income for their families. You might dream about running off to Bermuda and drinking martinis. But would you just sell your company to any random investor who came along? Would you risk all of those peoples' lives, people who had served you loyally for decades, to satisfy a whim of pleasure? It is more likely that you would research your options, map out a plan, and made a choice with suited both you and your responsibilities.

Medieval Women

In pagan days women held many rights and responsibilities. During the crusades, especially, with many men off at war, women ran the taverns, made the ale, and ran the government. In later years, as men returned home and Christianity rose in power, women were relegated to a more subservient role.

Still, women in medieval times were not meek and mild. That stereotype came in with the Victorian era, many centuries later. Back in medieval days, women had to be hearty and hard working. There were fields to tend, homes to maintain, and children to raise!

Women strove to be as healthy as they could because they faced a serious threat - a fifth of all women died during or just after childbirth. The church said that childbirth was the "pain of Eve" and instructed women to bear it without medicine or follow-up care. Of course, midwives did their best to skirt these rules, but childbirth still took an immense toll.

Childhood was rough in the Middle Ages – only forty percent of children survived the gauntlet of illnesses to adulthood. A woman who reached her marriageable years was a sturdy woman indeed.

You can see why fertility was so important to medieval people!

To summarize, in medieval days a woman could live a long, happy life, even into her eighties – as long as she was of the sturdy stock that made it through the challenges of childhood. She would be expected to be fertile and to have multiple children, which again weeded out the weaker ones. This was very much a time of 'survival of the fittest.' Medieval life quickly separated out the weak and frail. Those women who ran that gauntlet and survived were respected for that strength and for their wisdom in many areas of life.

So medieval women were strong - very strong. They had to be. They were respected. Still, would they fight?

Women and Weapons

Queen Boudicia, from Norwalk, was born around AD60. She personally – and successfully - led her troops against the Roman Empire. She had been flogged - and her daughters raped - spurring her to revenge. She was extremely intelligent and quite strategic. Her daughters rode in her chariot at her side.

Eleanor of Aquitaine, born in 1122, was brilliant and married first to a King of France and then to a King of England. She went on the Second Crusades as the leader of her troops - reportedly riding bare-breasted as an Amazon. At times she marched with her troops far ahead of her husband. When she divorced the King of France, she immediately married Henry II, who she passionately adored. He was eleven years her junior. When things went sour, Eleanor separated from him and actively led revolts against him.

Many historical accounts talk of women taking up arms to defend their villages and towns. Women would not passively let their children be slain or their homes burned. They were able and strong bodied from their daily work. They were well skilled with farm implements and knives, and used them with great talent against invaders.

Many of these defenses were successful, and the victories were celebrated as brave and proper, rather than dismissed as an unusual act for a woman. A mother was expected to defend her brood and to keep her home safe, just as a wolf mother protects her cubs.

Numerous women took their martial skills to a higher level. In 1301 a group of Italian women joined up to fight the crusade against the Turks. In 1348 at a tournament there were at least thirty women who participated, dressed as men.

This is not as unusual as you might think. In medieval times, all adults carried a knife at their belt for daily use in eating, chores, and defense. All knew how to use it. Being strong and safe was a necessary part of daily life.

Here is an interesting comparison. In modern times most women know how to drive, but few choose to invest themselves in the time and training to become race car drivers. In medieval times, most women knew how to defend themselves with a weapon. They had to. Few, though, actively sought the training to be swordswomen. Still, these women did exist, and did thrive as valued members of their communities.

So women in medieval times were far from shrinking violets. They were not mud-encrusted wretches huddling in straw huts. They were not pale damsels locked away in towers. They were strong, sturdy, and well versed in the use of knives. Many ran taverns, and most handled the brewing of ale. Those who made it through childhood and childbirth could expect to enjoy long, rich lives.

I hope you enjoy my tales of authentic, inspiring heroines!

Glossary

Ale - A style of beer which is made from barley and does not use hops. Ale was the common drink in medieval days. In the 1300s, 92% of brewers were female, and the women were known as "alewives". It was common for a tavern to be run by a widow and her children.

Blade - The metal slicing part of the sword.

Chemise - In medieval days, most people had only a few outfits. They would not want to wash their heavy main dress every time they wore it, just as in modern times we don't wash our jackets after each wearing. In order to keep the sweaty skin away from the dress, women wore a light, white under-dress which could then be washed more regularly. This was often slept in as well.

Drinking - In general, medieval sanitation was not great. People who drank milk had to drink it "raw" - pasteurization was not well known before the 1700s. Water was often unsafe to drink. For these reasons, all ages of medieval folk drank liquid with alcohol in it. The alcohol served as a natural sanitizer. This was even true as recently as colonial American times.

God's Teeth / God's Blood – Common oaths in the middle ages.

Grip - The part of the sword one holds, usually wrapped in leather or another substance to keep it firmly in the wielder's hand.

Guard - The crossed top of the sword's hilt which keeps the enemy's sword from sliding down and chopping off the wielder's fingers.

Hilt - The entire handle part of the sword; everything that is not blade.

Mead - A fermented beverage made from honey. Mead has been enjoyed for thousands of years and is mentioned in Beowulf.

Pommel - The bottom end of the sword, where the hilt ends.

Tip - The very end of the sword

Wolf's Head – a term for a bandit. The Latin legal term *caput gerat lupinum* meant they could be hunted and killed as legally as any dangerous wolf or wild animal that threatened the area.

Parts of a Sword

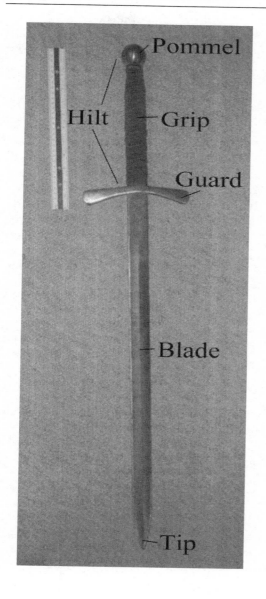

Medieval Clothing

Medieval people - despite modern stereotypes - did have noses and did like to stay clean. Public baths were popular, and people liked to swim as well. However, they did not have the luxury of bathing daily. Also, in medieval times people were often cold. Castles were damp and drafty. Fireplaces were not kept blazingly hot all night long. There is a reason that people wore many heavy layers including cloaks. That way they could add or remove layers as necessary to keep warm.

The basic under-layer was a chemise. This thin nightgown would be worn at night as well as during the day. Because it was against the body it kept the actual clothes clean from sweat. That way you could wash the chemise regularly and not have to wash your actual dress every day. Think of it like when you wear a turtleneck and a wool sweater. At the end of the day you would wash the turtleneck, but you would not wash the wool sweater after every wearing. If you wear a t-shirt under a jacket, you would toss the t-shirt into the washing machine but just hang the jacket on a hook again. The same is true for medieval outfits. The inner layer would be washed, while the other layer would be reused multiple days before it had to be washed.

The chemise was generally not meant to be seen, especially in colder months. It was underwear. There would always be an over-dress with a floor-length hem on top of that. Perhaps a glimpse of the chemise would show at the neckline or at the end-of-sleeve area. In hotter months the chemise might be more visible as the outer dress had short sleeves or no sleeves.

Men would typically wear a tunic over leggings. Men working in summer heat would sometimes wear simple linen "shorts" without anything else. Their chest and lower legs would be bare. This is a stark difference from how covered up women would be.

Both sexes would wear boots or shoes. There was no "left" or "right" - both halves would be made in the same oval shape.

Cloaks would be worn when going out into poor weather, to help keep you warm. These cloaks could be quite heavy if they were full circle cloaks, and incredibly warm.

Monks would wear similar clothing to non-religious men, but the monk's hair would be cut short and have a "tonsure" - or bald spot - shaved out of its center. The tonsure was a sign of their humility.

This illuminated image is from a 12th century manuscript at the library at Cambridge University.

Women's Clothing

     A number of readers had specific questions about women's medieval clothing so I created this page with those specific details. To illustrate it, I have included a drawing done by Andreas Muller, a famous German artist known for his work restoring ancient paintings. This drawing was published back in 1861, so it's now out of copyright. As you might expect the drawing shows German people, not English, but the fashions are from the 1200s and are quite similar in style.

     So, the basics. Women wore at least two layers of long dress. The bottom layer, or "chemise," was often plain white but could be fancier with nobles. This was what was against the skin, got sweaty, and would be washed. The chemise was often slept in, again especially if the person was poor.

The outer layer, what we would call the "dress," was the prettier layer. This would have the nicer stitching and designs. It could have embroidery or different fabrics stitched together to create designs. The outer dress could have long sleeves, short sleeves, or no sleeves, depending on how hot the weather was. In general, though, a woman's arms and legs were covered by the inner chemise and perhaps also by the outer dress as well. Women in medieval times did not tend to show skin from those parts of the body.

You might see images on the web with medieval women wearing long "trumpet" sleeves which made housework impractical. These were sometimes worn by French nobles who were showing off that they did not have to do menial labor. They were not a normal fashion in England or most other areas.

By the same token, women who had to work hard would wear shorter dresses - ending above the ankle rather than dragging on the floor. That was so their dresses did not catch or drag while they went about their work. Noblewomen who had a quiet day planned or a formal event would wear longer, floor-dragging dresses. These subtle differences helped to show off their status.

If it got even colder women would wear cloaks. These range from light, like the woman in the middle is wearing here, to heavy and full-circle, which could be amazingly warm. I have one of those.

Here is an illuminated image done between 1285 and 1292 which shows the famous poet Marie de France. Marie primarily wrote between 1160 to 1190 and was well known by nobility in France and England. Again, you can see how her outer long dress goes to the floor and the inner dress is visible at the arms. This copyright-free image comes via the National Library of France.

Women had an immense array of colorful dyes to choose from, some more expensive, some less expensive. So clothing could be quite bright and cheery. Just as in modern times, practicality had an aspect here. If someone was going to work in the pig pen all day long they'd probably wear something brown and old. If they were going to church they'd wear their best outfit they had.

In modern times we can sometimes think of dresses as "fancy" items we wear to "dress up" that are hard to move in. In medieval times, a dress was normal and natural! These were the outfits they wore every single day. Women made their dresses so they could do all their normal activities in them. To them a dress was like our modern t-shirt and sweatpants. So they're no question about "could they do chores in a dress" or "could they ride a horse in a dress." Of course they could - that's what the clothing was made for. Medieval women didn't generally hide out in tower rooms. Noblewomen would do archery and horseback riding for fun. Working women would scythe hay, ride to the market, and do a myriad of other chores in their dresses. It was what one wore. So those outfits absolutely were made to easily let them do those tasks. Dresses were loose to allow all of that. Women didn't ride side-saddle in medieval days - they simply put their legs on either side for stability. And their clothing was made for that. To ride, a woman could either tuck the skirt beneath her, like when one sits on a chair, or let it flow behind her. Either way works!

In terms of underclothes, most medieval women did not wear a bra. Their simple, straight dresses were meant to keep the body hidden rather than emphasized. A large breasted woman might wear a "binder" to keep the breasts from jiggling around while they tried to work. Current thought is that women didn't wear "underwear" (underpants) either. With their long multi-layer dresses it would be a challenge for underwear-wearing women to go to the bathroom. Instead, they would just move to a section of the field, fluff out their dresses, and go. Then they could get back to work. The same in the outhouses.

Even during the time of their periods, many researchers feel that the philosophy of the time was that binding or constricting a woman's flow would damage her fertility. So she simply bled into her underdress and that was washed. This free-flow practice continued long after medieval times. It was mentioned in doctors' journals in the 1800s. Even as recent as the 1900s there were cotton mills in the United States that had straw-strewn floors to absorb female workers' blood, so again this was not a short-term trend. And given that tampons can cause toxic shock syndrome, maybe those medieval women knew what they were doing :).

Let me know if you have any other questions about medieval women's clothing! I have a library of books here to help with research.

Dedication

To my mom, dad, siblings, and family members who encouraged me to indulge myself in medieval fantasies. I spent many long car rides creating epic tales of sword-wielding heroines and the strong men who stood by their sides. Jenn, Uncle Blake, and Dad were awesome proofers.

To Peter and Elizabeth May, who patiently toured me around England, Scotland, and France on three separate occasions. Elizabeth offered valuable tips on creating authentic scenes. Visiting the Berkhamsted motte and bailey was priceless.

To Jody, Leslie, Liz, Sarah, and Jenny, my friends who enjoy my eclectic ways and provide great suggestions. Becky was my first ever web-fan and her enthusiasm kept me going!

To the editors at BellaOnline, who inspire me daily to reach for my dreams and to aim for the stars. Lisa, Cheryll, Jeanne, Lizzie, Moe, Terrie, Ian, and Jilly provided insightful feedback to help my polishing efforts.

To the Massachusetts Mensa Writing Group for their feedback and enthusiastic support. Lynn, Tom, Ruth, Carmen, Al, and Dean all offered detailed, helpful advice!

To the Geek Girls, with their unflagging support for my expanding list of projects and enterprises. Debi's design talents are amazing. I simply adore the covers she created for me.

To the Academy of Knightly Arts for several years of in-depth training and combat experience with medieval swords and knives. I loved sparring with Nikki and Jo-Ann!

To B&R Stables who renewed my love of horseback riding and quiet forest trails.

To my son, James, whose insights into psychology help ground my characters in authentic behavior.

To Bob See, my partner in love for over 19 years and counting. He enthusiastically supports all of my new projects.

About the Author

Lisa Shea is a fervent fan of honor, loyalty, and chivalry. She brings to life worlds where men and women stand shoulder to shoulder, steady in their desire to make the world a better place for all. While her medieval heroines often wield a sword, they equally value the skilled use of their intelligence, wisdom, courage, and compassion.

Lisa has studied the Middle Ages since she was quite young. She has trained in medieval swordfighting for several years. She studied medieval dance and music with the SCA. She has been to England numerous times and loves exploring old castles and churches.

Please visit Lisa at LisaShea.com to learn more about her background and interests. Feedback is always appreciated!

As a special treat, as a warm thank-you for reading this book and supporting the cause of battered women, here's a sneak peek at the first chapter of *Believing Your Eyes*.

Believing   Your   Eyes
Chapter 1

England, 1180

"Full wise is he that can himselven knowe."
The Monkes Tale
Geoffrey Chaucer

The forest landscape undulated innocent and pristine beneath the frosted white of a fresh blanket of snow. Sunlight glinted mischievously through bare branches of oak and chestnut. Stephen drew in a lungful of the crisp late-January air, riding with lighthearted ease along the narrow path, keeping just in front of his younger companion.

Ian pulled ahead suddenly, his blonde hair shining in the sun. The wintry air made his breath puff in clouds of glittering lace as he cheerfully shouted out, "A pound says I beat you to the clearing!" He kicked his sleek, alabaster horse into a gallop.

Laughing, Stephen spurred his black mount and raced after him, his horse ploughing up the snowy trail with its hooves. It was only a matter of moments before he had caught and passed his friend.

The woods stretched on in a sea of twisting branches and sparkling icicles. Long streaks of clouds drifted far above, wafting across a pale-blue sky. The steeds flew across fallen logs and narrow streams. The distance between the two horses grew until Ian's horse had fallen far behind. Ian's challenges echoed distantly from the hollow depths of the woods.

The opening drew into view, and Stephen smiled. His younger friend was improving, but it would be a while before Ian could keep up with him through the twists and turns of the wooded path. He slowed the horse – and then as he drew in closer to the clearing he pulled harder, sliding to a stop in the dense snow. Every sense went on high alert as he scanned the area before him. He held up a hand, hearing Ian approach, and his friend was soon cascading to a stop beside him.

The horses snorted softly as they caught their breath. Echoes of the chase faded into silence. The pause lengthened as the men surveyed the woods with alert eyes. The two waited, watching, hearing only the distant sound of snow sloughing off branches.

The forest seemed, suddenly, very quiet.

Ian's voice came in a soft whisper. "What is it, Stephen?" He ran a hand through his short blond hair, then wrapped his brown traveling cloak tightly against a gust of crisp wind. Ahead to his left the sun was streaming through a gap in the trees, and the silence seemed almost palpable.

Ian shivered and looked around again. Gulping, his left hand lowered to the hilt of his sword, loosening the leather clasp on the scabbard with a deft twist of the thumb. "Do you think the Grays are finally turning south? Is that why you recommended we patrol the far north borders?"

Stephen's voice was soft. "Steady, Ian." Stephen motioned for Ian to be patient and listened intently again for a moment. He pointed to himself, and to the west side of the clearing. Then Stephen indicated for Ian to move to the east. Ian nodded, slipped off his horse and tied the reins securely to a nearby birch. He turned to Stephen, but dropped his eyes. Stephen saw in a glance the nervousness that added a tremor to Ian's movements.

Stephen looked with fondness at his friend. Ian had been trained well in the ways of arms, but although he was nearly twenty-five, he'd not been in many actual combat situations. Stephen gave him a nod of encouragement. The lad was long past ready for patrol. He reached out an arm, firmly clasping Ian's forearm, offering a smile. "Courage," he whispered.

Ian stood a moment to regain his composure, glancing over the sturdy, elegantly decorated breastplate and bracers he wore as if to steel himself. Then, taking a deep breath, he drew his sword and approached the clearing from the right.

Stephen watched him for a minute before slipping noiselessly to the left. Ian was Stephen's junior by five years, and Ian's father had routinely shielded his son from danger. Stephen knew the older man was nervous about risking the life of his only child. Still, surely the Lord knew it was critical for Ian to gain practical knowledge of how to defend his lands and home. When Stephen had been tasked with the training of the keep's forces, he had insisted that Ian join the patrols and put in his time on the wall.

The winter sun was bright against the open field of snow; Stephen gave his eyes a moment to adjust from the relative shadows of the forest. The cold seeped in through the leather armor he wore, but he preferred its flexibility and lightness over the heavy bulk that Ian gravitated toward.

Easing carefully through the deep drifts along the edge of the clearing, Stephen's eyes were drawn to a clutter of objects. He froze as their nature became clear. Sharp tension drew across his shoulders, and his grip tightened on his hilt. Ten snow-coated, rough looking men lay sprawled on the ground, their darkened blood marbleizing the pure white around them. To one side, hidden by trees until now, a cairn of ash sent wispy tendrils of smoke upwards, the melted snow around it languidly extinguishing the edges of the low flame.

Stephen's every sense went on high alert, attentive to the slightest movement, the faintest sound. The woods obliviously went on with its raspy sweep of branch on branch, the delicate flutter of snow easing from a passing breeze. At last he gave a calling wave to Ian, and the two moved into the clearing proper.

Stephen's brow creased as he drew close, taking in the gear on the fallen men. "Bandits by the look of it. All long dead. A few survivors ran off north." He glanced at a swath of tracks leading out of the clearing. "Those belong to the fleeing wolves' heads." He took in the signs of their lack of discipline; it was one of the few advantages they held against the bandits. He glanced up past the tracks with concern; a new wave of the storm was darkening the edges of the sky overhead, and a light flurry gently drifted down, slowly swirling into their prints.

Stephen motioned toward the glowing embers. "Whoever took them on, at least one person remained alive," he added quietly, walking toward the low mound of ash and stone. "Grays would leave their dead for the wolves. These bodies have been given a decent sending off." His eyes scanned the dead bandits for a moment, then moved again with curiosity to the cairn of ash. "I wonder who ..."

His voice trailed off as he gazed into the reddish glow. Something within gleamed and caught his eye. He picked up a stick and pushed the object out of the coals with it.

Ian's eyes lit up. "A bronze bracer!" He jumped forward and reached for the glowing object. The metal band was finely worked and glinted brightly as the clouds opened for a moment.

"Wait!" shouted Stephen in alarm, knocking Ian off balance enough that the blond fell sideways into a heavy drift under an oak. Stephen sighed and smiled fondly at his friend. "It is red hot - you would have burned your hand!" He shook his head as Ian ruefully climbed out of the snowbank and brushed himself off. "Still, do look at it," Stephen remarked, kneeling near the bracer to get a better look. "I have not seen lettering like this for years. An old language, but the engraving is new." He sat quietly for several moments, examining the markings.

A far-off horse's whinny snapped Stephen's head up, and he grabbed Ian by the arm. Together they sprinted toward the trees, coming alongside their own mounts to steady them, loosing their ties. A hush fell over the woods again; Stephen concentrated to hear any noise that seemed out of place.

Several full minutes went by without a sound. The light snow continued to fill their prints, melding them with the landscape.

Then, growing in intensity, the distinctive crash of hooves on dead branches approached from the north. Stephen drew back, pulling deeper into the shadows. The noise grew louder until two bearded men with wolfskin capes galloped thunderously into the clearing, broadswords held high. The redheaded man in front trampled through the edge of the cairn as he twisted the reins forcefully to slow his mount. He turned to snarl angrily at the second, who quickly spoke up.

"See, she ain't here," whined the smaller man, a greasy, unkempt redhead in a makeshift uniform. "We killed off her escorts, we did. Just like you ordered. Then Barney, yeah - it was Barney! He tried to wing her horse with an arrow, see, to make sure she didn't get away. But she was near the beast and the arrow got her in the side." His eyes furtively slid from side to side as he related his tale in a quick staccato. "It was poison dipped. It was an accident! He panicked and ran. I came back to tell you what happened. You wanted me to face her alone? Anyway, she didn't get far, it's sure. She's gone to her maker by now. What a tigress she was. Yeah, she put up a fight!" He licked his drooling lips, and his eyes glowed with some obscene thought.

The leader's face glowed crimson with fury at this news. "Your orders were to bring her in alive, fool," stormed the heavyset man. He cuffed the smaller man across the head, sending him tumbling off his horse.

"It was Barney!" pleaded the man, cringing in the snow.

"But you were in charge," shot back the larger man, "and Master was adamant about wanting her alive." A wolfish smile twisted his face. "I'll send *you* in to give him the news. Maybe you'll die more quickly than Barney did." He chuckled to himself. "You'd better hope so," he added with a sneer.

He looked around the clearing for a moment, then up at the sky. His brow furrowed. "With the storm, she won't last long, if she is even alive. We'll come back later to fetch her corpse." He glanced up at the gathering clouds again, then nodded. "That will have to do." Wheeling his shaggy mount, he galloped out of the clearing.

Gulping, the other scrambled onto his horse and spurred it on after his leader.

The hoofbeat echoed, faded, and then was lost in the valleys of the deep forest.

Ian let out a shuddering breath, creating a cloud of frost. "We had better get back to town," he whispered nervously, his hands shaking as he smoothed down his hair. "There could be more of them searching for the woman." He jumped as snow tumbled from a heavy branch.

Stephen retied his horse to a limb and circled the edge of the clearing, examining the ground. "This woman, whoever she is, is obviously wanted for a reason. She could provide valuable information on the Grays' movements. Search around to the west - see if you can pick up her tracks."

Ian made as if to protest, but seeing the set look on Stephen's face, he instead turned and set off hunting for any sign of the wounded woman.

Stephen moved with careful attention, his eyes scanning every drift of snow, every stray bent branch. His gaze moved past a shadow – and then swept back again.

There. Scattered drops of dark crimson – and the faintest of scratches, made by the sweep of a pine branch.

He kept his voice low, but pitched it to carry. "Here, to the east."

Ian ran to join him, and Stephen pointed out the signs. "Whoever she is, she has talent at covering her trail," he murmured as he eased forward. "Get our horses and follow behind me."

Soon they were tracking the tracing path through the wilderness, a light snow falling about their shoulders.

After an hour, they had traversed quite a distance. Many times the trail seemed to disappear in a stream or rocky area, but, with diligence, one of them was able to spot a broken branch or a smear of dried blood clinging to a sapling. Still, as twilight settled a violet cape over the forest, Stephen worried in earnest that they might lose all view of the faint signs under the gently falling snow.

Then, all at once, the way became clear. The pair came over the crest of a hill to find quite distinct footprints heading down the slope and ending under an ancient willow tree by a frozen stream.

Stephen stopped to survey the scene. Beneath the tree lay a roan stallion that turned his head protectively at their approach. Curled up against his flanks was a sleeping woman wrapped in a thick, black cloak, the hood pulled close around her face. She had apparently been there for a while; the snow had covered much of her body with a fine layer of white. The sun was setting behind them, and shadows were stretching across the hollow.

Stephen motioned Ian to stand guard and handed his own horse's reins over. He glanced around the clearing with a sharp eye, then he carefully worked his way down the snowy slope. The horse watched him steadily, but there was no other sound or movement. Stopping for a moment at the foot of the hill, Stephen then slowly moved toward the tree, careful to keep his hands away from his weapons so as not to frighten the woman. He grew concerned when she didn't stir at his approach, and, reaching her, he dropped easily to a knee at her side. He gently brushed off the snow to find a sign of the arrow the Grays spoke of.

In a flash, Stephen felt cold metal at his throat. The woman's eyes flew open; a pair of fever-bright green eyes burned into Stephen's own. He kept his body perfectly still despite the decidedly wicked edge on the dagger pressing into his neck. He looked steadily into that desperate gleam.

"I am here to help," he told her quietly. "We come from the keep at Penrith. We can take you there; you will be safe and cared for." He didn't move a muscle, willing her to trust him.

The woman seemed undecided, but her arm did not waver.

Stephen gently placed his fingers over the hand she held the dagger with. "You must know that you have been poisoned. If you kill me, it will not matter if I am telling the truth or not. You will die here in the snow."

This seemed to penetrate the fog behind her eyes; she nodded her acquiescence and reluctantly allowed him to take the dagger from her hand. He reached behind her and put the dagger in the leather saddlebag on her steed. Stephen then lifted the edge of her cloak to see the damage. Her blue tunic was ripped open and soaked through with blood. The scarlet rash flaring around a jagged wound on her lower ribs showed that some sort of poison - probably dwale - was already working its way into her system.

"We have got to get you back quickly," he explained as he worked. Examining the injury more closely, Stephen swore beneath his breath. The wound in her side was bad enough, but the poison was already taking hold of her. He could see how dilated her eyes were, and her body was trembling, although that could be the cold doing its own harm. Stephen looked back up the hill. "Bring the horses," he called to Ian. "She needs treatment as soon as possible." Ian led the steeds down the hill as Stephen lifted her in his arms. Her horse stood immediately beside them.

"Who are we rescuing? The lost daughter of a nearby Lord?" Ian asked in breathless wonder as he drew near. Stephen could almost see the puff in Ian's chest, the stories spinning in the man's mind with which he would boast to the serving wenches in the local taverns.

Stephen shook his head. Taking care not to jostle her, Stephen gathered the woman securely in his arms. He gently placed her onto his horse sidesaddle, then climbed up behind to steady her. Her roan moved close in, apparently prepared to follow. Ian reached for the horse's tack, but the horse only had a leather saddle and bags - no bridle or reins. He glanced around, shrugged, then mounted and turned his horse to follow Stephen.

Night fell quickly, and soon the winds were swirling the light snow into their faces, stinging their eyes. Stephen guided their horses back through the woods, moving with speed now that they could follow their own trail back. He held the woman tightly against him with one arm and tried to keep her warm despite of the dropping temperatures. Behind them, Stephen could hear Ian following close with the riderless roan.

Blinded by thick falling snow on this moonless night, Stephen struggled to see the path before him. Yet, when they drew near the clearing, the woman straightened against him and turned her face up to his. She tried to speak, but was unable to make any sound.

Understanding her need, Stephen turned the horse to face into the clearing and reined in to a stop. She raised her head and looked evenly out over the bodies, to the now dark cairn. She pulled the left side of her cloak back, revealing a long leather scabbard at her hip. It was made with high quality leather, but was simple in design - meant to last rather than impress. Down the center were stamped the letters 'Lucia'.

The woman took a deep breath, then drew her sword. It matched the scabbard - it was sturdy and well-made without being flashy. The sword bore the hundred small marks of frequent use. She solemnly saluted the cairn with her sword, paused for a wordless prayer, then kissed the hilt before resheathing it. Stephen watched the tears slide down her cheeks as she looked up at him and nodded. She was done.

"Thank you," she rasped softly, pulling her cloak around her body. Then she closed her eyes and slumped back against him.

Stephen wrapped her within his own cloak and moved off again at a quicker pace. They were still a half hour at least from the keep, and the temperature was dropping quickly.

Shivers racked her body, and he drew her even closer. His mind sorted through the possibilities as they rode. What woman would be traveling in the winter with the bandit attacks coming so hot and heavy? Where had she trained with a sword? He rode the remaining miles as quickly as he dared, pushing to get her to safety.

It seemed too long a time before the town's outer stone walls and main gate loomed ahead darkly, somber against the storm clouds. Stephen rode hard across the open meadow to the sturdy doors, pulling to a stop beneath the walls.

Ian's voice rang out in order. "Open the gates," he cried. "We've a wounded girl! Open up!"

Torches could be seen moving around in the windows by the stout wooden gate as the soldiers recognized the two men. The logs holding the doors secure made a low grating noise as they slowly slid free. The heavy doors were pulled open, and the three horses galloped inside.

Stephen led the way through the wide dirt streets of the town, galloping past the lights from windows and torches to the main building atop the hill. A few sleepy heads poked out of stone-lined windows to see who was racing through in the dense darkness. The streets were clean and the buildings well-kept; garden plots scattered in open areas were tended and neat.

Soon they had arrived at the main keep's gates, which stood open. Stable boys hurried with torches in hand to take the horses and guide the two companions inside. Stephen put his injured charge over his shoulder and hurried up the main stairs, taking a right in the great hall, down a narrow, twisting flight of steps to the healer's room. He grabbed a torch from the wall as he passed.

"It makes no sense to me why they heal down here in the dark," he muttered, balancing Lucia on his shoulder while carefully lowering the torch toward the bronze oil lamp on the side table. The wick caught, and suddenly the room flickered with light and shadow.

Ian came in behind him and lit the other candles while Stephen placed Lucia on the low central oak table, draping his own cloak over her for warmth. She lay curled up and motionless while Stephen moved to a cluttered bench beneath a tall set of shelves. Stephen reached for a pottery bowl holding a scant amount of yellow powder, a glass vial of water, and a marble mortar and pestle. All four stone walls were lined with shelves full of odd-smelling potions, drying herbs, and musty parchments.

Ian finished with the candles and stood by the wood table, apparently unsure of what to do next. Stephen let him be, carefully mixing the ingredients together, then adding in a pale yellow liquid from another glass vial.

A raspy voice called from the top of the stairs. "I am coming, I am coming." An elderly man in a rusty-brown robe hobbled down the flight, rubbing tired eyes beneath heavily sprouted brows. "I heard from the stable boys ... she has been poisoned?"

Stephen nodded, brow furrowed as he showed his results of his efforts to the tonsured monk.

"I know," sighed the monk. "It has been a long winter, and the Grays have been very active. Our supplies are running out. If only we could find more, and did not need to ration our remaining medicines. I guess this will have to do for her, though."

Lucia lay on the table, motionless now except for the slight trembling of her hands and feet. Her eyes were closed. Stephen gently drew the cloak back. In the light of the many candles, he now saw that she wore a long, blue tunic over a pair of black leggings. He heard Ian's snort of surprise, and smiled to himself. Not so unusual after all. He had met numerous women on his travels who preferred the warmth of pants for winter riding.

Stephen loosened the brown leather belt and gingerly slid the tunic up above her stomach, revealing her waist. The fabric was soaked with blood, and a long slice could be traced from her hip up to her lower ribs. He could also see that a speckled rash was spreading across her skin. He took a folded square of cloth from a shelf and poured some of the mixture into its center.

The monk turned to Ian. "Hold her wrists. She may struggle because of the pain," he warned the blond, gently pressing down on her ankles. "We have got to try and keep her from hurting herself. May the Lord calm her," he added to Stephen.

"Thank you, Matthew. Let us hope we have gotten to it quickly enough this time."

Stephen carefully cleaned the wound with a damp cloth, doing his best not to cause her further harm. She moaned softly while he worked, twisting beneath his hands, her body shivering more violently with every passing moment. As he wiped away the layers of caked blood, he found to his surprise that it was not deep after all; rather, a glancing slide along her ribs that had bled a great deal. Others he had worked on had been poisoned by far deeper wounds. With such a shallow injury, he didn't believe that enough poison could have gotten into her system to cause the spreading rash and bone-deep trembling.

Maybe the Grays were using something new, something even more vicious?

He held back the racing thoughts with practiced effort. For now he had to address the task at hand. Then he could have the luxury of dreading an even greater threat.

He quickly finished cleaning the wound, then put a clean cloth against it to hold back the bleeding. He used another cloth to wrap around her waist and hold the first one in place. A leather thong was tied to hold the bandage in position.

Satisfied that the wound was not mortal, he did a quick survey of the rest of her outfit while Ian looked away in embarrassment. In addition to the tunic and pants she wore high black, well-worn leather boots, which he removed, and simple stockings. He did not find any other indications of a wound beneath any of this, and his gentle examination of her arms and legs found strong muscle, but no obviously broken bones. This arrow wound seemed to be the only serious injury. Still, it should not have caused the rash that he could see on her stomach, nor the trembling that had seized her.

The reactions concerned him. What had happened?

Ian's eyes drew with curiosity over the woman's face. "She does not look familiar," he mused. "Who could she be?"

Stephen did not break his concentration, staring intently at the wound. "I think her name is Lucia," he replied, and glanced at the sword at her side. The Grays had deliberately sought her for some reason. They'd apparently poisoned her by accident, and had wanted her alive. As for the poison - it didn't seem to him like the arrow wound could account for her state. What, then?

He looked up at her face, at her closed eyes, down to the rosy lips. They were dark crimson against the paleness of her cheeks.

Dark crimson?

He looked more closely. There were flecks of blood around her lips. He took one of her trembling hands from Ian, examining it. He could see now that there was ash and blood mixed in with the dirt, and that they were singed, as if by fire.

Suddenly, the answer hit him clearly. She must have tried to clean her wound herself, of course, when her enemy had fled. She had gotten the poison on her fingers. His mind searched the possibilities. While building the cairn for her fallen comrades, she had burned herself. Naturally, she put her fingers in her mouth to soothe them.

The poison wasn't on her body - it was in her stomach.

"Sit her up," ordered Stephen, as he turned to the bench for his bowl of mixture.

Lucia half-opened her eyes as she was raised, and he could see again how dilated her pupils were. She tried to speak, but no words came out, and she gave up in exasperation and weariness. Stephen stood before her for a moment, holding the bowl. He looked across at the exhausted woman.

"You must drink this," he quietly requested, again willing her to believe him. She hesitated, looking up at him. "Please. Trust me," he added softly, holding her gaze.

She looked down at her tended wound, and at the rash that was visible even beyond the bandages. Looking back up at Stephen, she appeared to be weighing something in her mind. Finally, she nodded quietly.

Her hands were shaking too badly for her to hold the bowl herself, so he carefully poured the mixture into her mouth. She drank it down, closing her eyes at the taste of it. Almost immediately, she clutched at her stomach and moaned in pain. Matthew grabbed a nearby pail, and after a few moments, she vomited convulsively, gagging out the contents of her stomach. She continued to retch long after her belly was empty, the shivers wracking her entire body. All the while, Stephen wiped her brow with a cloth, keeping her long, auburn braid to one side. Matthew held her shoulders, and Ian kept her from rolling back.

When she was finally done, she slumped back onto the table, limp and exhausted.

Ian looked with concern at the still figure, but Matthew gave Stephen a pat on the shoulder. "I believe you were on the mark," he asserted. "She must have ingested some. That explains the symptoms." He put the pail to one side. "We have done what we can to get the base of it out – we will need to keep her warm now, and help her to stay awake, at least for a short while."

Stephen glanced around at the room, which, while bright with candlelight, was chill and damp. "It would be best if we could settle her in one of the rooms upstairs."

Matthew nodded in agreement. "With the seriousness of her symptoms, we should arrange a twenty-four hour watch too, for perhaps a week, until the symptoms fully fade." He glanced to the younger man. "Ian, could you arrange that?"

Ian brightened with a task to take charge of. "For my lovely lady, of course!"

An odd twinge ran through Stephen at Ian's possessive language, but he said nothing.

Ian continued, "I shall go wake my father right away. We can arrange for her to have one of the larger bedrooms." He looked over to Stephen, then his smile widened. "She should have great fun spending time with Anna once she recovers," he added with glee. "I need to get things ready!" He grinned with pleasure, then turned and ran up the stone steps.

Matthew turned to Stephen as Ian's footsteps finished echoing off the cold, stone walls. He chuckled, then looked down at Lucia, who lay with her eyes closed. "Aye, she is a pretty lass, though perhaps not the Lady that Ian is hoping for! Whatever she is, she is real enough. Call me a fool if he is not already smitten with her." Matthew smiled to himself at the thought, then gathered a woolen blanket off the shelf to wrap about her.

Stephen turned away from Matthew and gazed down at the exhausted woman. Lying there, she almost seemed to be a child, her arrow wound perhaps a youthful nightmare. He reached absently to her face and eased a stray hair back into the braided weave. She made a small noise, then lapsed back into silence.

Child indeed. Stephen could tell by the firm muscles in her arms that any appearance of helplessness was deceiving. She obviously knew how to wield that sword, and much else besides. Yes, it would be interesting to find out where she was from and where she had been headed.

His brow furrowed. For all he knew, she was the 'companion' of one of the wolves' heads and was being hauled back to pay the piper for some misdeed. Time would tell the truth, though.

Stephen took the blanket from Matthew and wrapped it gently around Lucia's body. He lifted her swaddled form easily, then snagged the handle of the oil lamp and headed toward the stairs. He could already hear muted footsteps and shouted orders as the great hall came to life.

Above it all, Ian's voice gave the commands.

Here's where to read Lucia's full story!

http://www.amazon.com/Believing-Your-Eyes-
Medieval-Romance-ebook/dp/B008RIBYTI/